The

ISBN: 978-1493741977
Copyright © by Telishia R. Berry
Strive Publishing, Inc. A division of Courageous Woman
Enterprises
For more information on ordering and author signings
please contact:
Courageous Woman Enterprises
P.O. BOX 7263
Flint, MI 48507
www.telishiaberry.com
www.courageouswomanmag.com
thecwmagazine@yahoo.com

This is a work of fiction. All characters, places and
events are from the author's imagination and should not be
confused with fact. Any resemblance to person's living or
dead, events or places is purely coincidental. Unauthorized or
restricted acts in relation to this publication may result in civil
proceedings and/or criminal prosecution.

Edited by Shonell Bacon
Proofread/formatted by Teresa D. Patterson
Proofread by Etta Brown
Cover designed by Keith Saunders, Marion Designs
First Edition

Acknowledgements

First and foremost I want to thank my Lord and Savior from whom all my blessings flow. Thank you for your favor and the provision. I know it's all YOU!

To my four reflections; Kendre', Tisha, Toya, and Kennedy. Thank you for believing in me and encouraging me to keep striving.

Thank you to my mother Paulette Wardlow and father, Keith Hall for giving me life! And thank you to the other dads in my life, Larry Jones, and Virgil Smoot.

Thank you to my grandparents, Robert and Dovie Wardlow, my God sent angels. R.I.P. Grandaddy!

My family of siblings, aunts, uncles, and cousins and BFF's that are always there no matter what. Aunt Lulu, Uncle James, Aunt Pam, Slick (Virgil Smoot III), Tonya Smith, Veronica Hood, Randy Lathan, Jared Hall, Sterling Hall, Donna Taylor, Natasha Cooper, Melecia Scott, Kevin and Kerry.

My spiritual mother, and sisters, Thank you for the encouragement and for praying me through my storms! Apostle Sandra Appleberry, Rev, Dr. Diva Verdun, Pastor Stephanye Wells, Evangelist Flora Sparks, Apostle Tiffany Baker, Rosina Baylor, Marlynne Cooley, Lisa Gray, Raquel Perkins, and Dr. Cheryl Appling.

Triple thank you to my editor, Shonell Bacon, for your expertise and for putting up with me during this project.

CHAPTER ONE

*I*t was the end of summer, 1968. Blacks were still mourning the assassination of Dr. Martin Luther King, Jr., Motown artists were topping the charts, US soldiers were being drafted to the Vietnam War, and Deacon John Wilson and his wife, Kadie, were trying to raise four, good, God-fearing children.

Of the four siblings, Johnny was the oldest at 22, and Al was just a year and a half younger than him. Their sister Maureen was eighteen and just two years older than Brenda.

The brothers spent most of their time away from the house, but when the four siblings were all together, an occasional board game was the perfect family entertainment.

"It's my turn," Brenda yelled.

"Well, then roll the dice, girl," Johnny said.

Brenda leaned across the board game, shaking the dice in her hand. She inhaled and blew on the dice for good luck.

"Papa's got a brand new bag!" she exclaimed and dropped the dice down onto the Monopoly board. "I got seven!"

"Naw, baby sis, you got craps," Johnny teased.

"Shut up. We ain't playin' no craps." Brenda chuckled.

Deacon Wilson stormed into the room. "I know y'all ain't up in my house shootin' craps," he bellowed.

"Nah, Daddy, it's just Monopoly," Johnny said, raising his hands in defense.

Deacon Wilson had already taken away a set of dice and two decks of playing cards he'd found in their rooms and threw them away.

"I done told y'all, I don't want no card playin' and dice rollin' in this house."

"But Daddy, it's just Monopoly. The dice came with the game," Brenda insisted.

"Y'all heard what I said. If you got to play this game with dice, then you just can't play it."

He believed playing any games using dice or playing cards was sinful and that good, saved church folk and their kids shouldn't do it.

Deacon walked right up to the table, and swooped the dice up into his hands. Johnny rocked on the back legs of his chair, chewing his gum on his front teeth. Al pulled the dark glasses he had resting on his forehead down over his eyes. Brenda sighed, smacked her lips, and folded her arms across her chest. Maureen, quiet as usual, never let her face reveal her thoughts.

"These are the devil's tools," Deacon said, raising his fist in the air, the dice gripped in his hand. "You play cards and shoot dice now, next, you'll be gamblin', drinkin', and smokin'."

Al smirked and held in his laugh that was about to blow.

"Then Jesus was led by the spirit unto the wilderness to be tempted by the devil, Matthew … four and one," Deacon recited from his memory bank of scriptures then walked over to the girls' record player and turned off Martha and the Vandellas' song, exited the room, and shut the door behind him.

"Now what does that Bible verse have to do with us playing a simple Monopoly game?" Al blurted, finally releasing the laughter he held in.

"That's exactly why I stay at Uncle Pap's most of the time," Johnny said. "Shoot, I win big money at his house playing poker."

"Johnny!" Maureen rushed toward the door to make sure it was closed tightly. "Shhh, you better keep your voice down before Daddy comes storming back in here and slaps you upside your head one good time, talking about playing poker!"

Brenda stood and began dancing. "Jimmy," she sang, "Oh Jimmy Mack, when are you coming back?"

"You better hush, too. You'll be dancing all right, while Daddy is Jimmy Smackin' his belt to your behind. Now cut it out, Brenda, before he comes back in here."

Brenda kept it up, singing, dancing, and laughing all up on Maureen until she saw that Maureen was cutting her eyes at her.

"Hump, Daddy kills me with all that holy stuff," Johnny said. He stood and pushed his chair up to the table. "He acts like he ain't never played cards before, like he ain't never committed no sins."

Johnny and Al exited the room. Maureen busied herself cleaning up the bedroom while Brenda continued sitting at the table playing with the Monopoly money.

"If this money was real, I'd hop me a train to Chicago," Brenda said. She brandished a handful of the play money.

"Yeah, Brenda, I'm sure you would, but it ain't, and you can't, so get to cleaning this room."

Brenda curled her lips and shot Maureen a look as if she couldn't stand her Goody Two-Shoes ways.

For Deacon and Kadie, raising four kids who were now all teenagers hadn't been an easy task, but Deacon referred to his Bible as his manual for *everything*. He even quoted scriptures at random from memory and had one for every situation.

"Train up a child in the way that he should go, and when he is old he will not depart from it" was the one he recited most often when it came to issues with the kids.

Deacon prided himself in being a model Christian. He knew the Bible from Genesis to Revelations. When he wasn't working first shift at the Chevrolet automotive plant, he studied the Bible, or taught it somewhere, either in Sunday school, mid-week Bible study, or at some annual Baptist convention, locally or out of state. Being the most upright and righteous man was his main objective. Most of the family, including the in-laws, respected him, but many thought he was overbearing and at times a bit of a fanatic.

Kadie, as much a Christian as he, but she was often annoyed by the way he used the Bible so much to dictate their lives.

"We were young once, too," she'd often say to Deacon.

Deacon and Kadie both played cards, smoked cigarettes, and even dipped snuff a few times when they were young, but they didn't want their kids to do it as Deacon was always on *sin patrol*, making sure his kids all looked and acted like they had some good Christian home-training.

Brenda—she was the youngest, and the one Deacon thought he'd better keep a closer eye on. It wasn't that she was a bad girl; she just had a tendency to cross the boundaries that Deacon placed before her.

4

He constantly reiterated his beliefs to anyone that would listen. Usually, Kadie became his captive audience.

"Times are different now," he'd say to Kadie. "You got to keep a grip on your children, or you'll end up pickin' 'em up off the wayside."

She believed just the opposite.

"No, the tighter you try to hold 'em, the more they want to break free. And then they start actin' up, and that's when you *will* be pickin' 'em up off the street corners, haulin' 'em out of the whorehouses, and everywhere else you tried to keep 'em from."

Kadie fussed at him real good for interrupting the kids' game like that and reminded him of when they were young before he became so saved and sanctified. After he thought about it, Deacon didn't feel bad for his reasons for doing it; he just felt a little sorry for being so harsh about it. He went to his small workspace in the basement and handcrafted a cardboard number spinner similar to the one the girls had for their Twister game. The four siblings all sat in the living room when he returned an hour later with it.

"You can use this in the place of the dice," he said as he tested it in front of them, flicking the spinner twice before placing it down in the center of the marble-top coffee table and walking out of the room.

Maureen picked it up, flicked it a few times, and sat it back on the table. The idea of a spinner in place of the dice for the Monopoly game just didn't sit well with them. Talking trash while shaking and blowing on the dice was the fun part of the game and helped keep the momentum. The other siblings were so tuned in to The Supremes who were guest performers on *The Ed Sullivan Show* that they didn't pay much attention to the spinner or the fact that

Deacon had tried to make amends. It didn't bother Deacon that the kids didn't understand his logic about things.

"I just want them to do right," Deacon muttered as he entered the kitchen.

"Yes, John," Kadie said, "and as you can see, with the liquor stores and bars open now, our children are all *right* here ... watching TV."

CHAPTER TWO

*"L*et's play that song again," Brenda said as she scurried across the bedroom floor to the record player. The sisters enjoyed themselves, laughing, dancing, and acting like typical teenage girls, playing records and performing as if on stage, one using a hairbrush, the other, a comb for microphones.

Deacon couldn't stand it. The way he'd seen kids dancing on television, he just knew that was the prelude to becoming loose women.

. "I ought to just rush right in there and snatch the cord right out of the wall socket," he said as he lay in bed next to Kadie with his arms folded across his chest.

"Let 'em alone, John, they're just being teenagers," Kadie insisted. "Don't you remember when we were young? We used to dance, jitter buggin' all over Miss Callie's juke joint."

Deacon sighed and quieted his emotions as his mind traveled back to the days when he and Kadie were just courting, when he could twirl and swing her from one hip to the other as they twisted, tapped, and danced the jitterbug as teenagers.

"It wasn't no juke joint. It was her living room," Deacon added just as he rolled over and went to sleep.

"Whatever you say, John, whatever *you* say," Kadie said, smiling as she sat up in the bed next to him and finished the hem she was hand stitching in her skirt.

They next morning the sound of Sunday morning spirituals blared from the small radio on the bookshelf in the basement. The soul-stirring voices of gospel singers like Reverend James Cleveland, Mahalia Jackson, and the Clara Ward singers echoed through all the heat vents in the house. Warm homemade biscuits waiting in the oven, the smell of bacon and eggs frying, and grits simmering filled the air, all reminding everyone in the house that it was Sunday, a day for the Wilson family to do nothing but worship and afterwards eat a good soul food meal.

As always, Deacon was up early studying his Bible at his rickety cherry wood desk in the basement. It had been a few weeks since Johnny and Al had gone into the Army. Johnny got drafted, and Al volunteered just to get away from home; everyone seemed to know that but Deacon. They both went to Vietnam. It bothered Deacon that both his sons were away fighting the war, but he stayed in constant prayer over them.

Deacon kept track of the time, shifting his eyes from the words on the pages of his King James Bible to the small clock on his desk. He knew Maureen and Brenda would be tired since he'd heard them up late laughing and singing that *worldly music*, as he called it.

At five minutes to seven, he made his way from the basement to the girls' room.

"Rise and shine," he said like an energetic drill sergeant as he banged on the bedroom door. "It's seven o'clock, now get on up. I don't care if you stayed up all night listening to that rock-and-roll mess, you're still getting up and going to church. Get on up."

"We up, Daddy," Maureen yelled as she rose, yawned, stretched her arms toward the ceiling, and then pulled herself out of bed.

"I don't want to go to church. I don't feel like it," Brenda said. She pulled her quilt over her head, exposing her bare feet. "I don't want to go," she whined then tossed, turned, and pouted.

"You might as well get on up 'cause all that acting and throwing fits ain't gone change nothin'."

"Hump," Brenda responded, kicking the covers to the floor. She growled as she rose and sat on the edge of the bed with her feet dangling.

Maureen smirked and shook her head. Brenda stammered across the room toward the door, stopping short to compose herself and her thoughts before she slowly opened the door.

"Daddy, I don't feel good," she said in a sorrowful tone as she gripped her stomach with one hand and held her forehead with the other. "I think I should stay home today."

Deacon paused for a moment to take in what Brenda said. "Well, you thought wrong. In this house, we will serve the Lord and make our way to his house every Sunday, sick or not."

Brenda sighed, pursed her lips, and rolled her eyes.

"I'm sure your mama's got something for a stomach ache."

Brenda mocked him, silently framing his words on her lips, twisting her neck, and bobbing her head from side to side as Deacon trampled back down the narrow staircase.

"Sunday is the Lord's day," Deacon ranted. "When I was a boy, my daddy woke us up at four a.m. to milk the cows, feed the hens, cook breakfast, then walk five miles to church wearing shoes so raggedy that my feet got sun burned through all the holes in 'em."

Everyone in the family had heard Deacon's childhood stories a million times at least, but he told them over and over as if it was the first time. He mumbled and fussed through the house, preaching and babbling about obedience until he made it back to the basement.

"Sunday is the Lord's day," Brenda mocked in Deacon's voice.

"Uumph," Maureen said, shaking her head. She stood at the mirror over the dresser, pulling out the pink sponge rollers she had clamped in her hair.

"Brenda, don't you know as long as you live in this house, you got to abide by *his* rules? Seems like you woulda done figured that out by now."

Brenda ignored her and continued sifting through her drawer of pantyhose.

Maureen was wise to the facts. She had learned long ago what to do and say and what not to do and say when it came to Deacon.

"At least you don't have to sing in the choir anymore," Maureen said.

Compromising with Kadie, Deacon told the girls that once they turned sixteen, they didn't have to sing in the youth choir or be forced to join the adult choir, but they had to continue going to Sunday school, Sunday service, and youth meetings. The youth choir age limit was 16 anyway. And most kids joined the adult choir after that, but Kadie felt that by age sixteen their kids were nearly adults and shouldn't be forced into working in the church. She believed that she and Deacon had instilled enough morals and principles in them that they'd be able to make some of their own decisions, good ones. But as long as you lived in Deacon's house, going to church was non-negotiable. Making sure his kids were raised in church was part of training them up right.

After Sunday school, Brenda and Pastor Pearson's daughters, Terri and Darlene walked to the corner store across from the church to get some soda and chips before service started. They laughed on the walk back as they mocked Mr. Johnson, their Sunday school teacher that stuttered.

"Turn to s...s. St. John th...three...si...si...Sixteen. Fo...for God s...so lo...loved th...the world," Brenda joked. They all laughed.

"Come on, Terri. We have to hurry up and go put on our choir robes," Darlene said.

They both sang in the choir and had to be ready to do the two-step march in from the back of the sanctuary.

"Why don't you sing with us anymore, Brenda?"

"'Cause I don't want to."

"Oh," Terri replied.

Brenda wanted them to believe that her decision was her own declaration of independence. Truth was, she had recently turned sixteen and was glad she was no longer required to make it to Saturday morning choir rehearsals. She'd taken a babysitting job instead.

"Come on, Darlene, we have to be ready to march," Terri said.

"Instead of *marching* down the aisle, you think they'll let me dance? Do the mashed potato or maybe the shotgun," Brenda said, giggling and dancing.

"Naah, maybe the twist," Darlene replied, twisting her plump hips from side to side and joining in Brenda's laughter.

"We'll see you after church," Terri said, shaking her head at them and tugging at Darlene's shoulder.

Terri and Darlene walked toward the choir room.
Brenda trotted down the steps to the ladies' lounge in the
church basement.

"Jesus is on the main line. Tell him what you want,
you just call Him up and tell Him what you want," Mother
Jesse sang with feeling and inspiration, but clapped her
hands a little offbeat.

It was already eleven thirty-five, but members still
trickled in even though church supposedly started at eleven.
Many of the members came late purposely, hoping they'd
miss Mother Jesse's twenty-minute devotional song that
she led with the deacons every Sunday.

After she sat in the ladies' lounge chucking down her
snacks and drinking Dr. Pepper, Brenda peeked in the side
sanctuary door first, then tipped in, peering up front to see
if her father was there with Mother Jesse leading devotion.
The deacons rotated Sunday duties, and she never could
remember which Sunday was his to lead in prayer or any
other business the deacons were in charge of. She saw
Deacon Flynn, who some of the church ladies had secretly
nicknamed "Flirting Flynn" standing up front, wearing the
best one of his three shark skin suits that were all two sizes
too small. The church ladies called him "Flirting Flynn"
because he always grinned in their faces, showing off his
gold plated teeth as if the teeth gave him some financial
status. His flirtatious manners were charming yet
humorous since he stood only about four-foot-five and he
wore a size five shoe. He had no idea that he was one of the
most entertaining topics the women chuckled about
whenever they got together to cook for a church function or
occasion.

Mother Jesse stood up between the two deacons. By now, she was on her sixth chorus of the song and making up her own lyrics.

"If you're broke and all ya money's spent, tell Him what you want," she sang. The congregation repeated, hesitantly dragging their voices. Although Mother Jesse was often hoarse and her voice cracked when she sang, nobody had the nerve to say anything to her about it. One of the founding members of the church, she made sure that every new generation of members knew it. She'd been leading the devotional songs for forty years, and was not about to be relieved from her self-appointed position. Even in her eighties, she could get around and strut like the best of them with the exception of an occasional use of a wooden cane. Most times, she'd walk around with the cane dangling across her wrist.

"This just old folks' decoration," she'd say.

Folks marveled over her amazing strength when the spirit would hit her. She'd jump and run up and down the sanctuary aisles like an Olympic track star for a good fifteen minutes.

"Hallelujah" and "Thank you, Jeeesus," she'd shout over and over until Pastor Pearson would get up, clear his throat, and say "Amen" at least a half dozen times.

All in all, Mother Jesse was a well-respected member and mother of the church. She didn't hesitate to get any youngster straight, that is, to her, anyone under sixty years of age.

It was obvious that the congregation grew tired of singing along with Mother Jesse. Most continued standing out of respect, but the noisome expressions on some of their faces indicated they wanted Pastor Pearson to hurry up and intervene.

"Let the church say amen," Pastor Pearson firmly interjected.

The congregation responded with an array of more "Amen."

"Thank you, Lord," Sister Abernathy said, flickering her eyelids as she sighed.

The members who sat in the pew in front of her snickered. They knew she couldn't stand Mother Jesse. She, too, was a feisty old lady who had her share of disagreements with Mother Jesse. For years, the two squabbled over trivial issues like decoration colors for the church anniversary and the dinner menu for the pastor's birthday celebration. Pastor Pearson once had to counsel the ladies and had insisted that they not be part of the same committees because they just couldn't seem to get along.

It took a few more "amens" from the deacons before the musical director, Brother Derrick, completely ended the song.

"Thank you, Deacons Mays and Flynn, and Mother Jesse, who is one of our beloved founding members here at Mt. Moriah Missionary Baptist Church," Pastor Pearson expressed respectfully, his short stocky frame barely visible behind the podium without the step stool one of the deacons made especially for him. He looked back at the associate ministers with a concerned eye, wondering why someone didn't have the step stool from his car since he had used it at another church he'd been invited to preach at. He noticed Deacon Simmons rushed in holding it in his hands.

Mother Jesse smiled up at him as Deacon Mays gripped her arm and escorted her to the second center pew, which was designated as the honorary Mothers' seats.

Everyone except the Mothers and those cradling small babies remained standing until assistant Pastor Pearson had led the responsive reading and a prayer that was so long and emotional he had to gasp between sentences to catch his breath.

Sighs of relief permeated throughout the sanctuary as Pastor Pearson finally waved his hands, gesturing everyone to sit down. Behind the deacons, the deaconesses sat flapping their paper fans and turning up their noses as the stench of flatulence that loomed into the air. The odor came from some of the lactose intolerant deacons who refused to admit it and deny themselves any of the buttermilk pancakes the women served at the General Assembly breakfast every fifth Sunday.

Brenda sat up straight, stretching her neck to see if her mother sat where she usually sat when it was her Sunday to serve on the nurse's guild. She noticed Deacon sitting on the first pew on the right side of the sanctuary, where all the deacons sat, slept, and sometimes snored loud enough for one of the deaconesses to give him a nice nudge. Sister Sherman would just outright smack her husband, Deacon Sherman, right in the back of his head. He'd wake up coughing and clearing his throat like he had a cold.

Maureen always sat on the end of the fourth pew so she could be close enough to get to the podium quickly to do the announcements. She enjoyed the announcement clerk position and thrived on the compliments members gave her.

Deacon Wilson got up and exited the side door while the choir sang. Brenda assumed the frustration on his face was due to the choir. He'd always complain, saying they sang too loud and the songs were just too long. He'd wait until he heard the pastor speak before he came back in to start the choir right up again. He didn't want to step in when the choir director was directing some fancy sing-and-pause. Deacon couldn't stand that. "Why don't they just end the song?" he'd ask.

After the third selection from the choir, the second offering, and the atmosphere being calm and settled, Pastor Pearson began his sermon.

"I'm not gonna hold ya long today since our young people are expecting you all to come back for the Youth Day program and dinner this afternoon," Pastor Pearson affirmed.

"Amen," said Deacon Mays as he nodded off to sleep.

"Today, I'm gonna talk about raising Godly children," Pastor Pearson said, opening his sermon. "There are rewards to raising God-like children."

Those words were like a slogan Brenda had heard over and over most of her life. She smirked as her mind recalled the mild dispute she had with Deacon that started the morning.

"Must I hear this again?" she said under her breath, twisting her lips. All she could think about was Deacon and his strict ways, counting the days to when she could get married and move out of the house.

CHAPTER THREE

*A*nother Saturday evening approached, and Kadie was tired. She'd spent most of the day in the hot kitchen getting a head start on Sunday's meal. She cooked fresh turnip greens that she'd picked from her garden the day before, fluffy hot water cornbread, that good sticky macaroni and cheese, and of course Deacon's favorite candied yams.

"I'm going over to Cheryl's house," Brenda announced as she slipped her feet into her freshly polished white pointed-toe sneakers.

"First, I want you to walk this food over to your uncle, Pap's, house."

Kadie placed two aluminum foil covered plates down into a brown paper bag.

"Ah Mama, can't Daddy just drive it over there?"

"Look girl, your daddy is teaching at the Great Lakes Baptist Convention all this week, and he won't get home 'til late."

Brenda huffed and sighed as Kadie turned her back.

"Hurry up now. Your aunt Bessy is sick, and you know Pap ain't hardly gonna cook for her. He's liable to let her sip on some Jack Daniels first." Kadie chuckled.

Brenda paused, wondering what her mother knew about liquor since she never saw anything remotely resembling liquor in that house.

Pap was Deacon's oldest brother by seven years. He lived only a few blocks away with his wife Bessy. He and Bessy didn't have kids, so Pap took to his nieces and nephews like they were his own.

Deacon and Pap were as different as night and day. While Deacon spent most of his time in church teaching the

Gospel, Pap spent most of his time raising hell at pool halls, all-night poker games, and an occasional evening with a loose woman that hung around the pool hall.

Brenda was tired by the time she made it to Hamilton Street. Beads of sweat flowed down her hairline. Continuously, she wiped it away with her fingers. As she strolled up the driveway carrying the paper bag that smelled of southern soul food, she could hear loud talking and cursing through the open front windows. Creeping up the back stairs toward the back door, she glanced over at Aunt Bessy's vegetable garden that looked like it hadn't been tended to in a while. She pushed the unlocked door open since no one heard the knocking over all the commotion. The stench of cigar smoke drifted up her nostrils, drawing wrinkles in her forehead. Billie Holiday played in the background on a small record player in a corner of the living room while a room full of middle-aged men sat around the dining room waiting to get into the poker game that was the center of the commotion.

"Hey, Uncle Pap," Brenda yelled, trying to be heard over the noise.

He looked up and spoke quickly, keeping his attention on the game.

"Hey there, baby girl. Whatcha know good?"

"Oh nothin' much. Mama sent this food over here for you and Aunt Bessy."

"Bessy's back there in…" He stopped mid-sentence. "Hot damn, there it is. Put the money on the table!"

Charged with excitement, he slammed his spread of winning cards down in the center of the table, then reached out to rake the pile of money he'd won toward him. His body jiggled as he exerted a hefty laugh and a toothy grin while the other players sighed with frustration. Two disappointed players got up from the table and switched places with two others waiting to play.

"Dammit," the shortest player exclaimed.

Pap was known for being a hardball card shark who didn't play about his money when he won a card game. Like Deacon Wilson, Pap had many amusing life stories to tell, only Uncle Pap's were mostly about the Korean War that he fought in or some street thug he had to strong arm.

"I'll put a cap in a nigga," he said. That had to be one of his most used phrases.

Everyone loved to listen to his stories like children listened to nursery rhymes. They'd laugh, but they knew they had some truth to them. He often told the story about Donald Stacks. He made sure he told it whenever he played poker with those he hadn't played with before. Donald once tried to cheat Pap out of some money in a poker game. Being new in town, he didn't know Pap that well. He'd heard that while Pap served in the Korean War he'd lost his left leg and two toes on his right foot. He figured since Pap had a wooden leg that he could outrun him. What he didn't know was Pap kept a pistol on his lap at every poker game he played, and he could hop as fast as he could run.

"I shot that nigga in his a...a...butt," Pap said, catching his tongue, respectfully glancing at Brenda standing against the wall.

Pap shot Donald once in the butt and took his money back while Donald lay in the middle of Dakota Street bleeding, begging, and pleading for his life. Pap was no killer though. Being in the armed services, he learned just where to shoot.

"I know how to break 'em down without killin' 'em," he said.

He did, however, have a sensitive side. Only Deacon knew that Pap had lost his leg when he'd hesitated to shoot a Korean woman in the field during the war. He would never kill anybody. He just took drastic measures to make anybody who cheated him remember never to do it again.

"I didn't want to make his mama cry," Pap bragged and laughed. "He wasn't the last fool I shot." He bit the tip off his cigar and spat it into an ashtray as he glared into the eyes of a new player sitting at the table.

Brenda loved her uncle Pap. She adored his brave spirit and magnetic personality. She was intrigued by all the action that took place at his house and at the barbershop where he set up poker games.

"Pull up a chair, baby girl. Let me teach you how to whip a nigga and take all his money."

Brenda grinned, gleaming with enthusiasm. She put the bag that dripped juice from the turnip greens on the kitchen counter. Pap nodded to a man who stood in the room and he quickly pulled a chair up to the table for Brenda.

Jake was the youngest player at the table at 28. His father Jacob Sr. and his uncle Blu were both Paps good friends and army buddies. After they both passed away, Pap looked after Jake like he did most of his old friends' kinfolk.

Jake eyed Brenda from head to toe, admiring her youthful, butterscotch complexion, and her wavy black hair. He could tell she was young, but how young, he wondered. He kept his inquisition discreet since he'd just listened to Pap's story about Donald Stacks. He definitely didn't want to get into any disputes about him fancying his young niece.

"Turn on some Retha," another player yelled from the table.

"What?" a voice yelled back.

"I said turn on some Aretha Franklin!" A rough voice repeated.

Brenda had totally forgotten she was supposed to meet her friend, Cheryl. She became so focused on the intensity of the poker game.

"See that," Pap whispered, showing Brenda the cards he had displayed in his hand.

He nodded and winked at her. She nodded and smiled back. The cards enthralled her. She envisioned herself laughing hysterically, winning and raking a pile of money into her bosom. She was elated by the acknowledgment Pap gave her and loved the nickname *Baby girl* he'd called her since she was the youngest of Deacon's two girls. It made her feel loved and protected. Not the kind of love and attention her parents gave her. It was different.

Pap was noted for pinning infamous nicknames on his peers. Sitting across from him was his childhood friend P. Willie. Most people thought the "P" was his first initial and Willie was his last name. His real name was actually Willie Banks. Pap gave him the name Pee Willie when they were kids growing up in Dyersburg, Tennessee. Willie had a weak bladder and would stop to urinate all the time when they ran around playing. He'd do it whenever and wherever he felt the need. They joked about all the "White only" signs on most of the public rest rooms around town so Willie felt defiant. He'd pee in parking lots on white folks' clean white washed tires and in flower and vegetable gardens white folks had planted in their yards. Pap started calling him Pee Willie. The name just stuck with him. P. Willie never complained about it either. He liked the name.

Folks often asked Pap how he got his nickname since his first name was George. Since he was the oldest of four siblings, he looked after his brother and two sisters.

The white, general storeowner where they lived once said, "Boy, you act mo' like the pappy than the brother." Since the storeowner didn't care to know his name, he called him "Pappy" when he wasn't calling him "boy." People around town thought that was his name and some called him "Pap" for short.

Carefully, Brenda continued observing the game and the other players, too. She caught a glimpse of Jake staring at her. They both looked away quickly.

Earleen and Velma, Pap's sisters-in-law, came through the back door. They were both big husky women known for being tough and rough highly-skilled poker players. Earleen was the biggest and the loudest. She stood about six feet tall, stout, with big hands and feet, broad shoulders. Her big breasts perked straight out like a bookshelf. Her gold tooth sparkled when she smiled, and she talked more trash than the city dump could hold. She wouldn't hesitate to tell any man how far in hell he could go or which one of her private parts he could kiss if he pissed her off.

"Hey everybody," Earleen announced, entering the room breasts first. "I need to get in this game and win me some money, honey."

P. Willie got up and Earleen sat in his chair. P. Willie was Earleen's ex-husband, and they couldn't be around each other too long before she would curse him out and belittle him. She was known to curse Willie so bad some said the house would shake and paint would peel off the walls.

"Don't leave on my account, Willie." Earleen smirked. "You owe me some money anyway. As a matter of fact, you owe me for twenty years of misery."

"All right, all right, you want in this game?" Pap said, intervening. He flipped and turned the cards, shuffling them creatively like an artist at work. Earleen continued her rude remarks at Willie. She enjoyed grandstanding in front of people, especially when he wouldn't respond.

Willie had already spent some days in jail for whipping on Earleen and some other days on bed rest from getting whipped by her. Willie hastily backed out of the game, slamming his hand of cards down on the table. He knew from their twenty-year marriage that he had no wins when it came to anything involving her. He divorced her because she'd made him feel like an abused child. Agitated, he flipped his wrist at her and bolted out the back door.

"Ah, Willie, you ain't gots to leave," Earleen said, grinning with satisfaction.

Brenda chuckled. She loved Earleen's spunk. She studied Earleen meticulously, from the way she mixed the cards in her hand to the way she tilted her head to one side surveying each player's moves. The sounds that came from her mouth when she licked her teeth, to the way she curled her lips and blew rings of smoke into the air when she puffed her Lucky Stripes cigarettes all fascinated Brenda.

"Pap, you know your sanctified brother would kill you if he knew you was over here teaching that girl how to gamble," Earleen said, tapping her cigarette ashes into the small glass ashtray. Pap eyed her scornfully and ignored her comment. They were known to argue as much as she and P. Willie did, but Pap wasn't in the mood, and he didn't want Brenda to witness them arguing. He was teaching her to play the game with people like Earleen, whose number one strategy was distraction, and Pap knew it. He kept playing, his lips fixed with a half-smile, and one eye focused on Earleen while still making eye contact with Brenda.

Although Deacon had some idea of Pap's gambling activities, he didn't know the extent of it, and surprisingly, he never banned his kids from being around him or visiting his home. Deacon knew all of his kids loved their uncle Pap. He and Pap had a brotherly respect for each other, and Deacon knew Pap would never allow any harm to come to his children.

Pap didn't have to ask Brenda not to mention the poker game to Deacon. He wasn't worried about it either. He knew how Deacon was trying to raise his kids, but he thought all people should learn something about life outside the church even if they never intended to live it.

"Learning to play poker ain't never hurt anybody. It's when you don't play fair that it gets dangerous," Pap said, projecting a cunning smile.

His opponents all winced, believing his words.

"Gone in the kitchen and get you a soda pop, Baby girl," he added.

Brenda returned to the table with her Dr. Pepper, feeling exuberant and fulfilled as if she had just been given a prize. She was proud of the card tips she'd learned and was anxious to replay the game with Maureen, but the thought quickly vanished when another thought of Deacon's no card, no dice rules entered her mind. She knew her daddy would have convulsions if he found his girls playing poker. *I'll have to play cards at Cheryl's house*, she thought.

"I'm gonna get on home," Brenda said, pulling away from the poker table.

"You got any money in your pockets?" Pap asked, pulling a wad of money he had rubber banded together from his pocket.

"Unh unh," she replied, shaking her head and smiling bashfully.

"Here you go, Baby girl. I want you to always keep some money in your pocket, and when you get old enough to get a man, a real man, make sure he got plenty of money to keep your pockets full, too."

"Thank you, Uncle Pap," she said, accepting the twenty-dollar bill and sliding it down into her pants pocket.

Jake smiled, examining her once again. She noticed his dark wide eyes slowly cruise her body from her small breasts to below her tiny waist. Naively, she paused, returning the stare. Her slight grin and bright eyes revealed her innocence. She was not ready for the advances of a man, especially one nearly twice her age. She quickly turned and made her way out the back door. Jake's eyes followed, trailing her petite frame and developing curves.

Jake's short silky black hair was combed back, the kind they called "Good hair" that black women loved to run their fingers through. He'd been blessed with smooth, blemish free, cocoa brown skin that glowed with one deep dimple on his left cheek. His hypnotic smile and perfectly shaped lips drew women to him. He wore a neat, expensive-looking black and white double-knit sweater. It coordinated with his black, professionally pressed, tailored slacks, and his freshly polished Stacy Adams. He was well put together.

Pap caught Jake's eyes and sharpened his own. For two seconds, their eyes met. Pap squinted, sneering at him with concern. Jake looked down. His eyes leveled only with the top rim of the cards he had spread in his hand. Pap focused on him, pinching his bottom lip between teeth. Pap was a good judge of character. Silently, with a stern eye, he assessed Jake carefully. He knew Jake was much older than Brenda, and Jake's noticeable admiration didn't alarm him too much; it just drew up some caution. He hoped Jake didn't have ill thoughts or intentions regarding his niece, for his own sake. Still, Pap, being the protective uncle he was, felt he needed to keep a close watch on Jake. He kept his mind on Jake, but returned his focus on the card game, puffed his cigar, and exhaled calmly.

CHAPTER FOUR

*B*renda sat with her best friend, Cheryl, on Cheryl's front porch, chatting and giggling like they had done since they were in fifth grade. They'd met when both their families moved from St. John Street to a predominately white, middle-class neighborhood on the North Side, Brenda's family lived in the poor black area across the railroad tracks. Cheryl's family, already on the Northside, had just moved to a bigger house located a few blocks from their last one. As fast as the Colored families moved in, the White residents moved out.

Cheryl and Brenda noticed the big moving truck pull in front of the house across the street.

"Look at them. My daddy said they lived there for twenty years. As soon as we moved in, they put up a for sale sign in their yard. I don't know what they're scared of," Cheryl said.

"I should run over there and say BOO!" Brenda said.

They both laughed.

"Better yet, I'm just going to exercise my civil rights," Cheryl said sarcastically.

"What?" Brenda asked.

Cheryl began punching her closed fist into the air.

"Black power. Power to the people. Say it loud, I'm black and I'm proud," Cheryl said as she pranced around the porch and yard until she collapsed on the grass in laughter.

"Girl, you better stop." Brenda laughed.

"Well, what they gone do, beat us?" She giggled.

"No, but your daddy will."

"Daddy's at work and Mama's at church. I can't wait until Friday. They're gonna be gone to Toledo for the whole weekend to visit my aunt Tilley in the hospital. Me and my brother are staying home. I already told William he could come over."

"Girl, your mama's gonna kill you. You know you can't have boy-company when your mama's not home," Brenda said sarcastically.

"Who's gonna tell her? Not Joseph, 'cause he's always sneaking girls in his room when they're not home." Cheryl shot Brenda a look.

"You know I'm not gone tell." Brenda smiled.

"I know because I told William to bring Karl, too."

"What?" Brenda exclaimed.

"Sure did."

"But I."

"But nothin'. You know you like him, and he likes you, too."

"I do like him, but he has too many girlfriends," Brenda said.

"Those are not girlfriends. They're just girls that like him."

"What about Deniece Nickson?" Brenda asked.

"Humph, them boys just like to look at them big jugs she got bouncing on her chest. I saw her all in his face, walking around, jiggling that big, nasty booty of hers."

Cheryl walked around on the sidewalk in front of her house, imitating Deniece's walk.

Brenda joined in, poking her chest and butt out. "Left, left, right, left."

They both burst into laughter. At the same moment, they noticed Deacon driving past in his Cadillac on his way home from the church a few blocks away. Deacon smiled and waved at them. They waved back at him, holding in their laughter. As soon as he passed them, they burst into laughter again.

"I wonder if your daddy saw us acting a fool." Cheryl giggled.

"Look Cheryl." Brenda tapped Cheryl on her shoulder as she noticed another car coming up the street. It was her friend and classmate, William, driving his dad's Chevrolet. Karl was on the passenger's side. The car slowed down in front of the girls. Karl leaned against the passenger door with his arms dangling outside the car.

"How y'all doing?" Karl smiled as he eyed Brenda from head to toe. The sunlight beamed on Karl's hair, a fresh Caesar cut with natural waves in the crown.

"What y'all doing out here?" William asked.

"Minding our business," Cheryl said.

Brenda smiled bashfully at Karl, looking around at the shrubbery, the street, everything to avoid his eyes. Cheryl stepped off the curb and walked around to the driver's side to talk to William.

"I have to get the car back to my dad," William said.

"I will see you this Saturday?" Cheryl said, smiling at William as she made her way back to the sidewalk. William smiled.

"You gone be here, too?" Karl asked Brenda.

Hesitant to speak and answer his question, Cheryl quickly answered for her, "Yeah, she will be here."

CHAPTER FIVE

*B*renda got up earlier than usual so she could get her Saturday chores done. She didn't want anything to stop her from hanging out with Cheryl or Karl. As soon as she finished mopping the floors and completing her long list of assigned chores, Brenda got dressed, slapped a coat of white shoe polish onto her white sneakers, and rushed out the house to meet up with Cheryl. She was anxious to get together with Karl. They'd laughed and talked all week in the math class they shared. Karl had a sensual smile and a magnetic personality that made Brenda blush and grin from ear-to-ear each time she was in his presence. She couldn't forget the soft kiss he'd planted on her cheek after school.

As soon as Cheryl saw Brenda, she sensed her best friend's excitement and chuckled. "You know," Cheryl said, "other than buck-tooth, Henry, from the fifth grade, Karl is about the only other boy you've liked."

"I didn't like buck-tooth, Henry!" They both laughed.

"I kind of like Victor Simmons. He is handsome, but he is just so wild. He flirted with me, but since he's graduating this year, I don't think he's paying me much attention," Brenda said.

Cheryl heard William and Karl laughing and talking as they walked up the block.

"Here they come," Cheryl announced as she looked outside the screened-in porch. Quickly, they both primped and patted their hair. Cheryl brushed the loose hairs from her shirt. Brenda licked and sucked her teeth, hoping she had rid any evidence of the chocolate cake she had just eaten.

William walked up the steps first. He stood a tall, slender six-foot-three with extremely long arms and big feet; one curl of his chemically straightened, shiny hair flipped down on the right side of his forehead. Karl, much shorter with a stocky physique, carried his hair brush in his hand and brushed his hair every few minutes.

"Can I have one of those?" Cheryl asked William, shifting her eyes toward the Winston-Salem cigarettes protruding from his shirt pocket.

"Girl, you know you don't smoke," William said.

"How you know what I do?" She grinned. "I'm grown and old enough to do what I want to do. Now, give me one."

"All right, grown lady." He chuckled, tapping the tip of the box twice, tilting it forward, and allowing a few cigarettes to stick out.

Cheryl pulled out two cigarettes then handed one to Brenda.

Brenda glanced over at Karl then accepted it willfully. Karl pulled out his own cigarettes then offered everyone his matchbook.

"Come on, y'all," Cheryl said. She glanced to her left then to her right before waving her hands and gesturing them to come inside the house to smoke.

When they finished smoking, Cheryl dashed through the house, squirting her mother's Pearls and Lace perfume into the air, hoping to mask the smell of smoke even though her parents were away for the weekend. Brenda and Karl took a seat on the brown chenille sofa that Cheryl's mother stated she didn't want any kids sitting on while Cheryl and William disappeared into the small den located off the dining room. A small porcelain lamp lit one side of the living room as The Supremes' song "Baby Love" played softly on the large television/stereo that took up the entire left side of the room.

"Why are you smiling so hard?" Karl asked.

"I'm not," Brenda replied, giggling. "Oh yeah, thanks for helping me with my math in class, although I got them ALL wrong!" She smiled, pursing her lips. Karl looked baffled since he considered himself a math whiz.

"Really?" Karl asked, concerned.

"No, I'm just kidding."

Karl sighed with relief.

"You played a good game," Brenda said, praising him on his scores and his skillful moves in the big high school football game between Northern High and Central High that he'd played in the day before.

Karl grabbed her hand and clutched it inside of his, tickling her palm.

"Your hands are so soft," he said, rubbing both her hands between his. Brenda blushed. "And you're so pretty."

"Thank you," Brenda replied in a soft bashful tone.

He leaned in closer to her. She inched back, smiling nervously.

"I know you're not gonna play shy."

"No," she stuttered, nervous. "I'm not."

Playfully, he pulled out a small section of her naturally wavy hair near her temple and twirled it in on his finger, making a ringlet.

"You're messing up my hair," she said, swiping her hair back into place.

He smirked, then inched closer, fidgeting with her ear, gliding his finger along her cheekbone as she blushed. He moved closer, cornering her on the end of the sofa, pressing his chest against hers. He planted his lips firmly against hers, sending a shot of heat through them both.

"Stop," she said, snickering. She pushed him away, but he went for her again, attempting to slide his tongue into her mouth. She had never kissed him or any other boy like that, so she wasn't sure if she was doing it right.

Karl's sixteen-year-old hormones raged, and he didn't waste time talking. His hands led the conversation as they wandered, touching and fondling Brenda. With time, she gained confidence in the kissing process, and they flowed with it pleasurably. Karl's hands found their way inside her white cotton blouse, and then found their way up Brenda's skirt. Brenda panicked and pushed his hands away.

"I don't want to do this," she said nervously, shifting her eyes toward the doorway of the den where Cheryl and William were.

Karl ignored her and continued kissing and pecking her neck hungrily as she squirmed.

"Stop," she said faintly.

Karl persisted with lustful intentions. His hands swarmed her body swiftly. As she closed her eyes and passionately kissed Karl, flashes of her father's lectures engulfed her mind, interfering with the heated moment. Tense, she pushed Karl away and pulled herself up off the sofa.

"Let's play some records," she said, trying to sway Karl's heated mood and calm down.

His faced was smeared with disappointment. She ignored him and put on The Temptation's "Get Ready," and they both got up and sang and danced.

"I love that song," he exclaimed as the music faded off.

Heated and anxious, he grabbed her left hand and twirled her into his arms, embracing her firmly up against his pounding chest and bulging pants.

"Why don't we walk down the street to my house?" he whispered in her ear.

"I don't know." Brenda smiled.

"I got all the jam records at my house."

She smiled as he began naming some of the Motown records he owned.

Suddenly, Cheryl and William erupted from the room.

"Come on, man, it's almost time to go to my little brother's basketball game," William said.

"Ah man, I forgot. Why don't we just hang out here," Karl said, thinking about how far he could get with Brenda.

"Naw, man, I told him we'd be there, and my dad is waiting for us."

Karl sighed with more disappointment as his plans to get Brenda to his house were sorely interrupted. And she was relieved. Kissing Karl and letting him feel her up was one thing, but going all the way with sex was another. She was not ready for that.

"I'll see ya later," Karl said and kissed Brenda on her cheek.

William kissed and hugged Cheryl before he and Karl left.

"Girl, why you look so pale? What did you do?" Cheryl gasped. "What did you and Karl do?"

"Nothin', we didn't do nothin'."

"So you just talked? Yeah right." Cheryl laughed.

"We kissed."

"And that's all?" Cheryl asked suspiciously.

"He was feeling all over me. Then we danced and then…"

"And then what?"

"His..." Brenda said, trying to get the words out.

"His What?"

"His thing was poking me," Brenda whispered.

"His thing?"

"You know what I mean! His...his penis was pressing against his pants. Girl, I thought it was gonna pop out."

They both laughed.

"Girl, if your daddy heard you say that word, he'd beat you 'til Jesus came and tied him up. Say it again, girl." Cheryl chuckled.

They both said the word together."P...P...Penis."

They fell all over each other, laughing hysterically.

"Well, what did you and William do?" Brenda asked. "I didn't hear no talking in that den. All I heard was breathing."

"We kissed."

"Did you ..."

"No," Cheryl replied, cutting into her words.

"Why not? You've already lost your virginity to him."

"'Cause I'm on the rag," Cheryl said sarcastically in that old lady voice she often used.

"Me too." They both buckled over with laughter. "That's funny how we have our periods at the same time."

"I told William to come over next weekend."

"Hmmm," Brenda responded.

"And Karl's coming, too," Cheryl continued.

Brenda didn't say anything; she just looked a little bewildered.

"Why are you looking like that?"

"You know what Karl wants to do."

"Well, why don't you just do it?"

"'Cause I don't want to."

"You scared?"

"Yeah, plus… it might hurt." Brenda folded her arms across her chest.

"You chicken," Cheryl said,

"Well. I ain't fast like you." Brenda shot Cheryl a look.

"Right," Cheryl said. "You like Karl, don't you? Well, don't forget Barbara Collins that's always in his face or Deniece with her big stanky booty. They throw themselves at him, but he likes you."

Brenda thought about the way Karl made her smile when they were in class and the nice words that twirled off his lips and the stars that she saw when she kissed him. Mostly, Brenda thought about the tingling feelings she got when his hands wandered about her body and how much more she liked him.

CHAPTER SIX

*B*renda sat with Cheryl on her front porch as they often did. Just as they were giggling Karl walked up to the house bouncing his basketball.

"Why y'all giggling?" Karl chuckled, still bouncing the ball. "Y'all laughing at me?" The girls tried to contain the snickering. "I'm on my way to the park. Why don't you walk with me, Brenda? It's right down the street."

"I know where the park is, Karl."

"Well, c'mon walk with me."

"No, you go ahead," Brenda said.

Karl kept asking and wouldn't take no for an answer.

"Girl, just go," Cheryl said, giving Brenda a nudge. After a few minutes of hesitation, Brenda agreed to go.

Karl and Brenda stood together in the center of the basketball court since there were no other players around.

"Let me show you some moves," Karl said before showing off his best moves intending to impress Brenda. He laughed as she tried to mimic him.

"This is hard work," Brenda said, wiping the sweat from her forehead with the back of her hand. Karl grabbed her by the hand and escorted her over to a tree where they sat, talked, and laughed. Brenda showed her shyness as Karl kissed her on the cheek. Before long, she gave in to his sensual kisses.

"C'mon, let's walk to my house," Karl said, taking Brenda by the hand. "My mom's cleaning some white folks' house out in Grand Blanc, and my daddy's workin' second shift at Buick."

"I don't know if I should be going to your house," Brenda said as they continued strolling down the sidewalk, approaching his house. She ignored the little voice in her head that told her not to go and kept right on walking. With her hand clutched in his, she walked a step behind him as he cut through a path in his neighbor's yard that led right to the side door of his house. Suddenly, Brenda stopped and let go of his hand.

"I-I don't think I should go in," she stammered. "Your parents are not home."

"C'mon." He grabbed her hand again, grinning mischievously as he pushed open the door, nodding to her to walk in first. She waited in the kitchen while Karl tipped around the house, double-checking to make sure no one was home.

"I'll wait right here," she confirmed.

"Wait for what?" Karl smiled and looked at her for a moment then he kissed her passionately. After that, she no longer hesitated.

Leading Brenda by the hand, Karl headed straight for his upstairs bedroom. They passed through the living room and dining room. The neatly kept home reminded her of her own house. A host of family portraits lined the living room walls above the floral printed sofa. She took special notice to the big portrait of a man in a decorated Army uniform in the middle of the others.

"Is he your brother?" she asked.

"Yeah, that's my big brother, Wallace."

He reminded her of her brothers, Al and Johnny. "Your sister's in my English class," she said, noticing a photo of Karl's younger sister, Victoria.

Karl pushed the door open to his room and flicked the light switch. Brenda looked around the room, admiring his sports trophies before she plopped down in the middle of his twin bed that was covered with a worn handmade quilt.

She worried about what Karl's parents would say if one of them came home and caught her in their house, especially in Karl's bedroom.

Brenda sat quietly, trying to convince herself that all they would do was listen to records.

He took a few minutes sifting through his stack of forty-five records before he played Smokey Robinson and the Miracles' "Tracks of My Tears" on the small record player. Brenda chuckled as he danced comically across the room, attempting to ease her tenseness. Without warning, he shut his bedroom door and turned the skeleton key that clicked and locked loudly. Brenda's expression shifted, and her smile faded. She wanted to get up and run, but at the same time, she wanted to play *big* girl although she was terrified.

Next to Brenda, Karl laid sideways across the bed with his feet dangling off the edge. His hands initiated their true intentions. Brenda's sense of fear enticed him. Her conscience wanted to deny him, but her heart didn't want to disappoint the popular high school star athlete. She knew many foolish girls wouldn't hesitate to give him what he wanted. Plus, he was cute, funny, and he'd told her he liked her a lot.

"Just relax," he said.

Nervously, she gave a half smile as Karl's hands crept slowly up her skirt, frisking her between her legs. She lay stiffly, afraid, but enjoyed the tingle she'd begun to feel between her legs. She tried to relax, taking deep, short breaths, but her anxiety persisted. Instead of sugarplums, visions of her daddy danced through her head. The stuttering words of her Sunday school teacher Mr. Johnson and his lessons on fornication buzzed in her mind. That infamous phrase her mother repeated constantly, "Keep your legs closed," haunted her. She tried hard to erase them all, but the images continued to invade her thoughts. A few scriptures that Deacon recited even bounced in her head.

Oh Lord, what am I doing here? she thought.

She gripped Karl's hands firmly, forcefully pushing him away, but he was stronger and overpowered her.

"Stop pushing me," he whispered.

"But, I'm scared," she admitted, whispering back. The big girl persona was silenced as the sweet church girl was revealed.

"I'm not gonna hurt you. You do want to be my girl, don't you?"

"Yeah," she responded, hunching her shoulders.

"Well, be still and let me have you," he demanded.

Frozen, she glared into his hungry eyes as he worked her pink cotton panties down her legs. They stopped at her knees as she locked them tightly, shivering. Karl yanked them hard one good time and maneuvered them from around her ankles, slinging them to the floor on the side of the bed.

Stressed, she settled her body underneath his. Wet with perspiration, Karl's manhood throbbed against her unopened gift. Her eyes watered. She closed them tightly, grinding her back teeth together in fear. Cautiously, she gave in to his urges, inhaling and exhaling rapidly, embracing him tightly, sinking the tips of all of her fingers into the arch of his back. Within minutes, that to her seemed like hours, those invasive thoughts of her daddy, mama, and Mr. Johnson slowly vanished. She breathed easier, caressing him, massaging his back, but lying still like a frightened little girl. A single tear flowed from the corner of her eye into her soft sideburns. She knew she would never be the same again. Her innocence melted away as her virginity disappeared.

CHAPTER SEVEN

*F*or the past few months, Brenda enjoyed being the live-in babysitter for her aunt Lois, especially during summer vacation. It gave her a chance to be away from all the rules at home. While Lois and her husband, Marshall, worked nights at the Fisher Body Plant, Brenda stayed with their daughters, Sophia and Dawn, after they got out of school since Brenda got home earlier than they did. Her only gripe was that she had to go home on the weekends because Deacon demanded she return to attend church with the family on Sunday.

Lois sat quietly at the kitchen table, peeling potatoes and listened to the irritating sound of Brenda gagging and vomiting in the bathroom located just off the kitchen near the back door. She could hear Brenda sighing heavily each time she flushed the toilet.

With her eyes watery and red and her light complexion pale pink, Brenda walked back into the kitchen.

Lois paused and stared up at her. "Are you pregnant?" she asked bluntly.

"No, noooo," Brenda replied assuredly.

"You don't look well at all." Lois stopped her potato cutting, planted her right elbow on to the table, and rested her hand under her chin.

"Maybe I have the flu or something," Brenda said.

"Hmm," Lois replied suspiciously. She eyed Brenda with concern, doubting that she had the flu.

Uncomfortable with her staring, Brenda turned away. She could tell Lois was thinking something. Lois had been pregnant twice, so she was familiar of all the telltale signs and symptoms.

Lois and Marshall were much younger than Deacon and Kadie and definitely not as strict. Still, Brenda didn't want Lois to know that she'd relinquished her virginity, and the thought of ever getting pregnant had not crossed her mind until that moment. Having an irregular menstrual cycle, being weeks late or even a month late for her period was not unusual, so she hadn't been concerned.

Now fear set in. She thought back on the one intimate experience she had with Karl weeks earlier.

I only did it one time, she thought. *I couldn't be.*

She stood gazing out the kitchen window, her hands fidgeting, twisting the side seams of her plaid, pleated skirt. She tried hard to appear confident that her vomiting could only be from a stomach virus, but she could barely look at Lois.

Brenda occupied herself, removing the dishes from the counter and placing them into the sink. She could feel Lois gawking at her from behind. She cringed.

"I'm going to take you to get a pregnancy test tomorrow," Lois said..

"For what? I'm not pregnant. I couldn't be," Brenda lied.

"Humph." Lois rolled her eyes and resumed peeling the potatoes.

With no further response, Brenda continued washing the dishes.

The next morning, Lois drove Brenda to a medical clinic across town. After an hour wait, the nurse called for Brenda.

Brenda anxiously sat in a chair in the patient room, waiting for the results of the urine test the nurse gave her when she first walked in. She took a deep breath when the door opened and the doctor walked in.

"Congratulations," the tall, slender doctor spoke. "You can go home and tell your husband that you are expecting." Although Brenda looked like a teenager, the doctor didn't question whether she was old enough to have a husband. In the sixties, it wasn't uncommon for teens to wed, especially during the war.

Expecting? Husband? Brenda thought. She sat expressionless as the doctor's words faded, and her face blurred as she imagined herself with a big belly, wearing an old pink bathrobe and run-over slippers. She quivered as images of her daddy with smoke blowing from his ears and fire from his mouth skipped around in her mind.

Without words, Brenda walked back into the waiting room in a daze. Brenda's face said it all, confirming Lois' fears. Together, they walked down the long hallway out the door in silence. To Brenda, the short distance from the building to the car seemed like miles. She had barely enough strength to open the car door. Her face crumbled into a whimpering cry as Lois helped her in the car and made her way back around to the driver's seat. Lois drove home pondering on the situation, shaking her head in disbelief.

"Lawd have mercy," Lois whispered to herself.

"What am I gonna do?" Brenda asked. "Mama and Daddy are gonna kill me. I'm only sixteen, and I'm pr ... na ... I can't even say it."

Back at Lois' house, Brenda plopped down on the sofa, folded her arms, and rested her face on her lap. Lois walked around, looking just as worried as Brenda. She knew how disappointed her sister would be, but more so how angry her brother-in-law would be about his baby daughter being pregnant, out of wedlock. Lois thought about an abortion,

44

but knew that was not an option. She knew the only abortion procedures around there were illegal ones done by somebody's uneducated mama performing unsafe, medical procedures in a back bedroom on the low end of town. Lois had a friend who died during one of those procedures, so that was definitely out of the question.

"For now, I'm going over to Charlotte's house," Lois said. "She has those Quinine pills, and I have some Humphrey Elevens."

"Humphrey what and Qui what?" Brenda questioned.

"They are pills that help you miscarry."

Brenda's eyes bulged with curiosity. "They have pills for that?"

"Well, a...a...just stay here, and I will be right back," Lois replied.

She knew the pills were not medically designed for that purpose, but it was rumored women had success when they used these prescription drugs in efforts of aborting a fetus.

Lois grabbed her keys and rushed out the front door. Solemnly, Brenda sat on the sofa in front of the window. She noticed a young woman walk by pushing a baby carriage.

"Oh God, what have I done?" she yelled.

She felt anxious and jittery. She stood and paced the floor, weeping and mumbling to herself. All the things her mother said and her father preached over the years swam around in her head. The thought of her father finding out weakened her stomach. She rushed to the bathroom, barely reaching the toilet before she vomited. She gagged and cried all at the same time. Drained, she tried to revive herself, splashing cold water from the faucet onto her face. She grabbed a towel from the rack behind the bathroom

45

door and patted her face. Exhausted, she sat down on the rim of the bathtub.

"Lord, I am so sorry." She sobbed and sank her face deep into the towel and cried harder.

She pulled herself together enough to answer the telephone after the fourth ring.

"Hi Mama," she said nervously, hearing Kadie's voice. Her heart dropped and a piercing sensation flushed through her body, anchoring at the tips of her toes.

Oh no, does she know? Did Lois go tell her? Brenda thought.

The tension soared giving her an instant headache.

"I was just calling to remind you about the youth meeting at church this evening."

"OK, Mama." She exhaled slowly with some relief as she hung up the phone. Church was definitely the last thing on Brenda's mind.

By now, her headache was so intense that she desperately needed to find some relief. She scrambled through the house searching for aspirin, looking in the medicine cabinet and the kitchen cabinets to no avail.

Brenda searched Lois' bedroom, her dresser, neatly decorated with perfume bottles, fragrant powders, tubes of lipstick, and a large white jewelry box in the center of the dresser. Brenda pulled open the first dresser drawer. She noticed a brown prescription bottle with the inscription Humphrey Eleven typed on it. With the bottle in one hand, she paused, thinking. She remembered this was one of the pills Lois told her about. She was desperate enough to make her problem go away immediately. She figured since Lois had already told her she was going to give her the pills that she would go ahead and just take some without any instructions. Quickly, Brenda opened the bottle and poured two pills and then one more into her other hand.

"I have to do this," she whispered.

She rushed into the living room and looked out the window to make sure Lois had not pulled back into the driveway. She dashed back into the kitchen, turned on the faucet, grabbed a cup, and filled it with water. Without hesitation, she popped the pills into her mouth and gulped down the full cup of water. She gagged a few times, but swallowed them all.

"God, please forgive me," she sobbed.

Fatigued by the events of the day, she lay back on the sofa and pondered the situation before dozing off to sleep. She tossed and turned for nearly an hour as the pills began to take effect, elevating her body temperature. She felt light as if she was floating. To her, the sounds of kids playing outside, the traffic, and the neighbor's dog barking seemed to be right in the living room. She felt the room spinning and turning, slowly then fast. Suddenly, she sprang up in a cold sweat. Wired, she rocked back and forth, biting her thumbnail. She wiped the sweat from her forehead then wiped her hand on her skirt.

Lois sped into the driveway and rushed in the front door. She stopped and observed Brenda's condition. "What's wrong with you?" she asked. "What happened?"

"Nothing," Brenda answered, still biting her nails.

"You look dazed."

Brenda continued rocking. "I have the Quinine pills. You're gonna have to take this with gin."

"Gin, you mean like alcohol?" Brenda asked.

Brenda's eyebrows drew together with three creases on her forehead. The pills plus the gin were supposed to be part of the potion for a miscarriage. Lois went into the kitchen to pour Brenda a glass of Gorton's Gin and came back.

"Here. I'm only going to give you two pills for now. Let's just see how you take to them," Lois said as she handed her the glass. Brenda still didn't mention that she had just taken the pills she thought were Humphrey Eleven. She was willing to do whatever it took to get rid of the fetus. She took the pills, gobbled the gin fast, and let out a long sigh.

"I will give you the Humphrey Eleven's a little later," Lois said.

"Well, I... I... I took some of those already," she hesitantly admitted.

"What?" Lois sounded furious.

"I was looking for something for my headache and found them in your dresser drawer."

"Oh my God," Lois screamed.

The thought of slapping and choking Brenda raced through her mind. She squinted her eyes, tightened her lips, and gritted her teeth, standing with both hands resting on her forehead.

"You said you were gonna give them to me," Brenda said, "So I took them since I couldn't find any aspirin."

Lois exhaled in frustration. A truckload of profanity swarmed inside her as she inflated her jaws with air and then released it like a deflating balloon. She controlled herself, realizing that the expletive expressions would be useless.

"First of all," Lois chastised, "you had no business rambling through my drawers. Those pills are not Humphrey Eleven's. They are pain pills I just put in that bottle. I wouldn't have given you both at the same time!"

"I'm sorry," Brenda replied.

"How many did you take?"

"I ... took three."

"Three? Oh my God. How are you feeling?"

"Well, I did feel kind of funny, and I was sweating."

"That's it," Lois yelled. "I'm not giving you nothin' else. The last thing I need for you to do is die on me. Your mama and daddy are gonna kill me, and you! I can't believe I am even doing this for you. I'm gonna call Aunt Margie, and ask her what to do about this situation 'cause you gonna give me a nervous breakdown. I'm gonna have to keep an eye on you. I don't know whether I should get you to the hospital or let you sleep it off. Dammit, girl!"

Lois was real mad at Brenda, but she could understand what she was going through and how badly she didn't want Deacon and Kadie to find out. Lois hated to lie to her sister, but she knew she had to come up with something to get Brenda out of having to go to a special youth meeting at church that evening. Lois told Kadie she and Marshall had to go check on his mother who was very ill and that they really needed Brenda to babysit for them. Deacon reluctantly agreed and took Maureen to church as usual.

Lois propped herself up in the corner chair in the living room with three pillows and a blanket as Brenda lay on the sofa. She sat there all night monitoring Brenda. She wondered if all the pills would have an ill effect on her. She prayed about it. She knew that if Brenda gave any indication that she was ill from the pills, she would immediately rush her to the emergency room.

***

"My back hurts, and I can hardly move my neck, sleeping on that sofa all night," Brenda said, stretching and rubbing the sleep from her eyes.

49

"How are you feeling, any spotting?" Lois asked.

"Spotting?" Brenda questioned.

"Bleeding?"

"No," Brenda answered, disappointed.

"I talked to Aunt Margie this morning. She told me not to give you any more pills if they didn't work. She told me to take you to the doctor and have you tell him that your husband is coming home from Vietnam, and you messed around with another man and got pregnant." Baffled, Brenda's eyes widened and her mouth drew open. She couldn't believe how fast her life had turned so badly.

Doctor Southgate was known among the black women in the community as a doctor that gave injections or prescriptions to women that wanted to end an early pregnancy.

On the way to Dr. Southgate, Lois prepped Brenda on what to say.

"Fix yourself up, girl." Lois pulled her pressed powder and lipstick from her purse and handed it to Brenda. "And here. Put this on." Lois took off her wedding band and tossed it to her.

Brenda paused, staring at the ring before putting it on her finger. She was still baffled about the whole thing and all the trouble Lois was going through to help her through it.

"Here goes," Lois said as they entered the door of the small brick building.

Brenda was too nervous to look at the doctor. She fidgeted with the wedding band on her finger as she spoke in a quivering voice, telling Dr. Southgate word-for-word what Lois told her to say. He assured her the injection he would give her would deliver the result she wanted.

After the injection, he told her, "Now go home and sit in a tub of hot water."

As soon as she got back to Lois' house, Brenda rushed into the bathroom to fill the tub with water.

Later that night, Brenda got excited, and felt relief when she saw the small blood stains in her panties. She rushed into the living room where Lois was watching TV since she had called in sick that night.

"I'm spotting, I'm spotting," Brenda shouted. She realized she'd been shouting and whispered,"I'm spotting."

Lois didn't really know how to respond. She felt guilty knowing her suggestions were not the most positive, but she wanted the whole thing to be over as much as Brenda did.

"Just go lie down and we'll see what happens," Lois said. She felt exhausted from working long hours and from the sleepless nights dealing with Brenda. Brenda went to bed in one of the girls' twin beds and Lois waited on the sofa for Marshall to come home.

Brenda barely slept that night as she constantly went back and forth to the bathroom, checking her underwear for more bloody evidence. She rubbed her stomach, anticipating the painful menstrual-like cramps that Lois told her to expect, and waited and waited.

At six a.m. the rain came down hard. The broken rain gutter continuously slapped the aluminum siding at the rear of the house. To Brenda, each whack felt like it was beating her own the back. She was stressed and worried. Since Dr. Southgate told her to give it at least twenty-four hours to see some results, she waited well into the next afternoon. She had made at least fifteen trips to the bathroom, but there was no more blood, not even a drop, and no abdominal cramps. All she had was a "no sleep" headache and tattered nerves that made her fidgety.

Lois' bedroom was right next to the bathroom. Once she went to bed, she heard Brenda going back and forth, opening and closing the bathroom door all night, but she was so tired she didn't bother to get up. She knew Brenda would get her up if anything significant happened.

Lois pulled herself out of bed late to get her morning coffee. She met Brenda in the hallway. She noticed that Brenda's eyes and nose were puffy and red.

"Well?" Lois asked. Brenda shrugged and hung her head as she rested her back against the wall. She didn't have to say anything. Lois knew.

Gently, Lois took Brenda by the arm and escorted her to the kitchen.

"What are we gonna do now?" Brenda asked as she sat down at the table.

Lois turned on the water faucet and filled the kettle.

"*We* ain't gonna do nothin'," Lois said as she placed the kettle down on the left front burner. Lois knew there wasn't anything else she could do, or wanted to do, especially if it was going to jeopardize Brenda's health.

Brenda's eyes watered, as she sniffled and wiped her wrist across her nose. Lois reached for the matchbox on the wall shelf and lit the pilot on the gas stove and swayed back as the flame blew up fast.

"Looks like you're gonna be a mother," Lois said.

Brenda squeezed her eyes shut and allowed the tears to roll down her cheeks. Her heart pounded to the same beat of her father's footsteps whenever he rushed down the basement staircase. Her stomach fluttered like an ocean at high tide. She felt the need to cry out loud, but she held it deep in her gut, afraid she would wake Uncle Marshall and the girls.

"Ain't no sense in crying now. Sometimes life takes us on a train ride that we don't ask to go on, but we have to ride it to get to the next stop."

"But why did this have to happen to me? I should have never ..." Brenda stopped mid-sentence thinking back to the intimate session with Karl.

"I don't have all the answers, but I do know things happen for a reason, especially if you do all you know how to change them and they still don't change. Then that's just how God meant it to be."

"This can't be what God wants for me. It just can't be," Brenda said firmly as she stood in front of the table.

"Well what else you thinking about doing?"

"I don't know, but I got to do something."

The hail of tears that she fought to hold back finally gave way. Simultaneously, the kettle whistled and Brenda let out a howl, waking the sleeping girls and her uncle. She covered her face and tried to muffle the sounds of her tearful frustration.

"Is everything all right in there?" Marshall yelled out from the bedroom.

"Everything is fine," Lois yelled back. "Sit down," Lois said to Brenda, pulling the chair out to the center of the kitchen. "You better pull yourself together. Your daddy will be here to pick you up so that you can get ready for church tomorrow."

Brenda dreaded the thought of going home. "I'm not going to church tomorrow, and I'm not going home either. Please, tell him I'm sick or something."

"Huh?" Lois frowned.

Sophia and Dawn ran into the kitchen happy and energetic like they did every morning. "Ring-a-round the rosy, ring-a-round the rosy," they chanted as they circled Brenda sitting in the chair.

"Go play, girls, go play," Lois said, shushing the girls out of the kitchen. When the girls ran off, she added, "I am not gonna lie to your daddy. He's so holy he's liable to see right through me. And I'll get struck down right in the middle of the lie. No missy, you gone have to face your mama and daddy."

Brenda sunk her face into her hands and cried more. "I can't go through with this."

"It's nothing you can do, but deal with it. You gone have to tell Kadie."

A few hours later, Brenda pulled herself together and got dressed. Deacon pulled up and honked his horn. Brenda took a deep breath and exhaled. She looked over at Lois sitting in the kitchen chair and Lois shot her back a look.

"You're going to be OK, Brenda."

CHAPTER EIGHT

A week passed, and Brenda still hadn't told Kadie or anyone else about her pregnancy. She laid on her bed for hours listening to the radio that played softly from the nightstand next to her bed. She stood up in front of the mirror and gazed at her belly. Even though it was too early in the pregnancy to show, she knew time was winding down and she would have to break the news.

"How am I gonna explain this?" she whispered.

"You talking to yourself?" Maureen asked as she walked in their bedroom and caught Brenda in the mirror.

"No, I'm not talking to myself."

Brenda, not in the mood for a conversation with Maureen, wanted her to stop looking at her before she figured out the true reason she stood staring at herself in the mirror. Brenda lay back down on her twin bed, pulled the blanket up over her, and turned over as if going to sleep.

Kadie noticed the increase in Brenda's appetite, but she first passed it off as maybe she wasn't eating much at Lois' house. But then her mother's intuition kicked in. Brenda wasn't showing at all, but there were signs: Brenda's frequent bathroom trips, the oversized plate of roast beef and potato salad that revved up her suspicion, fullness of Brenda's face and breasts.

Her mind wandered from Brenda to the door as someone knocked. Seeing Teddy, Brenda's friend from church, Kadie smiled. She went to the bottom of the stairs and yelled for Brenda to come down.

Teddy visited Brenda a few times since she had her sixteenth birthday, the official eligibility age to receive company from boys, according to Deacon. Kadie was especially fond of Teddy since he was from a well-respected family and his father, Reverend Theodore Carter, was one of the associate pastors at the church.

Teddy and Brenda chatted a bit on the front porch, but Brenda wasn't much for company that day. Besides, she didn't feel the same attraction that Teddy felt for her.

Brenda went into the kitchen to cut herself a piece of the German Chocolate cake Kadie made. She tried to act normal, making small talk with her mother, but Kadie wasn't much for conversation that day either. She had spoken to Lois minutes earlier, and Lois admitted that Brenda was pregnant, confirming her suspicion. Kadie was furious and hurt since she believed Brenda was still a virgin. The thought of her baby girl pregnant and out of wedlock sickened her. She immediately needed to whip up a homemade antacid.

She opened the cabinet and grabbed a glass, filling it with water from the faucet. She pulled the box of baking soda from the refrigerator, and scooping out two tablespoons of it, she stirred them into the glass of water. She wondered how she'd deal with this and worse how would she tell Deacon.

"Lord, have mercy," she whispered to herself.

Kadie tried to stay calm, waiting to see if Brenda would come right out and tell her she was pregnant. Brenda had been a little fidgety when she spoke to Kadie. She hurried to get a glass of milk from the refrigerator to go with the cake. She talked to Kadie as she stood with the refrigerator door open where Kadie could only see her head as she spoke.

"Mama, Teddy's going into the Army," Brenda said with a nervous giggle, "and he says he wants to marry me before he goes." She closed the refrigerator door.

Kadie stopped, rolled her eyes, and released a long sigh.

"Humph, why would you marry him?" Kadie asked firmly. "He's not the one you're pregnant by."

Brenda's giggle halted and her expression paused as if her face had been dipped in cement. She nearly dropped the glass of milk and the saucer with the cake.

"Huh I ... I'm not. You know I don't do stuff like that," Brenda replied.

"Really," Kadie said, staring right into Brenda's eyes.

Brenda couldn't seem to muster another word. She sat the glass of milk and cake on the dining room table. She broke into tears and ran back upstairs to her bedroom and shut the door behind her. Maureen had left the room to do laundry, so Brenda was alone. Nauseated, she felt like she would fall face-first right down on the hardwood floor. She gripped the doorknob to brace herself. With her back pressed against the door, she slid down to the floor and buried her face between her knees, gripping her head with her hands.

"How can this be happening?" she rambled to herself.

She crawled toward her bed and lay on the small tweed rug on the floor. She heard footsteps and knew Kadie was coming toward her room. She sat up and wiped away the tears that had swelled in her eyes.

"Brenda, are you ready to tell me the truth?" Kadie asked as she opened the door halfway. Brenda sat in silence, her face red and swollen. "I know that you're pregnant," Kadie said in soft tone, shutting the door behind her.

"Aunt Lois told you?"

"Well, put it this way, she confirmed my suspicions."

"Mama, I didn't mean for this to happen," Brenda said tearfully.

"I know you didn't mean for this to happen, but it did, and now we have to deal with it." After a long pause, Kadie stuttered, "Well, who did ... I mean who is..."

"Karl," Brenda said, cutting into her mother's question. "Karl is the only one, and it only happened one time."

"Not only am I hurt, but I am also very disappointed in you." Kadie's eyes watered.

"I know, Mama." Brenda lowered her head.

"You're only sixteen. Having a baby ... out of wedlock." Kadie sighed and shook her head. "Lord have mercy." Kadie gripped her stomach.

"I know, Mama. I will go to one of those places where they get rid of the baby."

"I don't know about that, Brenda," Kadie said. She didn't want her to be pregnant, but an abortion was totally against everything she and Deacon believed in. Brenda didn't tell her about all the pills she had taken at Lois' house, and it appeared Lois hadn't told Kadie that part either.

"I don't know how your daddy is going to react to this."

"Please don't tell him," Brenda pleaded.

"Believe me, if I don't tell him, time will," Kadie said as she exited the room.

Brenda stayed put in her room. She knew it was just a matter of time before everyone would know. She slid out the Hershey bar she had hidden under her pillow and ate it quickly then she cried herself to sleep, worried about what Deacon would say when he found out.

CHAPTER NINE

*D*eacon Wilson came home from work early that day. Kadie waited until after he'd eaten his dinner and went into the bedroom before she told him about Brenda.

Maureen nearly dropped the dish she was washing when she heard her father's loud voice yell from his bedroom. Kadie tried to calm him, but it was obvious that he was extremely angry.

Maureen dashed up the stairs and stormed in the bedroom.

"What in the world did you do?" she asked. Her face was flushed. Brenda ignored her. "Answer me! I heard Daddy yelling *your* name. What did you do to make him so mad?"

"Brenda, get down here!" Deacon Wilson shouted.

"Oh, God," Brenda whined. Tensed, she clenched her fists and walked slowly toward the staircase. Maureen followed behind her, anxious to know what was going on.

"Speed it up, girl, before my shoes scrape the skin right off your ankles," Maureen said. Brenda continued to ignore her and kept walking slowly, hesitantly anticipating the showdown she knew she would encounter once she was face-to-face with Deacon.

"Have a seat, Brenda," Deacon Wilson said in a stern tone. He sat at the head of the dining room table. Kadie stood catty-corner in the doorway while Maureen stood guard with her back against the wall, her hands resting on her hips, eager to find out what Brenda had done.

Shaking, with her head down, Brenda pulled the chair back and sat down. Her eyes focused on the green linen placemat that sat neatly on the table in front of her. She placed her sweaty palms flat down on the placemat, hoping the linen would help absorb the sweat that seemed to pour from all over her body. Deacon Wilson shook his head a moment before he spoke. The silence drew a lump in his throat.

"Em, em, em," he said, his disappointment obvious. The anger and hurt were visible in his eyes and in his wordless expression. He stuttered, trying to find the right words to say. "W-why, how could you let this happen?" he asked. "How could you do this to us? You know what the Bible says about fornication and you done got yourself pregnant!"

Brenda cringed. Maureen gasped, and her mouth drew wide open as she covered her lips with both hands.

"Well, she didn't get that way by herself," Kadie interjected.

"Em, em, em," Deacon repeated, shaking his head again.

"Maureen, you can excuse yourself while we deal with Brenda," Deacon Wilson said. In silence Maureen stepped out of the room, to where she was out of sight, but nearby so she could still hear the conversation. She stood with her ear near the door.

"You're just sixteen. You know what they call babies of unmarried women? Bastards, that's what they call 'em!"

Brenda cried, breaking her silence. "Daddy, I'm...I'm sorry. I could go to one of those places to have an a ... abor..."

"Abortion?" he yelled, cutting into her words. Kadie hung her head.

"Lord knows I am very disappointed in you. You are ruined. You will never have what your mother and I wanted for you. You're not about to get any lower by having an abortion. Abortion is murder, and one sin can't cover another," Deacon responded. Deacon's words penetrated deep in Brenda's stomach, she felt the need to rush to the toilet to vomit, but she held it in. "The Bible says thou shall not kill, and that we won't do. You also won't have a bastard child." He pounded his fist on the table, startling Kadie and Maureen who stood outside the door.

"We gone have to let God deal with you, and I'm gone deal with … what's the boy's name, Brenda?"

Brenda was crying so hard she couldn't speak.

"Karl, Daddy," Maureen answered from the other room. She rushed back into the room. "His name is Karl, right?" she added, turning to ask Brenda. Brenda nodded her head and rolled her eyes at Maureen. Maureen heard Brenda and Cheryl on the telephone talk often about Karl, and she saw them walking together at school. "Karl Hamilton," Maureen added, handing Brenda a few tissues from the box that sat at the other end of the table. Brenda let the tissues drop on the table. Her hatred for her sister's meddlesome ways was apparent.

"Maureen?" Kadie said, eyeing her daughter.

"Yes, Mama?"

"You have five seconds to leave this room and not return. Stop being so nosy. This does not concern you."

The room remained quiet as Maureen shuffled her feet and left the room.

"I'm going to see this Karl and his daddy," Deacon said. "I want to know what they gonna do about this." Brenda's eyes widened as she lifted her head with concern. "Where about does this Karl live?" he asked, curling his lips and gritting his teeth.

Brenda was too stunned to speak. Finally, she muttered, "Down on Jackson Street near Bonbright."

"Don't you go down there starting no ruckus, John," Kadie said.

"What do you mean? That little ..." Deacon caught his words. "Done got my baby girl pregnant. It's only gone be ruckus if he don't do something about it."

"Well, what you suppose he's gone do now?" Kadie asked.

"Marry her! That's the only way," Deacon spoke firmly.

Brenda collapsed her upper body right down on the table and let loose a whirl of tears and moans.

"Oh Lawd," Kadie exclaimed, throwing her hands in the air. She slipped on her shoes and grabbed her purse. "I'm going with you. You're gone get yourself in a world of trouble going to folks' house like this."

Deacon snatched opened the second drawer of the China cabinet and pulled out his shotgun shells then disappeared to the basement. Kadie rushed behind him.

"John, we're not down south. There's a better way to handle this. Don't you go getting that shotgun."

"You just hope I don't have to use it," he said, making his way back to the dining room carrying his double barrel shotgun. Shooting an angry glare at Brenda, he said, "Come on. You're showing me where this boy lives."

Brenda twisted her face and sniffled as more tears flowed heavily from her eyes.

"Please Daddy, please don't make me go," Brenda sobbed.

"I said get your shoes, girl. You ashamed now, huh? Well, you wasn't ashamed when you was laying up with him."

Tears blurred her vision as she walked around dazed, looking for her shoes.

"I don't want no trouble, John," Kadie expressed.

He ignored her, took the shotgun out the back door, and secured it in the trunk of his car.

"Jesus," Kadie shouted, tucking her purse under her arm then trailing out behind him.

Brenda walked out last, slowly, and still trying to put the shoes on her feet.

Sensing the coast was clear, Maureen ran to the window to watch them drive away.

***

Deacon slowed down as he pulled onto Jackson Street. "Where is the house?" Deacon yelled to Brenda who sat in the backseat.

"Right there," she replied, pointing to the green house with the bright yellow trim.

Deacon pulled his blue '67 Cadillac into the Hamilton's driveway.

"John, now you supposed to be a man of God. Don't you get over here showing out like the devil."

Again, he ignored Kadie and bolted out of the car, slamming his door behind him. He started toward the trunk but the ride over had helped him to at least think rationally. He decided to leave the shotgun in the trunk and hoped the conversation turned out to be a good one so he didn't have to rush back to the car to get it.

Kadie walked behind him up the driveway. Brenda waited in the car.

"John, please … stay calm," Kadie said just as he drew his hand up to knock at the Hamilton's door.

Karl's mother, Lillian opened the door half way.

"Mrs. Hamilton?" Deacon asked.

"Yes."

"How ya do, ma'am? My name is John Wilson. This is my wife, Kadie. I'd like to talk to Mr. Hamilton, please," Deacon spoke hard and as calm as he could be.

"Your son Karl's been seeing my daughter," Kadie added.

"C'mon in." Lillian was a little hesitant, but opened the door for them.

Deacon Wilson took off his hat as he walked into the Hamilton's home respectfully, just as he did when he entered anyone else's home or church.

Lillian didn't know what this was about, but she knew she needed to get her husband in the room quickly.

Mr. Hamilton, a tall, slender man, entered the kitchen where Deacon and Kadie waited. His low cut hair was gray and receding with a shiny ball spot on the top of his head. His dingy, white T-shirt hung loosely over his brown gabardine slacks. His feet were noticeably large as he walked on the back ends of his black leather bedroom shoes.

Lillian shot him a look as to say he could have fixed himself up better before coming to the door.

His voice loud and rough, he asked "What can I do for you?"

"I'm here to talk to you about your son, Karl," Deacon replied.

Lillian stood near the door, anxious to know what Deacon and his wife had to say about their son.

"What is this about?" Mr. Hamilton asked, frowning.

"My daughter Brenda is … is pregnant, and she said your son Karl had something to do with it. Now I want to know what he plans to do about it."

Lillian's mouth dropped open. She rushed through the house, calling for Karl.

"Yes, ma'am," Karl replied from the top of the staircase.

"Get down here now," Mr. Hamilton yelled. Karl quickly dashed down the stairs to the kitchen. He had never met Brenda's parents, so he didn't know who they were.

"Boy, you've been messing around with their daughter?" Mr. Hamilton asked.

Karl was speechless.

"Brenda," Deacon Wilson confirmed.

"She's pregnant!" Mr. Hamilton said, tightening his lips.

"And I expect you to marry her," Deacon Wilson blurted.

Karl was stunned, standing there, stone-faced.

"Now, wait a minute. Why should we believe that our son got your daughter pregnant?" Lillian spoke firmly.

"So what are you trying to say?" Kadie asked, raising her voice, staring Lillian in her eyes.

"Hold on here. He hasn't opened his mouth," Deacon Wilson said, staring right at Karl.

"Well, speak up boy," Mr. Hamilton demanded.

"It only happened one time," Karl blurted.

"Obviously, that's all it took," Kadie interjected, rolling her eyes.

"I didn't mean for this to happen," Karl said, "and I … I don't want to get married." Karl's nonchalant response made Deacon Wilson angrier. He wiped the sweat that shined above his brow and blew spurts of hot air from his mouth. Kadie had never seen him this angry before.

"So that's it, huh," Deacon Wilson expressed, twitching his lips and staring into Karl's eyes. Deacon's skin was a caramel color, but at that moment, the anger that swelled up inside him caused his skin tone to turn a plum burgundy. He tried to contain himself, but the thought of the shame brought to his daughter and to himself enraged him. The thought of the respect he had from his family and from his church worried him.

"I'm graduating this year and going to college," Karl spoke firmly. Deacon Wilson was furious as he puffed up and lashed out at Karl. In that angry moment, Deacon's good Christian integrity was silenced and his flesh ruled. He was a hurt man, a father.

"John," Kadie yelled as she pulled Deacon away from Karl.

"You ruined my daughter," he yelled, spewing speckles of spit from his mouth. Anger and disappointment were heard clearly in Deacon's voice.

Kadie pulled Deacon back, securing her chest against his back and gripping her arms tightly around his waist.

"I think you all better be leaving," Lillian said as she stood guard in front of Karl, protecting him from the whipping Deacon was eager to put on him.

"Yes, we can deal with this later," Mr. Hamilton said.

"Later? My daughter is pregnant," Deacon started in loud, but quickly lowered his voice, trying hard to regain his good character.

"Let's go," Kadie said, pulling Deacon away, feeling their attempt to get any consolation was useless.

Deacon slapped his thin brim hat on his head as he exited the Hamilton's kitchen.

He stepped hard toward the car, but Kadie thought he was going for the trunk.

"No, John!" she yelled.

Deacon halted his vengeful thoughts and got into the car. Normally, he was a gentleman and opened the car door for Kadie, but not this day. He was just too mad.

"Calm down, John," Kadie pleaded as she slid onto the passenger seat of the car. She barely pulled her feet in all the way before he started the engine and shifted to reverse. Deacon Wilson fumed. Kadie knew it was best she just kept quiet. Brenda covered her face with her hands and lay down on the back seat. A swirl of emotions fluttered through her insides.

Deacon sped through the few blocks back to his house, barely pausing at the stop signs on the way. He barged into his own driveway, scraping the metal underneath the trunk on the pavement. Kadie and Brenda walked in the house first while Deacon took time to remove the shotgun from the trunk and put it back in the cabinet in the basement.

The rest of the evening was solemn as everyone in the house tended to his or her own business. In silence, Kadie and Deacon retreated to their bedroom. Deacon wondered to himself if he had been a good father and if he had *trained up* his kid's right according to the Bible. He imagined what the church folks would say once they found out. The gray hairs on his back rose with the thought of his baby girl walking around the house with a big belly. The thought of sending her to his mother's house in Tennessee during the pregnancy crossed his mind but quickly diminished. Mostly, he thought about Karl and how he wanted to wrap his hands around his neck and choke him for not wanting to marry his daughter. His mind flooded with negative thoughts of how he believed Brenda's future would be with a baby and no husband. Because she would have a bastard child, he believed that her life was ruined and that no other man would want her.

Silence loomed the air in their bedroom as Kadie took to folding the laundry she hadn't finished earlier, trying to ease her own mind. After Deacon undressed and put on his plaid cotton pajamas, he slipped into bed and propped up two pillows behind him. He pulled his Bible from the nightstand and flipped through it, searching for the Holy words that he knew could soothe him.

Kadie began to hum her favorite hymn until she couldn't resist voicing her thoughts. "John, you know this is not our fault. I know we've done well with our four children. We've been married twenty-two years, and I know how you think. You digging into that Bible, trying to find where you went wrong. Humph, you know that everything happens for a reason."

"I didn't want to see my baby girl having no babies before she was married, especially by a man that don't want her," Deacon said.

"But you know that the Bible says that all things work together for the good of them that love God. You just have to believe that. Who knows who this child is going to be and why the Lord allows things to happen the way He does. You just as well accept it."

Deacon paused and raised his eyes toward her. He smirked and offered no comment then returned his attention back to the scriptures on the page. Kadie smiled, believing that he had taken in what she'd said.

"I know who to trust in," she added as she walked out of the room, singing softly.

"Take your burdens to the Lord and leave them there," she sang, rocking her head back and forth to the melody.

Brenda lay in her bed, tucked under her blankets, curled into a fetal position. Maureen sat in the corner at the small desk, finishing up letters she had written to Johnny and Al. This was juicy family business that she knew they would want to hear about while stationed in Vietnam. She couldn't wait to drop them in the mail.

"Girl, you gone be a mama," Maureen said, grinning, licking the last stamp, and pressing it onto the envelope, "and I'm gone be an auntie!"

CHAPTER TEN

*S*aturday rolled around again. Seemed like the weeks came and went faster and faster. Already into her third month, Brenda's clothes began to fit a little snugly. With the X-large shirts she'd borrowed from Uncle Marshall's closet, she was still able to conceal any evidence of the precious being that grew inside her.

Brenda made herself, Sophia, and Dawn some bacon and eggs and helped the girls get dressed while Lois and Marshal slept in. She had missed the last few Sundays of church and the weekly youth meeting. Due to the circumstances, Deacon and Kadie hadn't made a big thing about it. They all knew it wouldn't be long before everyone outside of the family would find out about the pregnancy. They were still dealing with the fact themselves.

That day was also Kadie's birthday. Maureen and Brenda always made her a cake and cooked a special dinner for her, so Brenda knew she'd be going home that day.

Brenda handed Sophia and Dawn a cup of milk and cleaned up the kitchen. She removed the twenty-five, one-dollar bills from the table that Lois left for her as payment for babysitting the girls that week. She wiped her damp hands on the red and white checkered dishtowel and counted her money. She thought about buying new shoes since her feet had swollen so that her shoes were too tight. She slid the money down into her girlish black patent leather purse and wiped Sophia's and Dawn's hands and mouths before than ran off to play.

Deacon pulled up in the driveway and honked his horn for Brenda to come out.

"I'm leaving," she yelled out to Lois, gathering her things that were bagged and piled on the sofa. Lois came from her bedroom, tying the belt of the lime green bathrobe she had on. The pink scarf she wore on her head barely covered her silky long hair that dangled around her ears and down the center of her back.

"You be good. I guess it's kinda late to say that." Lois chuckled.

"I'm still good, just made a mess of things," Brenda replied.

"Everything is gonna be fine."

Brenda smiled and walked out the front door.

Lois locked the door behind her and hoped what she said to Brenda would be true.

The whole thing was still hard for Deacon even though he was trying to come to terms with what was to come. On the drive home, Deacon and Brenda both sat quietly in the car across from each other. Lately, whenever Brenda was in the presence of Deacon, her nerves balled up like hard rocks tumbling about inside her stomach. Brenda kept her eyes on the scenery outside the car and the cars passing by. She swallowed the excess saliva that insisted on forming in her mouth. She couldn't manage to muster a single word the whole fifteen minutes it took to get home, and Deacon didn't say a word either. As soon as he pulled in the driveway and put the car in park, Brenda grabbed her things and rushed into the house.

Maureen scurried around in the kitchen, wearing the purple apron she made in her home economics class. The smell of baked chicken and cabbage spread throughout the house. The chocolate fudge cake she made from scratch graced the center of the dining room table. She didn't bother making the cornbread since she could never seem to fix it right, but Brenda could. Brenda had her very own way of making the fluffiest golden yellow cornbread that raised compliments by anyone that ate it.

"I left the cornbread for you to make," Maureen said.

Brenda had felt so betrayed by Maureen that they hadn't spoken much lately. Kadie's birthday was always a big event in the family, and working in the kitchen together was a way for them to at least break the ice. Brenda dropped her bags on the floor in the corner of the dining room, washed her hands, and joined in the cooking.

Brenda worked silently, stirring up the ingredients for the cornbread. Maureen kept trying to make small talk to lessen the awkwardness between them. Brenda didn't want to say anything about the baby, but Maureen was itching to talk about it.

"I can't believe I'm going to be an auntie. What are we going to name our baby?"

Brenda frowned, hunching her shoulders. "How about Lydia if it's a girl and Raymond if it's a boy?"

"No, those are about the ugliest baby names I ever heard." Brenda chuckled, finally breaking her silence and the awkwardness.

"If it's a girl, I'm gone dress her up real pretty and comb her hair and put bows on her." Maureen chuckled.

"But what if it's a boy who acts like Johnny?"

"Well, I'll just be whipping his little butt!" They both laughed.

Kadie peeked into the kitchen from the door adjoined to the dining room. She heard her daughters laughing, and the sound pleased her. They pleasantly worked in the kitchen *together* using many of the recipes they'd learned from her, and she'd learned from her mother. Kadie did notice the oversized shirt Brenda wore and the thickness which now showed on Brenda's body, but she didn't comment on it.

Deacon occupied himself and sat in his favorite lounge chair in the living room with his feet up on the coffee table, reading the *Flint Journal* newspaper.

"Ooh, this frosting is very sweet," Kadie said after swiping frosting from the cake that sat on the dining room table. She licked her index finger.

"Mama, you're not supposed to be eating that cake until after we make your dinner," Maureen kidded, peeking outside the kitchen.

With Johnny and Al away, Kadie's birthday celebration was a quiet one.

When she was finally alone with her thoughts, Brenda thought about Karl and wished he would call her. They had spoken only a few times at school before his graduation. Brenda still had another year of school to go and would have to finish school at the continuation school for pregnant teens. The only thing she and Karl really talked about was the episode at his house when Deacon nearly snatched him up. Deacon had forbidden her to see him. He figured that if Karl didn't think enough of her to marry her, then she shouldn't waste her time seeing him. But Brenda couldn't help but to think about him each time she looked at herself in the mirror and whenever she felt a flutter in her belly. She still wanted him to love her and his baby in her womb. She often fantasized about the two of them being together, happy and married.

That was the right way, the best way, and the decent way. She heard those words often.

She prayed for things to change between her and Karl and between Deacon and Karl. She tried to dismiss the thoughts that ran rampant in her mind and cuddled up with a book about babies and breast-feeding until she dozed off to sleep.

Just as the evening wound down, Deacon went out to pick up his favorite ice cream from the store. He didn't like the vanilla ice cream they had for the party. Kadie sat on the sofa reading the birthday cards she'd received when she noticed a few church members walking up the steps to the front door. Kadie sat her stack of cards down on the coffee table and unlocked the screen door.

"How are you, Sister Wilson?" Sister Abernathy greeted as she entered the Wilson's living room. Deacon Mays and Deacon Flynn followed behind her.

"I'm fine, how are you all?" Kadie asked, curious to why they'd dropped by unannounced.

"We need to speak to you and Deacon Wilson, if we may," Sister Abernathy said.

"Well, Deacon just went out to pick up some ice cream. He should be back any minute."

"We'd like to wait a few minutes for him, if you don't mind," Deacon Mays said.

Kadie was a little suspicious about the visit and waited anxiously for Deacon to get home.

Deacon Wilson recognized Deacon Flynn's bright white Cadillac parked in front of the house when he pulled up. He hurried in so fast Kadie didn't get a chance to warn him about the guests that invaded their living room.

Deacon Wilson caught the first glimpse of his guests over Kadie's shoulder as he handed her the bag of ice cream. He was a bit surprised at their unannounced visit, but was eager to know why they were there.

"How are you, Deacon?" Deacon Mays asked, standing out of respect with his hand held out.

"We need to talk with you," Deacon Flynn said, offering Deacon a handshake.

"And Sister Wilson, too," Sister Abernathy added, crossing her legs and extending her forearm out with her satin purse straps tucked in the inner crease of her elbow.

"Have a seat," Deacon Wilson said, waving his hand, gesturing them to sit down.

Kadie sat in Deacon's recliner chair and he pulled a chair from the dining table.

Sister Abernathy scooted to the edge of the sofa, preparing to dominate the meeting. "Well, it was brought to my attention that your daughter, Brenda, is ... expecting, and we know she's not married."

Kadie's heart sank nearly to the bottom of her shoes, and Deacon frowned, cocked his head, and sat back straight in his chair. Viewing the Wilson's expressions, Deacon Flynn quickly interjected.

"You know that it is the church's rules and regulations that any woman sought to become pregnant out of wedlock has to stand before the church, admit her sin, and repent before the congregation," he said.

"It's in the church bylaws," Deacon Mays confirmed.

"Humph." Deacon Wilson smirked. The anger he had felt for Karl crept up his spine once again. He knew what was in the church bylaws and he knew that eventually the church folk would find out, but he hadn't anticipated this type of encounter with any of the members. He had witnessed many young girls stand before the church to apologize for fornicating and getting pregnant, but he didn't believe he'd ever be in this position.

Kadie focused on Deacon.

Oh Lord, she thought, praying he wouldn't lash out at either of the deacons. She braced herself, ready to yank him back if he did.

Deacon had never been a man to use curse words, even in his younger years before he was saved, but there, right in his living room, a heap of choice words danced around his tongue eager to be spat right out at their faces, but he held them back, remembering his faith and his integrity.

Sitting squarely in the chair, he moved his torso forward. After a deep breath and a hard swallow, he spoke firmly to the group.

"Well, I'm a Christian man, been studying and teaching that Bible for many years. I know there ain't nowhere in it that says a woman pregnant out of wedlock has to stand before man and be judged."

"Deacon, we're going by the church's rules and regulations," Deacon Flynn spoke.

"Yes, we're speaking about the BYLAWS," Sister Abernathy spoke firmly, shaking her head.

By now Deacon had heard enough. He couldn't sit anymore and had to stand up to exert his frustration. "Right now, I don't care nothin' 'bout the church's rules or bylaws or the fact that you all had the nerve to come to my house to confront me like this. Neither one of you have a heaven or hell to put anybody in. My wife and I serve God and we gone go by the Word. The Bible says that all have sinned and come short the glory of God."

"Oh, but in First John one and nine, the Bible says that we must confess our sins one to another," Sister Abernathy stated.

"Yeah, and the Bible also says that he that is without sin cast the first stone," Kadie added.

Just as Kadie and Sister Abernathy were revving up for a Bible scripture boxing match, Deacon shot Kadie a confirming look and finished the conversation.

"I'm not interested in battling you with the scriptures or *your* interpretation of God's words. All I know is that my daughter will not be standing before the church. This is between her and God! It's a matter that my family and I will deal with."

Kadie's expression didn't tell it, but inside she beamed with joy, proud of the way Deacon stood up for his family even though he had his own feelings about Brenda's pregnancy.

"Church folks too quick to judge," Deacon continued. "I have sat there in church listening to many young girls stand before the congregation, and I never felt it was right. "Humph, ain't it something in the church's rules about deacon's drinking?" He eyed Deacon Mays. "I do know what the Bible says about drunkards, and it ain't been a Sunday yet that I ain't smelled alcohol on your breath, Deacon Mays."

Stunned, Deacon Mays coughed himself to a fit, and Sister Abernathy flickered her eyelids like she always did when she was irritated.

"I … I think we ought to be leaving now," Deacon Mays managed to say, his voice muffled through the dingy white handkerchief he held to his mouth.

The familiar voices from the living room woke Brenda from her nap. The mention of her name had urged her to tiptoe down to the bottom of the steps and eavesdrop on the meeting. She'd heard most of the conversation standing in the hallway, her back pressed against the wall, her eyes widening as the group blurted scriptures back and forth. She cheered silently at her father's firm defense of her honor then tipped her way back upstairs, skipping the two bottom steps that squeaked when the weight of feet traveled them. She popped back into her bed as if she hadn't heard anything.

Deacon Wilson offered no handshake as he made his way to the front door, and the Deacons knew from the crumbled expression on his face not to extend their hands out either. With an obvious attitude, Sister Abernathy stood up straight like a soldier, turned up her nose, gathered her purse straps around her wrist, and walked out the front door without speaking another word.

Gladly, Kadie closed the door behind them. She peeked at them through her sheer curtains as Deacon Flynn helped Sister Abernathy into the front seat of the car and drove off.

Deacon moved his chair back up to the dining room table and stopped in thought, resting his hands and weight on the back of it while Kadie rubbed her hand up and down his back to console his anger. Too angry to speak, he swallowed hard and just shook his head.

"Don't worry, John, all things work together, remember…"

Again, Deacon just shook his head and gritted his teeth.

After gathering himself, he grabbed his Sunday school teacher's book from the top of the China cabinet and tracked his way to the basement. Kadie opened the ice cream, scooped some in a bowl on top of a thick slice of the birthday cake. She grabbed one of the big spoons from the utensil drawer and walked with the bowl downstairs to

Deacon and sat it on his desk. She hoped the cold sweetness would calm him.

Brenda made sure the visitors were gone and the coast was clear before she made an appearance. "Was Sister Abernathy here?" Brenda asked, already knowing who was there.

"Yes," Kadie replied with a sneer.

"Hmm," Brenda said, hoping Kadie would elaborate on their visit without her asking.

"They all know you're pregnant, and they want you to apologize to the church," Kadie said bluntly, cutting right in to her.

Brenda acted surprised.

Kadie was obviously very disturbed, swishing the dishtowel around the plates to dry them before she stored them away. "Humph, the nerve of some folks," she said. She had witnessed many pregnant girls confess to fornicating and getting pregnant in front of the church, too, but she hoped she wouldn't have to see one of her own daughters in that situation.

"I had a feeling this day would come. When all the church elders would rush over here with their stones," she continued on. "I remember when Lynette Dixson stood up in front of the church when she got pregnant. She nearly fainted after she vomited right there in front of the pulpit. Them church folks act like we got pregnant all by ourselves. Maybe they should make the boys that helped us stand up there, too! Ain't like I don't feel bad enough as it is." Brenda sighed and shook her head. She knew things would get worse before they got any better. That's just how things were at Mt. Moriah Missionary Baptist Church.

Brenda sliced a piece of cake and scooped some ice cream in a bowl for herself. She looked over at Kadie. "Mama, I don't want to stand up in front of the church. Do I *have* to do that?" she asked.

Kadie was a strong woman of God. She knew the Bible just as well as Deacon did. She didn't deny that Brenda's predicament wasn't in a Godly order, but she knew the way the church folks nearly crucified young girls in this situation wasn't right either. She knew of some of the rules in the church bylaws, but she believed what the Bible said, "Judge not yet you be judged."

It was funny to her how the church taught the Bible, but wanted to pick and choose what parts of it they wanted to live by. Kadie knew things were not going to be easy for Brenda and that Brenda was going to have to make some changes in her life.

She turned to look Brenda straight in the eyes. "No, Brenda, you don't. Your father and I don't agree with the church rules on this one. I never did like to see the young unmarried women confess to the church. You're gonna have to walk with your head up. No matter what anyone else says, only God can judge you. Remember that. This is between you and God."

CHAPTER ELEVEN

*T*he sun beamed through the colorful stained glass windows at the back of Mt. Moriah Missionary Baptist Church. Since it was Women's Day, one of the top events of the year, only the women ushers served. They stood post at all the sanctuary doors, the center aisle pews, and the last pews. They were all energetic and full of smiles as they darted around showing off the new powder blue uniform dresses they wore with white nylons, white gloves, and white low heel pumps. Many of them had their hair freshly pressed, curled and some dyed, putting an extra effort in hair grooming much like they did on Easter Sunday or Mother's Day.

Two of the senior ushers stood at the main entrance, greeting and hugging the members and visitors that entered. Women came draped in fur stoles with furball hats to match. Glittery costume jewelry, knotted strings of pearls swung around their necks as they walked, carrying dainty pocket books which dangled from their wrists.

Two more ushers happily handed each person a program, a tithe and offering envelope, a building fund envelope, and an Annual Women's Day envelope. The last two ushers in the greeting line pinned a pink paper carnation on each woman.

Brenda surprised Kadie when she wanted to go to church since she hadn't been in a few months.

Brenda barley showed, but she was nervous about coming to church. She'd missed quite a few Sundays, but she was ready to face her accusers head on. She had been so rebellious about attending church she felt in some ways that was why things had happened the way they did.

Although she had begun to dislike going to Sunday school and goofed off a lot when she did go, she remembered the lessons about God's forgiveness and repentance.

The night before church, she had awakened in a cold sweat after she dreamed about a swarm of church members chasing her down the street, gripping stones and black leather belts. A vivid picture of Sister Abernathy charging at her with a brick in her hand stayed in her memory.

"This is between me and God," she whispered, reassuring herself as she thought about the last talk she had with Kadie.

After all that happened with Karl and the showdown with the deacons and Sister Abernathy, Brenda felt the need to sit in the house of the Lord—not to apologize before the church, but for herself. If she was going to repent, she would do it on her own terms.

The Women's Day Choir rose for a musical selection as the directress, Sister James, rotated her fingers and signaled Brother Derrick to begin. He hammered the keys dramatically, with a five-minute prelude bobbing his head as Sister Patrice filed in smoothly, slapping the tambourine against her hand.

The fifty-member choir sang with enthusiasm as the congregation responded emotionally, clapping, singing, and shouting. Sister Campbell led the song, her voice heavy and strong. She was known for piercing the soul and stirring up the spirit when she sang. Nobody else in that entire church could sing like her. The choir directors had her sing in just about every choir in the church including the missionary choir, the gospel chorus, and on the first Sunday, the mass choir. They would have had her sing with the male chorus if they could have justified it.

Sister Campbell looked back at Pastor Pearson's youngest daughter Darlene and nodded her head, gesturing her to come down from the choir to share the song with her. Darlene was not as good a singer as Sister Campbell, but she was the pastor's daughter, so everybody doted on her, telling how well she sang mostly to stay in good with the pastor. She had a soft squeaky voice that could hit high notes and hold them long. Anytime she did that members of the congregation fell into an emotional tizzy.

Ushers and nurses, including Kadie, rushed over carrying paper fans toward those standing limp and faint, overcome by the surge of the Holy Spirit that shook up the service. Deacon always commented that most of them were just performing.

"The Holy Spirit wouldn't dare go anywhere near them," he'd say with a chuckle.

Like clockwork, Mother Jesse sprinted down the center aisle. "Hallelujah. Thank you, Jesus," she shouted.

After the congregation calmed down a bit, the ushers worked their way through the sanctuary, passing the gold plated collection plates while Brother Derrick played the organ softly. Coins hit against the metal of the collection plates. Dollar bills and envelopes stuffed with ten percent of the earnings of many church members filled the plates as they were passed down each pew. Pastor Pearson stood up at the pulpit waiting for Mother Jesse to stop running and catch her breath.

"Thank God for the ushers' new uniforms," he said, bucking his eyes and flipping his hand, hinting to the ushers to escort Mother Jesse to her seat so that he could bless the offering.

"How many know that God is a good God, a merciful God, and a forgiving God?" he asked.

"Amen," a ripple of voices from the congregation responded.

"I know there is someone here that wants to be forgiven. The Lord is faithful and wants just to forgive you. Is there anybody here?" Pastor Pearson said, staring out onto the congregation, panning the sanctuary from left to right.

Brenda's attention zoomed in on Pastor Pearson. Her heart jumped, skipped, and her stomach turned flips.

Is Pastor Pearson referring to me? she thought. *Mama and Daddy said I didn't have to do this.*

Her skin turned pale. She felt the need to gush out the oatmeal she had for breakfast. Even as adamant as she felt about facing some of the members that day, she didn't want to be on front-street, displayed before the entire congregation.

"God is waiting on you," Pastor reiterated.

Stiff, she pulled herself to the edge of the pew. Her damp palms gripped the back of the pew in front of her. Her knees spread apart underneath the extra-large dress she'd borrowed from Kadie's closet. Her shoulders curled down.

"I am not going to do this. I'm just going to walk out the back door," she whispered.

I can't believe Pastor Pearson is doing this to me.

Just as she raised her head, another young lady walked up to the front of the church.

"Praise God," a lady from the congregation shouted.

Brenda paused, her body halfway in the sitting position. Deacon Flynn handed the young girl the microphone. Brenda was relieved to see someone else up front, but she wanted to get out of there quickly. The girl could barely speak for crying. One of the nurses handed her

some tissue and stood nearby just in case the girl had a
fainting spell.

"I stand before you today to ask for your forgiveness."
The girl sniffled. Brenda did not want to hear the rest since
this scene had become a regular occurrence in the church's
order of service.

"Excuse me," Brenda said to the family seated next to
her as she slid past them trying to make a fast exit out of
the sanctuary. Deacon and Kadie were both seated up front.
All the maneuvering and feet shuffling caused Deacon and
Kadie to look back and notice Brenda exiting the side door
in the sanctuary.

She pushed open the swinging door to the restroom
and rushed into one of the stalls. She took a few deep
breaths and grabbed a wad of toilet paper to wipe the tears
from her eyes. When she stepped out the stall, Mother
Jesse was standing at the sink.

"How you doing, baby?" Mother Jesse asked.

"I'm … fine," Brenda answered nervously.

"Not feelin' too well?"

"No," Brenda replied.

Mother Jesse walked over to her, lifted her chin with
one hand and wiped her tears with the other.

"You hold your up head, girl. No need for all these
tears now. You've got to take care of yourself and that little
one you're carrying in your belly. Everything's gone be
fine. Don't you worry about what these church folks sayin'.
Half of 'em hypocrites anyhow. You just trust in the Lord.
You hear me?"

"It was a mi … stak…"

"Shhh, I said trust in the Lord. He's already forgiven
you," Mother Jesse said, cutting into Brenda's words.

"Yes, ma'am," Brenda answered. Brenda stared at her, wondering how she could know since she believed her stomach wasn't big enough to notice, plus she wore a loose-fitting dress. She wondered if the whole church knew and was that the reason she felt so many stares from church members.

Truth was, once a few members knew about something, everyone else would soon find out. Plus, Mother Jesse was old and wise; she knew what women looked like when they were pregnant even before their bellies showed.

"I birthed eleven children. I knows whatcha look like when you with child, the way ya skin glows, and the stride in your walk," Mother Jesse said as she stood imitating with her body movements. Brenda wiped her tears as she looked at herself in the mirror. "This here is a girl, a beautiful baby girl," Mother Jesse said as she stretched her hand out and touched Brenda's barely noticeable baby bump. Brenda smiled. "You gone back out there and hold your head up high and keep on walkin' with Jesus. Trust in the Lord with all thine heart and lean not unto thy own understanding but in all thy ways acknowledge him and he will direct your path." Mother Jesse smiled and opened her arms to embrace Brenda. Brenda wiped her tears and hugged her. "Don't you let this situation turn you around, you hear me, 'cause God don't make mistakes."

CHAPTER TWELVE

*M*onths moved by quickly. The wet brown and orange leaves blowing around in the streets showed evidence that fall was in full bloom. A sharp wind raced straight through the seams of the black trench coat that barely fastened around Brenda's growing belly. Brenda and Cheryl had been planning their weekend all week as they sat in the back of Miss McGreagor's class at the continuation school for pregnant teens they had both transferred to. They often talked about their plans to become mothers and joked about how ironic it was that they both became pregnant at the same time. Friends and family members joked about it, too, and drew their own conclusions that Brenda and Cheryl must have planned it, or they were all in the same bed together with William and Karl the night they conceived.

Brenda pulled the collar of her coat up over her ears, trying to keep out the cold wind. She stepped briskly with a pregnant woman's wobble down the sidewalk, looking up ahead for Cheryl who was walking to meet her.

"Hurry up, slow poke," Cheryl yelled as she walked toward Brenda.

"Well, you know I can't walk as fast with this baby swimming around in my belly."

"I can't either, but I still ain't as slow as you." They giggled.

Although they were both about six months pregnant, Cheryl didn't show as much as Brenda did.

"Your belly's so much bigger than mine. Maybe you got twins," Cheryl said.

"Mama says it's 'cause the secret is out," Brenda replied. "Baby ain't got to hide no more."

As they walked together, an old Chevy full of young men pulled up alongside them.

"What's happening?" one the young men yelled from the car window.

Another guy in the car noticed the roundness of both the girls' waistlines. "Looks like somebody done already got to 'em. They both got big bellies." The guys chuckled then rolled the window back up and drove off. Brenda and Cheryl laughed themselves to tears, mimicking the young man's words.

The smothered pork chops Cheryl's mom made sat covered on top of the stove. Cheryl hurried in the kitchen, grabbed a plate, and piled a lump of mashed potatoes right in the center. She then doused them with gravy that swirled on her plate. Brenda followed, scooping a hefty helping of potatoes onto her plate, too.

"Ugh," Brenda said, turning up her nose as she watched Cheryl spoon out Lima beans from a big silver pot.

"Girl, you don't know what you missin'. Beans, beans, good for your heart. The more you eat, the more you..." Cheryl said, fluttering her lips to make a fart sound.

"I don't need beans for that. This little baby is a definite gas machine."

They laughed. Cheryl pulled a large pitcher from the refrigerator and poured them both a glass of iced tea. They spent the rest of the evening talking about what was to become of them, their futures, and how much they resented William and Karl who were nowhere in their plans.

"You think we gone be good mothers?" Brenda asked.

"Yeah, shoot, we both done enough babysitting and changing diapers. I think we gone be fine."

"Yeah, I think so, too," Brenda replied though unsure. They spent the whole night talking about the what if's, their hopes, and their dreams. They wrote down dozens of baby names, a list for boys and one for girls.

"You gone name your baby after William if it's a boy?" Brenda asked.

"Humph," Cheryl responded, rolling her eyes.

Although they had talked trash about William and Karl all night, Brenda still wanted Karl to be part of her child's life. She fantasized about him coming by the house with a beautiful diamond ring and carrying her in his arms right out the front door. She just didn't want to be classified as an unwed mother or her baby to be titled a bastard like Deacon said. No matter what Deacon said about Karl, she carried the thoughts of them living happily ever after deep in her heart.

Maybe things will be different after the baby comes, she thought.

CHAPTER THIRTEEN

"*I* think it's time to go to the hospital," Brenda said. Her actual due date was still a few days away, but she knew it was time. Brenda grimaced as she wobbled her way into her parents' bedroom. At first, she thought the pains came from all the meatloaf she had eaten earlier until they began to come faster and stronger.

Kadie stared up at Brenda and stood up to touch her belly. "Oh, yes," she said. "I've seen that look before and your belly is hard as a rock. I'll have to call your daddy at work and leave Maureen a note."

Brenda hissed, inhaled, and exhaled as she gathered her small suitcase and pink wool coat. Kadie took hold of Brenda's forearm and helped her out the back door and into the car.

"Lay down across the back seat," Kadie said.

Brenda propped her suitcase up on the seat against the door and used her purse as a pillow.

"You all right back there?" Kadie asked, stopping at a traffic light.

"Uhm hmm." Brenda squirmed on the seat. Thoughts of what was about to happen flashed in her mind. She tried to imagine what the baby looked like and wondered if it was a pretty baby girl like Mother Jesse said or if it was a baby boy that looked like Karl.

The dozens of baby names that she and Cheryl came up with and the ones Maureen suggested whirled around in her mind. She cringed as the sharp pains pierced her belly. She thought about calling Karl and wondered if he would even care to see the baby.

Everything's gonna be fine—Lois' words flashed in Brenda's mind. With every good thought she had, she couldn't help but to think about the drastic measures she had taken to get rid of the baby when she first found out she was pregnant. The pills, the injection that Dr. Southgate had given, and the gin all weighed in her mind.

"Lord, please don't let nothing be wrong with my baby," she prayed softly.

A flood of warm fluid gushed from her body, dripping from the seat to the floor of the car.

Brenda groaned. "I think my water broke," she announced.

"Oh Lord," Kadie shouted, pressing harder on the gas pedal. "We're almost there."

Brenda squirmed as the pain increased. "Mama, it hurts."

"Just hold on. We're almost there."

Kadie raced into the hospital parking lot, barely putting the car into the park gear before she ran inside, waving her hands for help. The nurses rushed out to assist Brenda in getting out of the car.

"Just stay calm," a nurse said.

Kadie parked the car and grabbed Brenda's suitcase and purse. She searched through her coin purse for change to call Deacon.

Brenda moaned and cried for hours. Repeatedly, Kadie drenched the white washcloth the nurse gave her with cold water, squeezed it out, and wiped the perspiration from Brenda's face before laying the cloth across her forehead.

At the thirtieth hour of labor, the baby was ready to make its grand entrance into the world. Kadie, Deacon, and Maureen all waited in the waiting room.

"Push," Dr. Hyatt shouted.

"Just one more time," the blonde hair nurse added.

Brenda gritted her teeth, took a long deep breath, and gave one last push and the room filled with a squalling holler that was heard clear to the waiting room down the hall.

"It's a girl," Dr. Hyatt announced.

Brenda let out a sigh of relief, and a flood of tears followed. The baby girl opened her lungs and let loose a piercing scream.

"Is she OK?" Brenda asked, concerned.

"She's fine," the nurse answered.

"I mean her fingers…does she have all her fingers and her toes?" Brenda asked.

"Now why in the world would you ask such a thing?" Dr. Hyatt asked.

"I just … want to know if she is all right." The bad thoughts she'd had about the baby being deformed worried her.

"She's a beautiful 7 pound 6 ounce baby girl," the nurse said as she picked the baby up from the scale, wrapped her in a blanket, and handed her to Brenda.

"She's perfect. She's got a lot of hair, and she's so pale," Brenda said, marveling over the tiny infant. "Tia, her name is Tia. Tia Clarice…Wilson." Brenda smiled and planted a kiss on little Tia's forehead before handing her back to the nurse.

"I'm gonna get her all cleaned and ready to see your husband."

"I don't have a husband," Brenda responded.

The nurse shot Brenda a look of disgrace, shook her head, and pushed the infant bed out the room and down the hall to the nursery.

Brenda wanted so badly to pick up the phone and call Karl to tell him about their beautiful baby girl, but she didn't.

The doctor informed Deacon, Kadie, and Maureen of the delivery. "Congratulations, it's a girl," Dr. Hyatt announced.

They were relieved to know that Brenda was doing fine.

"You're a grandma, and I'm an auntie," Maureen said, giggling. She hugged Kadie.

"And somebody's gonna be callin' you Granddaddy," Maureen said to Deacon with a confirming smile.

Deacon was expressionless, but Kadie knew he was happy about their first grandchild. He just didn't want anybody to *think* he was happy about it.

They all walked to the nursery to see the baby through the big glass window.

"Which one is she?" Deacon asked. "They all look alike."

"There she is right there, Wilson, the name tag says Brenda Wilson," Kadie said.

"She's so tiny and she looks like a little white baby," Deacon said.

"Most babies are tiny, John, and she gone get some color," Kadie said, smiling.

"She looks like me," Maureen said proudly.

Brenda slept for hours, and when she awakened, she found Maureen sitting beside her.

"Where's Mama and Daddy?" she asked.

"They could only stay for a while, and I was just staying until you woke up."

"Is Daddy still mad at me?"

"I don't think so. He said the baby was so tiny and pretty, too. He wants you to name her Ophelia."

"Ophelia!"

"*I* think her name should be Vanessa."

"Vanessa is a pretty name, but I already named her Tia, Tia Clarice."

"Well, I guess Tia is OK, I mean she is your baby. You should name her what you want to name her."

"Yep."

"I'm going home, and I'll be back tomorrow. But first, I have a surprise for you." Maureen got up and pulled back the white curtain that divided the room. "Surprise," Maureen shouted.

Slowly, Brenda rose, shifting her sore body to see what the surprise was.

"Cheryl?" she said.

"Yep," Maureen replied. "She had her baby last night."

"Hey Brenda," Cheryl said softly, still exhausted from her delivery.

"I don't care what you two say. I think you two planned this whole thing. How in the world did you two end up pregnant at the same time and have your babies a day apart?" Maureen said, chuckling.

"No, we didn't plan it. It just happened that way," Cheryl said, joining in the laughter.

"I had a baby girl," Brenda said.

"I know. I had a girl, too. Her name is Tabya Lynette."

"Did you tell William?"

"No, but my mama called him, and my brother told Karl that you had your baby. So he knows, too."

"He probably won't come," Brenda said.

"Who cares? You have a beautiful baby girl, and I do, too. I told you, we gone make it without them fools."

Brenda smiled. She wanted to believe what Cheryl said. All the negative things Deacon had said over the last few months stayed on her mind. According to Deacon, Brenda was ruined. If Karl didn't want to marry her, he said, no other man ever would.

Two nurses walked in, pushing Brenda's and Cheryl's babies. Cheryl took Tabya in her arms and propped her up in the breast-feeding position. The other nurse handed Tia and a tiny baby bottle to Brenda.

"Why ain't you breastfeeding?" Cheryl asked.

"'Cause I don't know how."

"But you had a book, and we learned about it in class." Understanding babies and childbirth was part of a class they both took at the continuation school.

"Humph, I must have missed that day." Brenda smirked.

Cheryl laughed. "Girl, it just comes naturally for the baby."

"This bottle is fine for me."

The two teenage girls both sat, feeding and admiring their newborn daughters.

"How ironic, me and my best friend had our babies a day apart," Cheryl said.

"Yes, it is," Brenda replied then returned her focus back to Tia.

Cheryl gazed into Tabya's eyes, smoothing her silky black hair down and playing with her tiny fingers. "She is so precious. I don't ever want anything to happen to her. I want her to be smart, and I pray she don't ever run into a

no-good dog like William. I'm gonna make sure of it."
Cheryl wiped the tears that formed in her eyes.

"Now, how are you gonna do that? Our parents sure
didn't have any control of what happened to us, so how do
you think we'll be able to do that?

"Humph, as soon as Tabya turns fifteen, no, twelve
I'm gonna put birth control pills in her orange juice."
Brenda and Cheryl laughed. "But I'm serious," Cheryl said.
"My daughter won't ever have to go through this."

Brenda and Cheryl talked and giggled the whole day,
both trying to forget about the fathers of their babies.
Exhausted, they both slept on and off while their visitors
came and went.

Long after hospital hours, a male voice pulled Brenda
from her sleep.

"Wake up," the male voice whispered.

Brenda squinted and opened her eyes. "Karl?" she said
before yawning.

"I heard you had the baby, and I wanted to see her. I
looked at her through the glass in the nursery."

"I didn't think you would come," Brenda said.

"I wanted to see what she looked like."

"Well?"

"She just looks like ... a baby, all pale and stuff. She is
pretty though."

"You don't think she looks like you?" Brenda asked.

"Yeah, she's got my nose," Karl said.

"I haven't seen or talked to you in a while. I thought
you didn't care."

"Your father was so mean to me."

"Well, think about it, wouldn't you be?" she asked.

Karl shrugged. "I have to go, but I am going to buy her something, OK?"

"Oh … OK." As quickly and as quietly as Karl came in, he left.

Brenda lay there silently, thinking how wonderful it was that Karl snuck in to see his daughter and offer to buy her something. She thought about how nice it would be if they could be together and if they would get married. She wondered if that would make Deacon happy. She smiled with those thoughts and dozed back off to sleep.

"Girl, I heard you talking in your sleep last night. I guess you were dreaming," Cheryl said.

"No, I wasn't. Karl was here. He snuck into the hospital."

"Now, I know you were dreaming."

"I wasn't. He really was here. He saw the baby. Says he's gone buy her something."

"Hmm," Cheryl replied with a hint of jealousy.

Weeks later, Brenda sat at home enjoying her new baby and basked in all the fuss the family made over Tia, a definite change from the way they had all reacted when they learned she was pregnant. Despite the semblance of calm that evaded the house, Brenda grew melancholy over the passing days. She was unhappy with herself. Although the possibilities seemed a bit farfetched, Brenda still wished Karl and her would be happy in love, raise their child together, and live happily ever after.

That's how things are supposed to be, she thought. *Happy.*

CHAPTER FOURTEEN

*B*renda stuck her key in the back door and opened it. The sound of laughter in the dining room met her. Kadie smiled as she rocked back in the chair, slapping at the dining room table as she and Maureen exchanged conversation.

"What's so funny?" Brenda asked, stepping into the room.

"We're just happy," Kadie said.

"What you so happy about?"

"Maureen is getting married."

"Married?" Brenda asked.

"Yeah, Daniel asked me to marry him," Maureen gushed. She held out her left hand, showing the single diamond ring she wore on her ring finger.

"Well, congratulations," Brenda said. She was happy, but a little jealous that Maureen was getting married and starting a new life in the proper way, the way Deacon said it should be. She wished that she was the one getting married and *happy*.

Kadie and Maureen went on rambling about the wedding colors, guest list, and other details for the next big family event. Brenda didn't feel needed in the planning or the blissful conversation they were having. She picked Tia up off the sofa, wrapped her in a blanket, and headed toward the door.

"What are you doing?" Kadie asked, looking at Brenda.

"I am taking Tia to Cheryl's house with me."

"Just leave her. Let her sleep. She don't need to be out running around with you."

Brenda pursed her lips, but knew Kadie was right. She unwrapped Tia and laid her back down, grabbed her purse and a piece of hot water cornbread from a platter in the kitchen, and exited out the back door.

***

"Hey Brenda. Where's Tia?" Cheryl asked, holding Tabya in her arms as she opened the door for Brenda.

"My mama wanted her to stay home. I swear, sometimes I don't know if Tia's my baby or hers." Brenda plopped down on the chair in Cheryl's room and put her feet up on the ottoman in front of it.

"Maybe you should be grateful your mama cares enough to keep Tia as much as she does. I don't have that luxury." Cheryl put Tabya in her crib then shut and locked the door before turning on the radio.

"What becomes of a broken heart..." They both sang along with the radio.

"These are so pretty," Brenda said, sifting through the stack of new baby clothes Cheryl had lying on the bed. Cheryl unintentionally ignored Brenda. "I cannot believe William took that fat tail Gwen Carson to the prom," Cheryl said, rolling her eyes.

"At least I did get to go to the junior prom last year," Brenda said.

"He's only seen Tabya one time. He acts like she means nothing to him," Cheryl rambled on as if Brenda hadn't said anything.

"Well Karl hasn't seen Tia that much. He did buy her a dress, and his mother made her a blanket."

Cheryl pursed her lips and shook her head. "I'm tired of talking about his sorry butt," Cheryl announced, pulling out a shoebox she had pushed under the bed.

"What in the world?" Brenda said, bucking her eyes.

Cheryl pulled out a rolled marijuana cigarette, put it to her mouth, and lit it.

"Where'd you get that?" Brenda asked.

"Don't worry about that. Here, take a puff."

"I don't know how to smoke that," Brenda said.

"Like this." Cheryl took a long draw and inhaled it.

"Here," she insisted, handing the marijuana to Brenda. Brenda hesitated.

"C'mon," Cheryl said, moving it closer to Brenda. Brenda took it and inhaled it exactly the way she'd watched Cheryl do it.

They continued to dance and sing to the music, giggling uncontrollably as the marijuana took effect. At that moment, they'd forgotten all about William and Karl and all the resentment they felt toward them. Cheryl had forgotten about Tabya until she heard her crying. She staggered, trying to catch her balance as she held Tabya in her arms.

"Girl, you'd better sit down with that baby before you fall down," Brenda said with a slur.

"Shhhh," she said, kissing Tabya on her forehead. She floated toward the crib to lay her back down. Cheryl turned down the volume on the radio. "Well, I might as well tell you now."

"Tell me what?" Brenda asked.

"I'm moving to New Jersey with my cousin, Tootie."

"New Jersey?"

"Yeah, I am tired of being here, and I told you I want the best for Tabya. Now that I've finished school at that stupid continuation school, I'm gonna go live with Tootie and go to college there."

101

Brenda looked puzzled, still dazed from smoking the marijuana, but she heard clearly what Cheryl said. The thought of her best friend moving away worried her. The one person she knew understood her and whose life was almost identical was moving away? She wanted that thought to go away just like the thoughts of Karl had, so she continued to smoke the marijuana with Cheryl.

Brenda didn't feel as guilty about indulging in those sinful things Deacon constantly preached about like she used to. Her father's scornful words didn't invade her thoughts as much. If they did, she ignored them. As it was, she had already committed the ultimate sin in her father's eyes, so anything else couldn't be as bad unless she got pregnant again.

If I'm as bad as Deacon says I am, she thought, *and no man gone want me, why not do as I please?*

After she sobered a bit, Brenda stood in front of the mirror in Cheryl's bathroom re-styling her hair. She borrowed a washcloth from Cheryl and drenched it with warm water. She hoped it would help rejuvenate her as she swished it across her face and neck.

Cheryl was in no condition to walk Brenda halfway home like she usually did. She was too high from the marijuana since she'd smoked most of it. She lay limp across her bed. Brenda didn't bother her. She knew she'd have to walk by herself. She peeked in the crib at Tabya and pulled the small yellow blanket up over her little shoulders before leaving.

As she approached her street, a car drove up beside her. Brenda ignored it, thinking it was some young boys from the neighborhood.

"Hey Baby girl," a familiar male yelled from the driver's side window.

Brenda recognized the voice and the name she was called. Uncle Pap stopped his brand new yellow Cadillac, and Brenda stopped to admire the sparkling car with white wall tires. Deacon had a nice Cadillac, too, but Pap had a tendency to go to the extreme to really deck out his cars.

"This sho is a pretty car," Brenda said.

"C'mon. I'll take you for a ride."

Brenda slid into the passenger seat as she admired the car's interior. She glided her hands across the smooth leather seats.

Pap's bottle of Jack Daniels caught her eye. It lay on the front seat next to a paper bag. She patted her hair, glancing at herself in the side view mirror, hoping she'd prepped herself and she'd sobered up enough so that no signs of her marijuana smoking could be detected.

Pap pulled in front of an old building that Brenda had passed by many times and assumed it was just an old abandoned building. In a quick motion, Pap reached under his seat, pulled out his long barrel pistol, and stuck it down in the front of his pants. Brenda wasn't startled at all. She was used to seeing her uncle Pap with his pistol.

"I'll be right back," he said as he grabbed the paper bag that was full of money he'd won at a poker game. From the back seat, he grabbed his fancy carved, cherry wood walking cane.

Brenda grew impatient waiting in the car. She fidgeted with her hair and nails, glancing back and forth at herself in the rearview mirror. Her eyes darted back and forth at the bottle of Jack Daniels lodged down between the front seats. She'd heard folks comment about Jack Daniels many times.

She was curious and already opened for adventure considering the marijuana she'd just smoked. She turned back to view herself in the mirror and squirmed in her seat, trying to evade her curiosity. She looked around first, then quickly grabbed the bottle and unscrewed the top, tightening her lips around it to get a quick sip.

"Ugh," she said, frowning. She wiped her lips with the back of her hand and took another sip, then hurried to put the top back on the bottle and push it back down in the seats.

Uncle Pap had taken more than a few minutes inside the building, so Brenda decided to get out the car and go inside. Once inside, she walked down a long dark hallway. A large burly black man standing at the end of the hallway glared at her. He folded his big arms across his chest.

"I'm looking for Uncle Pap," Brenda said.

"Who are you?" he spoke with a deep rough tone.

"I'm his niece." The man pointed toward the area where Pap was. The redolence of cigarettes, cigars, and bootleg whiskey brewing filled the air. The lights were dim except in a room in the back where several men and a few women seated at card tables gambled, drank, and cursed. P. Willie and Earleen sat across from each other at a table in the corner. Although those two disliked each other so much, they were often seen together.

The smell of food urged Brenda to peek into the large kitchen where three heavy-set women stood preparing orders, one cleaning chicken, one seasoning it, and the one wobbling around, telling the other two what to do. Two big pots sizzled with hot grease, frying chicken thighs and legs. Small plates with slices of pound cake and sweet potato pies covered the table near the kitchen door.

Brenda was amazed to see all the activities taking place in this old building. Pap noticed Brenda as he stood in a hallway, talking to another man.

"What you doing in here, girl?" Pap asked.

"I thought you forgot about me," she replied.

"You go on back to the car. I'll be right out." Pap knew this place was not a good place for his niece to be since every wild thing imaginable took place in there. And he didn't have any control of what took place..

"OK." She turned and walked back toward the front door.

Brenda noticed a door slightly ajar and peered inside. Although she assumed things went on in that place, she was a little stunned by the naked women who danced on men's laps.

"Hey pretty girl," a soft male voice from a dark corner spoke. Brenda looked, but didn't see anyone."Hey pretty girl," the voice spoke again and a man stepped out into the soft light. It was Jake. Brenda remembered him from card games at Pap's house a few years earlier. Jake's skin was smooth and his smile was alluring, revealing his pearly white teeth. He had a face that not many women would forget. Even in the dim light, his eyes sparkled and his wavy black hair glistened. His dimples deepened with his smile.

"You talking to me?" Brenda asked, looking around, pointing to herself.

With a sparkle in his eyes and smooth grin, he looked around. "I don't see any other pretty girls standing here in front of me." Brenda smiled bashfully. "What are you doing here?" he asked. He knew this was not a place for good respectable women.

"I'm waiting on Uncle Pap to take me home."

"If you need a ride, I'll take you home."

"No, Uncle Pap's coming out. He'll take me," Brenda said, unable to control her blushing.

"All right, pretty girl," Jake said smiling, standing poised like a picture from a men's clothing catalog.

Brenda threw her hand up in a hurried wave and left the building while Jake stepped back into the dark corner he had been standing in.Brenda grinned at the thought of such a fine older man flirting with her. His debonair demeanor was tantalizing, and she was dazzled by his smooth voice and the amiable way he spoke to her. It made her feel special, the way Uncle Pap did. She didn't ponder too much on it since she was sure he was much too old to be seriously interested in her. Besides, Deacon's words of no man wanting her were still planted in her head. But she couldn't resist thinking about him. She smiled with every thought of him, but with every good thought about Jake or any other man, things Deacon said would invade her thoughts.

Pap got back into the car with another paper bag of money he had to pay a winner in the street lottery. They drove off. "So why haven't you been coming around?" Pap asked.

Brenda shrugged. "I don't know. I thought maybe you were mad at me for having a baby, like Daddy was," Brenda replied.

"No, I'm not mad at you. I'm mad at the nigga that got you that way then ran off and left you. He better hope I don't run into him. He's lucky I didn't look him up."

Brenda smirked.

Pap pulled into the driveway at Brenda's house and put the car in park.

"You just go on and take care of that baby and live your life."

"OK," Brenda said.

Pap shifted his body to reach into his pants pocket to pull out his money that was neatly clamped together with a gold money clip.

"Here," Pap said and handed Brenda a crisp fifty-dollar bill.

"Thank you." Brenda smiled.

"You remember what I said. Take care of that baby and live your life. Don't be fooled by none of these fools out here."

CHAPTER FIFTEEN

*I*t seemed like every time Brenda went out the house and came back, some sort of commotion occurred. It ranged from Deacon fussing about the church folk to Maureen's big wedding plans. As soon as she put her key in the door and opened it, she heard the loud voices and foot stomping.

What is it this time? Brenda thought.

Brenda walked into the living room and saw Maureen stomping with her arms crisscrossed around her waist. She was crying, her face soaked with tears. Kadie was buckled over, screaming and crying.

"Lord Jesus," she shouted. It was obvious that something was terribly wrong.

"What's wrong? What happened?" She dropped her purse to the floor.

Maureen could barely form the words. Tears dripped to her blouse. Kadie fell down on the sofa, holding her chest.

"Mama," Maureen shouted.

"Why God, why?" Kadie screamed.

Immediately, Brenda rushed over to Tia's playpen . She was awake, quiet, and playing with her fingers. Brenda sighed, pressing her hand to her chest.

"Did something happen to Daddy?" she yelled.

"No," Maureen said, shaking her head. "Al is dead."

"What? Al? Dead? My brother Al?" Brenda's head dropped, and her body crashed down on the sofa behind her and within seconds, she became just as distraught as Maureen and Kadie. She and Maureen hugged each other and tried to console Kadie. Brenda learned that two soldiers stopped by earlier to inform them of Al's death,

They stated he'd been killed in combat. Kadie knew many mothers whose sons went to war in Vietnam and didn't return. She had prayed that both her sons would return home safely. She'd been somewhat relieved when Johnny came home due to a gunshot injury to his leg. The news had her devastated.

The three women tried to pull themselves together.

"We have to call Daddy at work," Maureen said.

"I can't," Brenda cried, wiping the tears from her top lip.

Kadie cleared her eyes to see the chime clock that sat on top of the television. "He'll be home soon. We'll just wait until he gets here," she said

Brenda went into the kitchen to get Kadie a glass of water and took it to her.

"I can't believe this is happening. Are they sure it's Al?" Brenda asked Maureen.

Maureen handed Kadie a wet washcloth she'd got from the bathroom. Kadie's face crumbled as she opened her hand to reveal the identification tags the soldiers had given her. They all broke down crying again.

They all paused when they heard a car pull into the driveway. They waited quietly, unsure if it was Deacon or Johnny. The back door opened then closed. They heard the sound of keys hitting the dining room table. They all sat speechless with grim faces as Deacon stepped into the room. Kadie broke the silence, greeting him with a tearful embrace.

"What's wrong?" Deacon asked in a frantic tone when he saw their forlon expressions.

All three women broke into hysterics again. Kadie opened her hand to show Deacon the name tags she held. Deacon's lips trembled as he asked, "Albert?" Kadie

109

nodded and covered her face with the washcloth. "Oh Lord, not my son." He stood motionless, a single tear rolled down his cheek as he gripped his chest and stumbled backwards, plopping down in the dining room chair. He wept, tapping his balled fist on the table. This was the first time the girls had seen their father cry.

He removed his eyeglasses, pulled his handkerchief from his pocket, and patted his eyes. He rested his elbows on the table and dropped his head low, mumbling words and scriptures.

"God giveth and God taketh away," Deacon said, trying to justify his loss. Just then, Johnny came limping in through the back door. He was still healing from the bullet wound and needed to use crutches. The tears and expressions on everyone's face alerted him that something was wrong.

"Johnny," Deacon said, his voice a whisper.

Johnny's eyes grew wide as he answered, "Yeah Daddy?"

"Your brother is dead."

Johnny gasped and sighed, dropping the crutches to the floor. He grabbed the wall to keep his balance.

"Ah man, not Al," Johnny said as he collapsed in the chair across from Deacon, covered his face with his hands, and cried.

Maureen tried to recover herself as much as she could. She wiped her face with the tissues she had clenched in her fist. Her voice trembled as she repeated to Deacon and Johnny what the soldiers said happened to Al.

Deacon was silent as he stared at the photos of Al that hung on the wall in age sequence among all four of his children. Years of memories flashed in his mind. The loss of his second born was devastating, but he dared to question God. Prayer and the Bible was always his remedy to deal with any situation. He folded his arms across his chest and rocked back and forth in his chair, reciting scriptures. Johnny rested his arms down on the table and laid his head down on his arms. Kadie continuously cried as Brenda tried to console her. All the emotions in the room made Tia cry.

"Bring me the baby," Kadie said.

Brenda picked Tia up with her pink blanket still clinging to her bottom and handed her to Kadie. She cried louder as she hugged and kissed Tia. Brenda sat down at the dining table across from Deacon and Johnny. Normally when the family sat at the table it was happy times, but not this day. On this day the Wilson family was in mourning.

Deacon pulled out an ink pen from his shirt pocket and reached for the note pad that stuck out of the plastic fruit bowl in the center of the table. Quietly, he wrote some words on it, put the pen down, got up from the chair, and headed for the basement without saying anything else.

Maureen took a few deep breaths and pulled herself together. She knew someone had to be strong and take control of the situation. She pulled open the first drawer in the China cabinet and took out Kadie's telephone book. She unraveled the telephone cord that was plugged in behind the sofa so that she could take it back into the bedroom.

Aunt Lois was the first one she called. Lois' sobs could be heard clear over the phone line. "Mama's not doing well, and I don't know about Daddy," Maureen said.

"I'll be right over," Lois replied.

Maurene spent at least an hour calling family members. She cringed each time she had to repeat the dreadful words of her brother's death.

It took more than a week for Al's body to be shipped back to the United States. Deacon, Johnny, and Maureen, along with Sister Danner from the church's bereavement committee, took care of the funeral arrangements because Kadie couldn't bear to do it.

Although it was a nice spring day, it was sad in the Wilson home as the family prepared for the funeral.

"I will be glad when this is over," Brenda said as she dressed Tia in a frilly blue dress.

"It will never be over. This is something we'll always remember," Maureen replied as she pushed a tiny pearl earring into her ear lobe. She rolled up the last few tissues she pulled from the Kleenex box and pushed them deep down into her purse. She then straightened a wrinkle in her stockings, slipped on her black pumps, and walked out of the room.

Brenda twisted the ruffles straight on Tia's dress and propped her up in the center of her bed while she phoned Karl's mother. Karl's mother had recently started to show more interest in Tia and agreed to take care of her while Brenda went to the funeral.

Kadie was so weak from crying and barely eating that Lois and her other sisters, Anne and Margretta, from Chicago had to help her get dressed. The family called Margretta Margie for short.

"You're gonna be all right, Kadie," Margie said as she zipped up the back of Kadie's black dress.

Lois wiped the tears from Kadie's eyes and patted pressed powder on her face.

"Yeah, Kay. God's gonna give you strength to get through this."

"I know," Kadie whimpered.

Deacon hadn't said much to anyone about Al's death, and he didn't take any time off from work or teaching Bible classes that week before the funeral. That morning he was up earlier than usual. He sat quietly at his desk, his body squared in the ripped, burgundy leather chair. He stared at Al's army green duffel bag that sat on a chair next to the desk. The name Albert G. Wilson was sewn onto the front of it. The "G" was for George. George was Uncle Pap's first name. The duffle bag had sat there since being delivered days earlier by some of the army staff members. It reminded Deacon of how Al used to sit there to talk or mostly to be talked to. He smirked and smiled with thoughts of Al as a child. He remembered when Al used to tell everyone that he was going to be a preacher when he grew up.

Deacon pulled the heavy bag down off the chair and loosened the drawstring that held it closed. He reached down inside it and pulled out many of Al's clothes, including his favorite blue cardigan sweater, a bundle of letters, a small wooden keepsake box, and a deck of playing cards. Deacon looked at the cards, frowned, and then shook his head and smiled.

Inside the small wooden box, he found a clock on a chain that he and Kadie had given Albert for a birthday gift years earlier. His heart sank when he found a tiny picture of himself and Kadie when they were younger. He held back the tears that rained inside him. He sifted through the bag and found the Bible he had given him when he was much younger. A list of Bible scriptures he'd written down for him before he went to the Army was still lodged in the book of Psalms. As Deacon flipped through some of the pages, he noticed that some of the verses had been underlined. Deacon smiled. He felt glad to know Al had been marking in it, believing Al had been reading it.

He pulled out a pair of dress shoes and a tiny bag that held Al's shoe polish and shining cloth. Deacon paused, staring at the shoes. He took a moment to shine them and slip them on his own feet. The emotions that he tried so hard to keep inside released like a roaring river. He sobbed the way even a strong man would when something hurt so deep that he couldn't bear the pain.

The U.S. flag draped the closed casket that was set in front of the altar at Mt. Moriah Missionary Baptist Church. Two soldiers standing at attention flanked either side of the casket. Kadie's four sisters helped her to her seat while the church ladies and nurses stood around with tissue boxes and paper fans, offering extra care and comfort to Kadie since she was both a nurse and a deaconess at the church.

Johnny walked in on his crutches. He stood beside Deacon but kept a close eye on Kadie, Maureen, and Brenda. The church was packed with church members, relatives and Al's school friends.

"I didn't know Al had so many friends," Brenda whispered.

The ceremony began and everyone took it well, considering the loss. All that changed when at the end of the ceremony, the soldiers and pallbearers rolled the casket out of the church. Kadie and Deacon wept for the loss of their son. Johnny was like Deacon and didn't want anyone to see him mourn, but at that moment no one could hold back the tears.

After the burial, the Wilson family retreated to their home

Kadie's sisters Margretta and Lois helped Kadie to bed.

"You need to eat," Lois said as she handed Kadie a plate of baked chicken and green beans. Kadie took a few bites and sat the plate to the side.

Margretta and Lois eyed one another; they both hoped Kadie could pull through this horrendous event in her life.

Deacon didn't want to be around so many people although they were family. He politely bowed out to his own space in the basement.

Maureen walked around, picking up plates and cleaning.

"Why don't you sit yourself down somewhere," Margie told her. "I'll take care of all that."

"I can't help it. I can't just sit," Maureen said.

Brenda wanted to get away from all the people, too. Cheryl had been there with Brenda and the family during the week of the funeral. She was all set to move to New Jersey when she heard the news and decided hold off her trip to be there for her best friend.

Brenda followed Cheryl out of the house, and the two jumped in Cheryl's father's car.

"I need to pick up Tia," Brenda said once in the car.

"So Karl wants to see her now, huh?" Cheryl asked.

"No," Brenda replied. "His mother agreed to keep her while I attended the funeral."

They pulled in front of Karl's house and saw his mother Lillian on the front porch, rocking Tia.

"Was she crying?" Brenda asked.

"No more than any normal baby does," Lillian said.

"She's probably sleepy. There's been so much going on at my house, she probably just tired."

"I'm gonna pray for your mother. I know what it feels like to lose a child. I lost my daughter, Patricia, when she was just seven months old to crib death. Yeah, I know what it feels like." Lillian kissed Tia and handed her to Brenda.

"She's taking it pretty hard, but I know she'll get through it," Brenda said.

Lillian stared at Tia. "She is a pretty baby," she said. "She looks like Karl when he was a baby." Lillian smiled. That was her way of letting Brenda know that she believed Karl was truly Tia's father. Brenda returned the smile.

Karl walked out of the side door, drinking a glass of water.

"Go in the kitchen and get that pie off the counter," Lillian said.

Karl turned and went back into the house and came back with a warm sweet-potato pie.

"Take that home to your family," Lillian said.

As Karl handed the pie to Brenda, their eyes met. He posed a half smile, but there was something different about him. Brenda just wasn't sure what it was.

"I'm sorry about your brother," Karl said.

"Thanks," Brenda replied. Normally, whenever she saw Karl, her heart pounded just like it did the first time they were together in his bedroom, but not this time, not after all she'd experienced—carrying Tia with him not being involved, him not wanting to marry her. There wasn't so much different about him, she realized. It was her. Her feelings about him had changed.

"I took some pictures of Tia and used my daddy's movie camera," Karl said.

"Oh," Brenda said nonchalantly.

116

"C'mon, Bren, I have to get my daddy's car home before he gets the dogs out looking for me," Cheryl yelled from the car window.

"I have to go," Brenda said.

"All right," Karl said as he brushed his fingers across Tia's soft black hair.

"Don't you keep that baby away from us," Lillian yelled as Brenda walked toward the car.

"I won't," Brenda replied as she opened the car door. She sat in the passenger seat, and Tia rested against her chest wrapped in a pink knitted blanket.

"What's wrong with you?" Cheryl asked.

"I don't know."

"Sure is funny how Karl's family suddenly wants to deal with you," Cheryl said.

"It's not me they want to deal with, it's Tia. They want to see her. They know she's his baby."

"I don't think William or his family will ever want to know Tabya, but I don't give a rat's tail either," Cheryl proclaimed. Brenda stared out the window in silence.

"What are you thinking?" Cheryl asked.

"Karl," Brenda replied. "I don't know. It was as if all those feelings I had for Karl disappeared in a flash. He didn't even look the same to me. It was weird."

"Guess you don't *love* him like you thought," Cheryl said.

"I guess I have a lot on my mind right now, dealing with Al's death."

"Do you and Tia want to come over my house for a while? I got to get this car home. Besides, I know my mama is ready for me to take Tabya off her hands."

"Nah, I need to get back home to check on my family."

"OK." Cheryl slowed down. "Look girl," Cheryl said, pointing toward the basketball court at the park. "That's Jimmy and Pretty Tony. They were at the funeral."

"Yep, they're playing basketball in their church clothes," Brenda said.

Cheryl pulled the car into the lot near the basketball court and parked.

"Jimmy sure got some big feet, and you know what that means," Cheryl said, giggling.

"No," Brenda replied, like she didn't know then smirked.

"I'm just trying to cheer you up, girl."Brenda smiled slightly.

"Maybe this will help." Cheryl pulled out a rolled marijuana cigarette and lit it. "Tia sleep?"

"Yep," Brenda said, looking at Tia sleeping on her chest.

"I'll lay her down on the back seat," Cheryl said, taking Tia from Brenda's arms.

Brenda hesitated a moment since she had just come from her brother's funeral, but smoking weed had become a regular thing she and Cheryl did, and she thought it just might ease her grief "C'mon girl." Brenda laid Tia on the back seat, covering her with a blanket.

Cheryl handed the joint to Brenda. "Here girl," she said, "get you a nice long puff of that."

Brenda gripped it between her thumb and index finger and inhaled it like a pro. She choked and coughed, glancing back at Tia. After she finished, she passed it back to Cheryl.

"This ought to help you get your mind off your troubles," Cheryl said, taking her hit then passing it back to

Brenda. Cheryl glanced at her watch, knowing she needed to get home with her father's car.

Brenda glanced back at Tia again before inhaling once more.

"Damn girl, save me some," Cheryl said.

"So this is what it takes to ease my troubles?" Brenda stated, staring at the marijuana cigarette. She inhaled again as she felt a numbness take over all the pain.

CHAPTER SIXTEEN

*A*lthough the family still grieved Al's death months later, they mustered up the strength to pull together and make it through the next big family event: Maureen's wedding.

Maureen and Brenda sat in their bedroom and shared a conversation as they both made last-minute preparations for the wedding.

"That is a pretty dress," Brenda said.

"Thanks, but now I think I should have bought the one with the puffy sleeves," Maureen replied as she patted, pulled, and straightened the wedding dress she wore.

Brenda sat on the end of her bed, pulling threads from the hem in her baby blue maid of honor dress.

Brenda decided to be blunt, "You sure you love Daniel?" she asked.

"Yeah, I'm sure," Maureen answered, smiling at her reflection in the mirror. She glanced at Brenda, wondering why she asked that question

"Well, how you know you love him?"

"I just know. I mean we get along so well, and we have fun together."

"That's it? You mean that's all it took, and you're in love?"

"It's just a feeling, something you just know in your gut."

"A feeling? I mean you ain't had no other boyfriend, how you know if you love him?" Brenda asked, hunching her shoulders.

"I do love him, and he loves me, too. He asked me to marry him, didn't he?"

"You just want to get out of this house." Brenda smirked.

"That is not true," Maureen exclaimed. Maureen carefully pulled off the dress and hung it on a large hanger, attached it to the top of the closet door, and exited the room without saying another word to Brenda.

Brenda sat on the end of the bed, staring at the wedding dress. She imagined herself wearing it at her own wedding. She laid the maid of honor dress she was holding on the bed and walked toward the wedding gown. She heard the front door close as she ran her fingers across the pretty white lace, pearls, and sequin embellishments. From the bedroom window, she watched Maureen leave with Daniel.

Hurriedly, she kicked her shoes off across the room, took off her skirt and top and slung them onto the bed, pulled the wedding dress down, and stepped into its opening. The dress fit a little snug since she was a few sizes larger than Maureen after giving birth to Tia. She couldn't zip up the back on her own, so she let it hang open. She spun and twisted around in the dress, gazing at herself in the full-length mirror that sat in the corner of the room. She imagined herself gracefully floating down the aisle in the church sanctuary as the music to the wedding march played. Only she could no longer imagine herself with Karl. Those feelings were not as strong as they had been before.

"Who's gonna marry me?" she whispered to herself as she angrily, but carefully took the dress off. She made sure she pulled the silk straps over the hanger and hung it back over the door exactly where it hung before. She tried to be happy about Maureen getting married, but deep down she wished it was her wedding the family was all giddy about.

Maureen seemed to be doing everything right and in the right order.

"Won't be no babies out of wedlock for her, no shotgun wedding, no man telling her he don't want to marry her, and no Daddy telling her she ain't worthy of a good man 'cause she's ruined," Brenda whispered.

What is love supposed to feel like? Brenda's mind wondered as she lay back on her bed. She wanted to know what love really was, what it felt like. She knew it wasn't what she felt for Karl because the feelings she had felt for him before weren't the same anymore. Those thoughts often ran through her mind.

Her mind focused on Uncle Pap. To her, he was the model man. He showed her affection and love. She loved the way he treated her, the way he talked to her so sweetly, the way he would do anything for her or do anything to anybody who even thought about bringing her harm. She wanted a man like her uncle Pap. A man that would treat her like a princess, protect her, and give her anything her heart desired.

"That's the kind of man I want," Brenda whispered as she curled up under a blanket, but her good thoughts were taunted by the many statements Deacon had made in the past: "You're ruined. Ain't no man gonna want you, not no good man. No man wants to take care of another man's child." Though it had been awhile since Deacon made any of those negative statements, they still haunted her.

The wedding day had finally arrived, even after so much grief and indecisiveness on whether or not to postpone the wedding due to Al's death.

"I sure wish Al was here to see you so all dolled up," Johnny said. "You know he would have something to say."

"Yeah, he'd say, Maureen, where you going with that dress on? You gone have me whip some niggas 'bout my sister!" Maureen teased.

"Yeah, it was unbelievable how much he was turning into Daddy and Uncle Pap."

They both laughed. "I'm gonna always miss my knuckled head brother," Johnny said as he embraced Maureen.

"Me too."

"Today is your day, lil sis."

Maureen smiled, sniffled, and wiped the tears from her eyes before planting a kiss on Johnny's cheek. This was supposed to be a happy time and everyone tried to make it that way for Maureen.

At the church, Kadie busied herself strolling through the sanctuary, making sure the decorations were fashionably placed and the flowers were arranged to her liking. She couldn't help but to think about the day Al's casket was rolled down that same aisle she walked. She tried hard to replace those thoughts with thoughts of how he would look as a groomsman wearing a nice black tuxedo standing at the altar at his sister's wedding.

Deacon sat at the back of the church, having a few laughs with Daniel's father. One by one, the wedding party arrived. Maureen picked six bridesmaids, including Brenda who was her maid of honor. Her friends Katherine, Peaches, Delora, and cousins Lucinda and Dovita, were prepping for the ceremony. They all gathered in the small Sunday school room near the choir room that doubled as the bridal quarters whenever there was a wedding. Daniel and the groomsmen gathered in a room in the church basement. His brother Richard was down the hall shaving in the men's restroom.

The Baptist Junkie

"What in the world is that smell?" Kadie asked, covering her nose as she walked past the men's restroom.

"Oh, sorry, Mrs. Wilson," Daniel said with a chuckle. "My brother didn't have time to shave this morning, and he uses that smelly shaving cream."

"My goodness," Kadie said as she rambled through her small satin purse for her perfume. She pumped a few squirts into the air from the tiny bottle and fanned the air with her white gloves.

"You boys 'bout ready?" Kadie asked.

"Yes, ma'am."

Kadie took that time to reiterate a few words she'd already expressed to Daniel when he and Maureen announced they were getting married.

"Daniel, I trust you gone take good care of my daughter," Kadie said, slightly tugging him to the side.

"Oh, yes ma'am. I got things all planned out," Daniel replied.

"Good, 'cause Maureen's a good girl, and she deserves a good man. John and me ain't never seen nothing but good in you. You just stay that way and don't prove me wrong, you hear?" Kadie stared right into his eyes with her hands gripping his upper arms gently.

"Yes, ma'am. I will," Daniel said.

Kadie softened her expression with a smile and a hug. "Now, will you get your brother out of that men's room? He's gonna scare all the guests away with that smelly stuff." Kadie chuckled, covering her nose.

Brenda finished pinning the curls in her hair while her cousin Dovita held Tia. "What have you been feeding this baby?" Dovita asked. "She's so fat." She bounced Tia on her lap.

124

"Mama's been feeding her smashed potatoes." Brenda chuckled.

"You mean mashed potatoes," Dovita said.

"Hey, hey," Lois said as she barged in excitedly. "I brought you big Mama's pearl necklace she gave me for your *something borrowed*."

"Thank you," Maureen said, glowing with happiness. "Mama gave me her blue handkerchief, her old good luck coin, and Brenda bought me a rhinestone pendant that I pinned right here on my brassiere."

"So you have your something old, something new, something borrowed, and something blue?"

"Yes, ma'am." Maureen smiled.

" Awww, Maureen, you look so pretty."

"Thank you, Aunt Lois."

"You and Danny planned this wedding pretty quick. Girl, you ain't knocked up, are you?" Lois asked playfully.

"No, I am not," Maureen responded firmly. "Folks do get married when they're in love, not just when they've gotten knocked up. I want to spend the rest of my life with Daniel."

"Well, good. I am happy for you. I wish you the best," Lois said hugging Maureen.

After the bridesmaids were all dressed, they lined up in the hallway. Brenda stayed in the room with Maureen.

"I really am happy for you," Brenda said. "You're the prettiest bride I've ever seen." She smiled.

"Thank you, baby sister."

"Don't you go having babies and forget about Tia." Brenda smiled.

"Humph, Tia ain't just your baby," Maureen said. "She's mine, too."

Maureen and Brenda smiled and held each other in a warm embrace.

"Oh, we almost forgot about this," Brenda said as she pulled out the baby blue garter belt from a bag. Maureen sat down in the chair while Brenda helped her slip it onto her leg. Brenda patted, smoothed, tucked, and pulled on Maureen's dress, preparing her for the big entrance.

A familiar knock sounded at the door. "That must be Daddy," Maureen and Brenda said simultaneously.

"You ain't got to worry about hearing that knock *no* more," Brenda said.

They both chuckled.

"Y'all ready in there?" Deacon yelled from outside the door.

"Yeah Daddy, she's ready." Brenda gave Maureen a once-over and straightened her veil."You ready?" she asked.

"I'm ready."

"I really am happy for you," Brenda repeated. Brenda blew her a kiss and backed out the door.

Deacon peeked in the room. "Is my daughter in here?" he said, looking around the room.

"Daddy, I am your daughter." Maureen blushed.

"Girl, you look like one of those girls in a magazine."

"Thank you, Daddy."

"Now, you know," he began, "if things don't go right for you, you can always come back home."

"I know, Daddy."

Deacon smiled. "But I know things gone be just fine for you. If I didn't believe that, I would have said you couldn't marry him."

"I know that, too, Daddy." Maureen smiled.

"All right, we better get you out there before Kadie starts raising sand. Ready?" Deacon opened the door and extended his elbow. Maureen smiled and took a deep breath.

"I'm ready, Daddy."

Maureen tucked her arm into Deacon's as they walked out. The organist began the wedding march. Deacon was so proud. He and Maureen both grinned from ear to ear.

"Daddy, Daniel is a good man," she whispered. "We gone be fine. We *all* gone be fine."

CHAPTER SEVENTEEN

*B*renda finally got around to cleaning and rearranging the bedroom since Maureen moved. She worked all day, cleaning and disassembling Maureen's twin bed, and moved her desk to make more room for Tia. Aside from Tia crying, the house was rather quiet. There was no laughing, no feet traveling the stairs, and no sibling rivalry. As usual, Deacon spent most of his time at the church and in the basement. Kadie went in and out of depression mourning Al's death.

Maureen was enjoying married life until Daniel got drafted into the Army. Johnny and his girlfriend, Reatta, had recently eloped. Kadie and Deacon weren't happy about it, but they had already endured so much that year they didn't have the energy to object.

Even after moving all the furniture in the bedroom, Brenda wasn't satisfied.

"This is just not it. Everybody's gone on with their lives but me."

Brenda walked around the room, picking up Tia's toys as she thought about what she wanted to do with her life. She pulled the postcard that Cheryl sent her off the dresser mirror and read it again. Frustrated, Brenda tossed the postcard on to the dresser and stood there gazing at herself in the mirror. The few pounds she'd lost were noticeable.

Tia had fallen asleep with the nipple of her baby bottle still clutched between her eight teeth. Brenda plopped down on the bed and curled up next to her. Most nights, she couldn't sleep. She simply lay in bed, thinking about her life. She thought about going to cosmetology school. She thought about going to night school like Cheryl did before she moved away to at least finish high school since she hadn't returned to school after Tia's birth. She wondered about Karl. She hadn't heard from him since he'd left to attend college at Wayne State University. She knew she had to do something. She just had to figure out what that something would be.

Deacon, wearing one of his favorite plaid suits, stood at the dining table. He sifted through the mail and took out the letter addressed to him and tucked it in the drawer of the China cabinet. He, looked through a few books he had stacked on the table and shoved the ones he needed to teach his Wednesday morning Bible class into his briefcase.

"It's about time for you to be giving up that bottle, lil girl," he said, bending down to talk to Tia. "You're a big girl," Deacon said.

She stood there sliding her bottom back and forth against the wall, smiling back at him. Brenda headed straight for the refrigerator.

"Brenda, I've been meaning to talk to you," Deacon said. Brenda sighed quietly and stood in the doorway to hear what he was going to say. "I think you done missed enough church. I understood how you was feeling 'bout how some of them church folks was actin', but we passed all that now. The Lord forgave you and that's all that matters. As long as you in this house, you gonna have to be in church regularly." Deacon locked his briefcase, grabbed his black trench coat from the chair, and slapped his black brim hat on his head. "Bye lil baby," he said as he walked toward the back door.

"Bye bye," Tia said, waving and grinning, still gripping her bottle.

Brenda didn't say a word, just stepped out of the way to let Deacon through the doorway. He knew that Brenda understood him clearly.

"Come on, let Grandma put you in your high chair so you can eat," Kadie said. She spread butter on a slice of toast, ripped it into small pieces, and fed Tia the eggs and bacon. Brenda sat down at the table and began to read the newspaper Deacon left sitting there.

"Mama, I'm gonna get me an apartment," Brenda blurted as she pulled the newspaper up in front of her face.

"Apartment? Humph!" Kadie kept feeding Tia.

"Yeah, Mama an apartment. I'm almost nineteen now. It's 'bout time I got out on my own…me *and* Tia." Brenda slowly pulled the newspaper down to see Kadie's reaction.

Kadie twisted her lips, and batted her eyes.

Although Brenda had her own baby, Kadie still saw Brenda as the baby of the family. After Al's death and Maureen's wedding, the last thing Kadie thought about was Brenda leaving, too. Tia was like her own child and caring for her helped her through her time of grief and moments of depression. She didn't feel Brenda was ready to move out on her own and definitely not responsible enough to totally care for Tia.

"How in the world would you take care of yourself…*and* Tia without a job?"

"Mama, Karen Scott got a new apartment. She went to Social Aid and they gave her money. I can do that, too."

"Social Aid," Kadie shouted. "Girl, you know good and well your Father will have two fits and a hen!"

"I just got to get out of here. I'm tired of Daddy always on my case about something. Now he's talking about church. Humph, I'm grown!"

Kadie shook her head and continued feeding Tia. As bad as she wanted to keep Brenda and especially Tia, right there with her, she knew it was a possibility that they'd both be leaving her sometime or another.

Brenda knew Kadie was not happy about what she said, but she was ready to put her plans in motion.

"C'mon Tia. Let's go get us a bath," Brenda said as she used a napkin to wipe Tia's face and hands before lifting her out of the high chair. Kadie didn't say a word. It was at that moment that Kadie felt powerless, realizing that Tia was Brenda's daughter and not hers and that Brenda wasn't going to stop until she got what she wanted.

***

"I can't wait to get out of here," Brenda said, her voice muffled by the sound of the running water. Brenda sat Tia down in the water. Tia wasn't always excited about bath time, so Brenda often had to sing to her in order to keep her calm.

Hands on my heart what is this here. This is my thinking box,
Mommie, my dear. Thinking box, thinking box
Inky, Inky do, that's what I learned in the school...

Brenda pointed and tapped on Tia's head then her nose and other parts as they related to the song. She continued singing the song while getting Tia dressed. By the time she was finished with her, Tia wore a pretty pink ruffled dress, ruffled panties, socks, and white lace bows in her hair.

"We gone get our own house," she whispered to Tia as she adjusted the straps on Tia's tiny white patented leather shoes.

131

Brenda's mind was set. She would do exactly what she said she wanted to do no matter what Kadie said or how Deacon would feel about it. She just had to figure out how, though.

***

It was late in the afternoon. Brenda glanced at her watch. She and Tia had been sitting in the welfare office for over three hours after Brenda filled out some forms.

"I wish they'd hurry up," Brenda complained, rolling her eyes. They sat and watched as social workers called people, mostly single women with their children, through the big brown door.

Finally, a tall slender white women,wearing a red hairpiece and a navy blue polyester dress came through the door.

"Brenda Wilson," the woman called.

Hastily, Brenda got up, flung Tia on her hip, and walked toward the door.

"Are you Brenda Wilson?"

"Yeah," Brenda replied.

"My name is Mrs. Pero. I am a caseworker. I'm going to be going over your application."

They walked down a long narrow hallway to her office. The smell of oldness and musk masked by cleaning fluid was strong in the air. Brenda plopped Tia down on her lap as she sat down at the desk across from Ms. Pero. Immediately, the caseworker began reading and marking on the forms Brenda had filled out while Brenda sat quietly and waited.

Mr. Pero asked Brenda a series of personal questions, from where and whom she lived with to how much money did everyone in the household earn and have in their bank accounts. She asked many questions about Deacon and his income.

The caseworker eyeballed Brenda and Tia, scanning their clothes from head to toe. "That's a beautiful dress," she said, noticing the fancy dress Tia had on.

With her red ink pen, Mrs. Pero took a few more notes before she spoke again. Brenda sat there, biting on her bottom lip with sheer anticipation.

"I don't think we can assist you," Ms. Pero said bluntly.

Brenda swallowed hard and responded equally blunt, "Why not?"

"Since your father is employed by General Motors, he certainly should be able to support you and your one daughter."

Brenda's mood quickly turned to anger. Her infamous eye rolling and lip smacking gestures revealed she was pissed. She sighed and realized that she had gone about this the wrong way and had given up more information than she should have.

The caseworker smirked as she noticed Brenda's apparent attitude and looked down at the forms pretending she was still reading them.

"C'mon Tia," Brenda demanded angrily. As she picked up Tia, she noticed the caseworker staple the forms she'd filled out and tossed them onto a pile of others. Brenda was visibly angry, her light complexion, red as she mumbled a few choice words under her breath. She didn't even consider saying, "Thank you," "goodbye," or anything.

"Dangit! Ain't this about a…" Brenda exclaimed, catching her tongue.

What am I gonna do now? she thought. She believed welfare would be her lucky break. She was angry, at the caseworker, and at herself for getting pregnant so young and not having the money to move on her own and even more angry at Karl whom she felt abandoned her. Instantly, thoughts of him annoyed her even more.

"I hate that bastard!"Although her feelings for him changed, she never resented him more than on this day. She gritted and grinded her teeth as she visualized him having fun with his friends in college while she had to stay home to care for their child with no support from him.

***

Several months later, Brenda was even more anxious to get out on her own. She thought she'd try the welfare system again. "I know what to do this time," she said assuredly as she dressed for the second venture. With sheer deception as her main objective, she plotted carefully. She remembered how the caseworker looked at their clothes and commented on how nice they were.

"If you have to look poor and destitute in order for them to help you, then poor and destitute we shall be."She pondered only a moment before her creative energies surged and she was ready to work, like a scientist working on a new invention. First, she sifted through a bag of clothes Tia had outgrown."This is perfect," she said as she pulled out a stained, ivory colored dress two sizes too small for Tia. She had clothes and shoes from that bag scattered on the bed and on the floor. Tia sat watching as she pranced confidently around the room.

Brenda gave no consideration to tidiness whatsoever. Using a kitchen knife, she cut the toe ends out of a pair of Tia's black patented leather shoes that were too small. She put on an old snagged, dingy white dress from a bag of clothes the white lady Kadie did housework for gave to her.

134

She ripped the leather on some old slippers and wore them. Forcefully, she pulled the little dress over Tia's head losing two buttons in the struggle. The long sleeves, barely past her elbows were tight under her armpits restricting her movement. Still calculating, she panned the room for more ideas.

"Aha," she said as she pulled a fingernail clipper off the dresser and clipped holes in the knee areas of Tia's white tights then enlarged the holes, stretching them with her fingers.

"Now get down on the floor and play," she said, hoping Tia would accumulate dust from the wooden floors to make her look more dingy and needy. Brenda brushed her black wavy hair back and didn't comb Tia's at all, all part of the illusion. Finally, with Tia on her hip she stood in front of the full-length mirror admiring their costumes as if they were a works of art. She tugged and pulled on their clothes like a fashion designer would prepare models for a fashion show.

"Perfect," she said devilishly.

***

Children ran rampant in the welfare department..With all the commotion in the room, Tia got the urge to get down and play. She squirmed then slid backwards out of the chair. Brenda was already tense and jittery. She did not want to see Tia running among all the disruption in the room. She snatched a hand full of the back of Tia's shirt and pulled her back, sitting her firmly on her lap.

Minutes later, the big brown door opened again. The same caseworker as before appeared at the door.

"Brenda Wilson" Brenda inhaled, released two quick breaths, and got up as if she was preparing for a Broadway performance, making her way to the stage and Tia was her prop, fastened to her hip.

"I'm Brenda," she said as she approached the lady.

They followed the lady to her office, down the same odor filled hallway. Tia sat on Brenda's lap at the desk across from the caseworker. As the caseworker looked over the paperwork, Brenda sat quietly. She cleared her throat, preparing to answer the intrusive questions she knew would follow. Brenda wasn't sure if the caseworker remembered them and the case worker didn't act as if they were familiar either. The silence in the room was beginning to make Brenda a little nervous. She felt it was time to expedite her illustrious plan and demonstrate her theatrical abilities.

Just short of tears, in a humbling, sincere voice Brenda began to speak.

"I just don't know what else to do," she began. "My parents put me out, and I have no place to go. I've been staying from house to house with friends."

The caseworker lifted the box of tissue from her desk and offered them to Brenda. She pulled out a few and dabbed her eyes. Once again, the caseworker scanned them up and down, appraising their apparel, but there was no doubt that as a result of Brenda's less fashionable coordinates, they definitely looked needy. They were well-costumed for this show that Brenda and Tia could have been models for a "help the poor" poster.

They sat in silence as the caseworker took notes with her famous red ink pen. Without hesitation, she handed Brenda some forms to sign.

"Given the circumstances," the caseworker said, "I will approve your application. I would not want to see you and your daughter without a place to live. Now all you need to do is find you a place. I'll set you up for your food stamps."

136

"Food stamps?"

"Yes, so you and your daughter can get food."

Brenda didn't know anything about food stamps. She had no idea they were included in the deal. She just figured she'd get food from her parents' house. Brenda was ecstatic, but dared to express it. She signed the forms and handed them back to the caseworker.

"You come back once you've found a place," the caseworker said as she escorted them out of her office.

"Thank you," Brenda replied with humbling gratitude. Once they got past the big brown door, Brenda exhaled in celebration. Her expression was a combination of victory and relief. "We did it," she whispered. As they exited the building, she shouted, repeating it over and over, "We did it, we did it."

CHAPTER EIGHTEEN

*K*adie was sad that Brenda was leaving and taking Tia, but she knew there was nothing she còuld do about it. Deacon was outright furious.

"Welfare is not the way to raise a child," he said. "I worked two and sometimes three jobs before I got the job at GM, and your mama washed, ironed, and scrubbed white folks' floors so that all of y'all didn't have to worry about nothing." He slammed his glass of iced tea down on the table, spilling some on the placemat. "I'll tell you what … since you want to get out into the world so bad, you go right ahead, but you leave that baby right here."

Brenda paused, shocked by his suggestion. "Tia is my baby," Brenda said, "and I'm gonna take care of her." Brenda picked Tia up off the sofa and carried her upstairs. Tears streamed down her face.

"John, you can't make her leave her baby," Kadie said. "God knows I want nothing more than to keep both of them right here in this house, but she's over eighteen now. She is grown. You think we can hold her here forever? You're the one always quoting scriptures, *Train up a child in the way he should go…*" Kadie pursed her lips.

"Yeah, but I'm just not so sure about Brenda. She never listened. She done already messed up."

"All I know to do is pray about it. Brenda's gone be fine. She found an apartment just a few blocks over on Buick Street."

Deacon sighed, shook his head, and hoped that Kadie was right.

***

"This is perfect," Brenda said as she pranced through their upstairs apartment. Tia totted around, playing and giggling, enjoying the sound of her hard walking shoes clacking against the polished dark wood floors. The two-family duplex had two bedrooms and a large backyard.

"It's so small," Deacon said.

"Well, Daddy, it's just me and Tia. This is fine for us. There's a bedroom for me and one for her."

"Oh, it's plenty big enough," Kadie said.

Deacon shot Kadie a look. It was still hard for him to accept Brenda living on her own with Tia.

"Maureen has some extra furniture that Daniel's mother gave them," Brenda said. "She said I can have it."

"No, we're gonna help you get some furniture," Kadie said.

Deacon sighed and eyed Kadie again. He looked around at the carved moldings in the ceiling and the glass doorknobs on both the bedroom doors.

"I ... guess we can't let you stay here ... without at least something to sit on ... and Tia needs a bed to sleep in," Deacon admitted.

Brenda grinned from ear to ear. She was excited about getting new furnishings, but mostly, she was happy to hear Deacon say that he would help.

"I'm gonna pay her first month's rent, but she has to get a job. I just don't want her dependent on welfare."

"Ok, John," Kadie said. She still hadn't told him that Brenda went back to the welfare office and was approved. "Daniel said he will help her get a job in the plant."

Brenda managed to furnish their apartment within a few weeks. She had new bedroom suites for Tia and for herself along with used furnishings from family members.

She was so happy, but wished Cheryl could be around to help her celebrate and decorate. With her gone, Brenda began spending time with a new group of friends which included Lorraine Jackson, a loud and wild woman that she loved hanging out with.

She had met Lorraine at a barbecue at Lorraine's cousin Joe's house. Like Brenda, Lorraine was in her early twenties, single, and had two sons, Brian and Mario.

"Girl, this is a nice place," Lorraine said as she relaxed in Brenda's living room.

"Thanks."

"Go on back in there and play," Lorraine said to her sons, who ran back and forth through the living room. "Can I get an ashtray?" Lorraine asked.

"I don't have an ashtray."

"That's ok." Lorraine pulled the napkin from under her glass of soda and spread it open on the table. She took an envelope from her purse and dumped the contents of it on to the napkin. "This is some good stuff," Lorraine said as she pulled out a pack of cigarette papers and began to scoop some of the marijuana into the paper. "C'mon and roll you a joint, girl." Lorraine waved the brown envelope in the air.

"I don't really know how to do that," Brenda said, hunching her shoulders.

"I thought you said you smoked weed before."

"I did, but it was already rolled up."

Lorraine pushed her boys' coats and her purse to the side and slid over on the couch, making space for Brenda to sit down. She sat beside her as if she was taking a lesson in joint rolling. Lorraine pinched some of the marijuana up in her fingers and sprinkled it into the cigarette paper she held in the other hand. She glided it past her nostrils before she licked the paper's edge like an envelope and sealed it closed. Brenda followed the same procedure and rolled up one for herself, only she hadn't done it as smoothly and dropped some of the marijuana on to the floor.

"Don't be wasting it," Lorraine said. "Girl, that cost money ... and honey." She laughed.

"Honey?"

"Girl, you ain't hip on nothin' is you? See ... this is what you call a nickel bag. That means it costs five dollars, get it ... nickel, and when I ain't got no money, I got to give Bones a lil something extra, that's *honey,* if you know what I mean." She grinned.

Brenda shook her head as if she understood what Lorraine meant.

"Bones?" she asked.

"He helps me out with the boys sometimes."

"Oh, he's their father?"

"Nah. I ain't seen neither one of their no good daddies in a few years. I don't even worry about it either." Lorraine put the joint between her lips and inhaled herself a long serving. Brenda watched and copied her motions. The scene reminded her of the first time she smoked marijuana with Cheryl. "Wooo wee," Lorraine said as she sucked at the air.

Brenda nearly choked as she laughed and inhaled again. They both laughed all night and rolled up the rest of the marijuana and smoked it until it was gone. The brand new cherry wood coffee table was covered with cigarette papers, marijuana seeds, and a tin pan of crumbs from the sweet potato pie Kadie had made for her and Tia.

Tia and Lorraine's boys had worn themselves out playing into the late hours of the morning until they just couldn't take it anymore. All three kids were sprawled out on the hardwood floor in Tia's room fast asleep.

Brenda shared a few joints with Cheryl before, but she had never gotten that high. The feeling reminded her of the time she took the Humphrey Eleven pills when she was pregnant. She laid back on the sofa and allowed that high to spin her around the room like a carnival ride.

Lorraine swayed her way over to the record player that sat on a small end table in the corner. "Girl, we got to go out," Lorraine said as she staggered and danced, grooving to the rhythm of her high.

"Out where?" Brenda's words dragged from her mouth.

"Not tonight. We got to get somebody to keep these kids and then we go out."

"Uh huh. I want to go." Brenda replied, the only words she could muster.

She had never been to a club before, but she was ready to venture into new things.

***

The following weekend, Kadie had already planned to keep Tia, so a baby sitter was not a problem. "I ain't never been to no dance hall," Brenda said as she stood in the mirror wearing the skirt Lorraine loaned her, adjusting the split in it that ran up close to her rear end. "I ain't never worn no skirt this short before either."

"There's a first time for everything, and it's called a club not a dance hall. You sound so southern." Lorraine stuffed two joints into the lining of her purse. "Bones works at the club. He's gone let us in for free, so you don't have to worry 'bout that. You ready?"

142

"I guess." Brenda shrugged.

They pulled up to the club in Lorraine's rusty white '63 Buick Riviera that her father had given her before he moved down south with his mistress. A big sign on the front of the club read Poppa's Pad Night Club. Lorraine pulled her knitted shawl down to expose her boney shoulders and the thin spaghetti straps of her dress that crisscrossed on her back then glanced at herself in the rearview mirror.

"C'mon girl," Lorraine said, yanking her small beaded purse from the front seat and slamming the squeaky car door behind her.

Brenda got out the car, wiped at the wrinkles in her skirt, and popped a peppermint in her mouth. She walked a few steps behind Lorraine, trying to stay balanced in the high-heeled shoes she'd borrowed from Lois. "Don't know how long I'll wear these shoes. I shole don't think I can dance in them!"

"Hey Bones," Lorraine said, smiling at the heavyweight black man guarding the front door of the club.

"Bones?" Brenda whispered under her breath, eyeing his large physique. She had assumed he'd be a slender man since his name was Bones. Sweat dripped from his side burns, and his expensive looking shirt had large wet spots under his armpits. His large belly hung jolly over his mustard yellow slacks, causing his black leather belt to disappear under his belly. His large cheeks poked out and jiggled when he spoke, and his double chin blended in with his neck. Bones was a known hustler, and women tolerated his gluttonous ways because he was smooth and paid good for their affections. What women didn't know, until later,

143

was that Bones' good pay was only temporary since he had an agenda.

"This is Brenda." The words twirled out Lorraine's mouth as she pulled herself up to Bones' cheek and kissed him.

"Hi," Brenda replied softly. She tried to conceal it, but her expression glowed with a tinge of disgust.

Bones nodded and handed Lorraine a small brown envelope, and she quickly slid it into her purse. As they walked inside the club, Bone's licked his lips lustfully as his eyes trailed every inch of Brenda's body.

Lorraine stepped into the club, dancing to the sound of Isaac Hayes's "Shaft." Two of her friends, Pam and Diane walked up to greet her.

"What's happening, girl?" they both said. They were dressed similar to Lorraine. They surrounded her, excluding Brenda as if she wasn't standing there.

"C'mon Brenda," Lorraine said, taking hold of Brenda's hand as she and her friends floated out to the dance floor.

"Nah, you go ahead," Brenda said, waving the trio off.

Brenda found a table in a dark corner and sat down. She paid attention to her surroundings and the many characters that walked by. She noticed the disproportioned ratio of men to women. Many of the men had an entourage of women, with women draped on each arm. She swayed and snapped her fingers to the beat as a skimpy-dressed waitress weaved her way past the crowd of tables and chairs and sat a drink down on her table.

"I … I didn't order this."

"I know, Bones did," the waitress replied.

"Bones?"

"Yeah," the waitress said, pointing to the area where Bones stood. Bones nodded and grinned. Brenda posed a half smile and accepted the drink. She took a few sips of the liquor and tolerated its strong taste in order to finish it.

Bones walked over to her table and sat down. "You want another drink?"

"No, thank you." Brenda noticed, but tried not to stare at his large body that overlapped the wooden chair he sat in across from her. His belly pressed against the table's edge as his meaty arms rested across the table top. "Why did you send *me* a drink?"

"Beautiful lady, over here by yourself. You looked a little tense. I thought a drink might be good for you," he said.

Brenda tried to be cordial, but her expression showcased her non-interest in conversing with him.

What Brenda didn't know was Bones knew how to get the heart of a woman to make her see past his unattractiveness. He smoothly moved his way in charming her with compliments, and she giggled from his flattery.

"How come I ain't never seen you round Lorraine before?"

"We really just started hanging out."

"Oh." He sucked his teeth, rotating the toothpick he held in his mouth from one side to the other.

Some time had passed during the conversation, and she noticed Lorraine wasn't in her view. Brenda squinted, scanning the darkness of the club for Lorraine.

"You looking for Lorraine?"

"Yeah, I'm ready to go."

"She in the poker room in the back."

"She playin' poker?"

"Humph, Nah," Bones replied. Brenda looked confused. "I can take you home."

"I ... I'll just wait for Lorraine."

Bones shrugged. "You might be waiting a long time," he said. He pulled his keys from his pocket and yelled to one of his flunkies standing off to the side. "Junior, bring my car around to the front."

"Really, I'll just wait for Lorraine."

Bones was persistent as he used much effort to pull himself away from the table to stand up. "It's cool, mama. I'll get you home. I'm not gonna hurt you. It's cool, I'll have one of the fellas tell Lorraine," he said, smiling.

Brenda was reluctant at first, but agreed to let Bones take her home. They talked and laughed in the car on the way. Brenda found him to be quite a gentleman, smooth and charming despite his appearance. He turned off his headlights as he pulled his long black Cadillac into Brenda's driveway.

"Thank you," Brenda said as she reached to open the car door.

"Let me get that for you." Bones wiggled his way out of the car and walked around to the passenger's side to open the door for Brenda. "Ain't you gone invite me in?" he asked in a smooth tone, sliding his finger around the brim of his hat.

"It's a ... kind of late, and I have to get up early."

"Aaw, just for a few minutes. I won't stay long."

Brenda could not understand how just a few hours ago the man she thought was the most disgusting looking man she had ever seen was now so charming and persuasive and a guest at her apartment.

Bones shifted his pants legs and braced himself to sit down. His body nearly spread across the entire sofa."Pretty lil girl," Bones said, noticing the many pictures of Tia placed on the wall and tables around the room. "Your daughter?"

"Yeah."

"I'ma lil thirsty. Can I have something to drink?"

Brenda stepped into the small kitchen and poured herself and Bones a glass of cola. Bones slid a small bottle of rum from his inside jacket pocket and poured some into his glass. He poured some into Brenda's glass without asking her if she wanted it, but she drank it without complaining.

Bones took notice of everything in the room. A picture of a man in his Army uniform sat on her end table.

"That your ... man?"

"No, that's my brother. He died in the war."

"Oh, sorry. That Vietnam is a motha. I lost a brother, too."

Brenda walked over to her stereo.

"I see you got a nice record collection," Bones said. Brenda pulled out a Gladys Knight and the Pips record and played it. Bones bobbed his head to the beat. "I love that song," he said as he sang a few of the lyrics to "Midnight Train to Georgia." "Can I get a little more of that cola?" Bones asked. She refilled both their glasses, and he poured more rum in them. Brenda sat down beside him and drank her rum and coke.

"Can I check out a few of your albums?" Brenda handed him a few of the albums she was sifting through. She played a few of his song requests. In addition to the drink she had at the club, the two glasses of rum and coke had her drunk. Brenda yawned and glanced over at the wall

147

clock, shooting hints that she was ready for him to go. Instead of taking the hints, he placed the album cover on his lap and pulled out a small brown envelope from his jacket pocket and poured white powder from it onto the album cover. Brenda had seen Lorraine with brown envelopes filled with marijuana and recently she saw her with envelopes filled with cocaine. Obviously very intoxicated, Brenda stared at his movements.

"You want a hit?" Bones asked.

"Ah … A, no," Brenda stuttered.

"Aw … C'mon. Take a hit."

Brenda shook her head. "It's late and I'm tired." Her words slurred.

Bones sifted and divided out four lines of the cocaine with the smooth edge of the envelope then sniffed one full line as Brenda watched. Bones ignored her gestures and kept talking and sniffing. "Where's her father?" Bones nodded, looking at Tia's picture.

Brenda shrugged, trying to avoid the question. She began to clean up. She reached for Bones' glass.

"Sit down," he said as he caught her hand and gripped it gently. Brenda was startled, but cautiously sat down on the tiny space left on the sofa beside him. "I'm not gonna hurt you. I would never do that. You seem like a good girl. I like good girls." His words floated smoothly into the air as he smiled.

Brenda sat quietly, slouched on the sofa hoping that his next words would lead him out the door, but he just kept talking. The smoothness of his voice was soothing and hypnotic. Bones reached into another pocket and pulled out a folded stack of crisp dollar bills. "I like kids. Here, take this and buy your daughter something nice from Uncle Bones." He handed her a hundred-dollar bill.

"I, ah, I can't take…"

"Take it," he whispered, cutting into her words. He pulled a second hundred-dollar bill from the stack. "Take this … for you."

"I … I don't know," Brenda said hesitantly.

"Relax … here, do a line." He lifted the album cover up in front of her face.

"I don't … I … I," Brenda stuttered.

"Go 'head. It'll help you unwind."

Brenda hesitated, staring curiously at the white powder. She saw Lorraine sniff cocaine, but always turned it down when she offered it to her.

"C'mon try it. It's easy," Bones said. He scooped a small amount onto his index finger and sniffed it then scooped more for Brenda. "Try it."

Being in such a vulnerable state, Bones' charming personality outweighed his unattractiveness. He smiled as Brenda stared into his eyes, lowered her nose to his finger, and quickly sniffed it off his finger.

"See, this is real good stuff," Bones assured, scooping his finger into it a second time, once again feeding it to her nose. She sniffed, laid her head back against the back of the sofa, and wiped her nose with the back of her hand.

"Wow," Brenda responded, blinking her eyes and shaking her head from the dizziness that came over her.

"Go ahead," Bones said, pushing it at her again, urging her to do more.

She sniffed the rest by herself as Bones enjoyed the scene of his accomplishment. He had a vindictive agenda. He loved pretty women, but he hated them, too. He had deep psychological issues about them. When he was a young boy he felt it was the pretty women he liked that taunted him for being so big. He knew his smooth talk and money could lure women, but he felt that's all the women cared about, so he got a thrill out of introducing them to drugs and turning them into junkies and sometimes even prostitutes.

Brenda changed rapidly. She was hyper and fidgety like a little girl. Her voice was slurred as she rambled out words. She became loose and unlady like, slinging her bare legs open as she spoke, slouched on the sofa.

Bones laughed as she told him stories about her family and how it was growing up in a religious household. He laughed more as she mocked her father and his favorite quotes and scriptures.

"For God so loved the whole wide world," she mumbled, giggling, high and numb to the touch of Bones' fat fingers traveling up and down her bare legs.

Brenda was dazed as Bones slowly removed her blouse and massaged her breasts without her resistance. She went from being hyper and fidgety to sluggish. When she finally fell asleep, Bones laid her down on the sofa and stared at her from head to toe, her bare breasts, thick legs, and the short skirt that was bunched up around her waist, revealing the silky white panties she wore. With heavy breaths, he thought about satisfying his sexual urges as she lay there so vulnerable, but the brightness of the new morning sun that beamed through the thin curtains halted his thoughts like a vampire that strikes in the darkness and hides in the light. Bones smirked and picked up her blouse that was slung across the back of the sofa and dropped it down on her chest. He scooped up the money he'd given her that was lying on the coffee table. His first thought was to shove it in his pocket.

I'll see her again, he thought. With a devilish expression on his face, he dropped the two hundred-dollar

bills back on the table, slipped on his jacket and hat,
grabbed his rum, and tipped out the front door

CHAPTER NINETEEN

*B*renda woke up, frantic and paranoid and in a cold
sweat. She looked around at the messy coffee table and the
cocaine residue left on the album cover. Confused, she tried
to remember what happened. As she pulled herself up from
the sofa, her blouse fell off her chest and onto the floor.
Shamefully, she picked it up and covered herself. Her bare
feet pressed against the wooden floor as she rocked back
and forth cradling herself. She rubbed her hands up and
down her arms and shoulders as a cold chill rattled her
body. Dazed and unclear about what happened and why her
blouse was off, she looked down at her bare chest and dug
deep into her memory, trying to recall whether she had
been intimate with Bones. She hoped she hadn't. The
thought of any sexual contact with him sickened her.

She did remember him giving her the money as she
picked it up off the table and balled it up in her fist. She
though back to what Loraine said about Bones and *honey*.

Still a little woozy, she stumbled and made her way to
the bathroom, turned on the water faucet, and stared at her
reflection in the mirror. She felt ashamed for not
remembering what happened after she snorted the cocaine.
Hastily, she yanked off her skirt, examining herself,
touching her vaginal area for any evidence of a sexual
encounter with Bones. She believed nothing could have
happened.

She didn't realize that there were other things just as
damaging as a sexual encounter that had been set in motion
with her one reckless night.

A few months passed, and hanging out and getting
high became a regular endeavor for Brenda and Lorraine.
Their nights usually started the same, the pair at Brenda's,
taking in lines of cocaine before one of them suggested
they head out to see what they could get into.

This night was no different. After spending a few
hours at the Tip of the Rock Club where most of the high-
class hookers and well-known pimps frequented, Lorraine
and Brenda ended up at Poppa's Pad, where Bones always
worked the door. Brenda never mentioned to Lorraine the
night with Bones or the little brown envelopes he'd been
giving her. She thought Brenda's first and only cocaine
experiences were with her. She didn't know that Bones had
supplied Brenda with cocaine several times since that night
he'd driven her home from the club. The more Brenda did,
the more she wanted, and she never had a problem getting
it.

As they entered the club, Lorraine greeted Bones with
a hug and a kiss on his fat cheek as she always did. She
looked back and caught a glimpse of Brenda also giving
Bones a hug and kiss, but quickly dismissed the negative
thoughts that ran through her head.

"C'mon girl," Lorraine said, tugging at Brenda,
locking her arm into hers.

Bones locked his eyes on both their backsides,
devilishly dipping his imagination into a ménage trois with
them. He licked his lips and sucked at his teeth as Big Ray,
one of the club bouncers shut the door behind them.

The club was packed that night. As usual, the man to
woman ratio was disproportioned. Some of the women
stood around near the dance floor hoping to be chosen by
one of the three-piece suitors who already had an entourage
of women trailing them. Other women didn't care about the

shortage of men and took themselves to the dance floor. The D.J. catered to them, playing the songs that kept them twisting and turning, celebrating their independence.

Lorraine was always wild and uncaring; she sang and danced her way through the crowed on the dance floor. Brenda occupied a seat at a table in a dark corner. She wasn't so big on dancing in the club. If she wasn't standing around bobbing to the beat, she was sitting at a table sipping on a drink.

Just as Lorraine emerged from the dance floor, she noticed Brenda and Bones standing in the corner talking. She frowned when she saw Bones slide a brown envelope into the front of Brenda's bra and walk away. Immediately, Lorraine walked over to her.

"Was that Bones you was just talking to?" she asked knowing already that it was Bones.

"Uh huh," Brenda replied, staring out onto the dance floor, swaying to the music as if it was her favorite song.

"Ooh girl," Lorraine said, "all that liquor got me going. Come go with me to the little girls' room."

Brenda followed Lorraine down a dark corridor to the ladies' bathroom. Lorraine checked the stalls, making sure no one else was in the restroom as Brenda stood in the mirror picking at the new afro style she wore. Her hair was so soft that the afro kind of dropped and swayed on the sides.

Abruptly, Lorraine snatched a handful of Brenda's hair and slammed her up against the wall, then gripped her throat with both hands.

"What's going on with you and Bones?"

"Nothing!" Brenda shouted, gagging and struggling, trying to break free of Lorraine's grip.

"I told you Bones was my man, and you better stay away from him."

"No, you didn't. You said he was just a…"

Lorraine cut into her words. "Like I said, stay away! What is this?" Lorraine ripped the brown envelope from Brenda's bra, exposing her cleavage.

The two ladies wrestled and fought over the envelope, slapping and punching at each other, ripping at each other's clothes and hair.

"Give me that," Brenda yelled.

"You hussy!" Lorraine screamed. Lorraine was furious and it wasn't that she cared so much for Bones; she felt Brenda was moving in on her supply man. She knew Bones dealt with other women, but she felt privileged, and the possibility of being pushed aside for Brenda frightened her.

Another lady walked into the restroom and ran out. Big Ray rushed in and pulled Lorraine off Brenda, wrapping his big arms around her waist and tugging her backward out of the ladies' room.

"You stay away from him, you whore!" Lorraine yelled, her feet dangling in the air and her hand gripping the brown envelope of cocaine tightly.

Brenda took a moment to gather herself, using a paper towel to wipe the blood that trickled from the corner of her lip and her nostrils. She splashed water on her red swollen eyes. Her eyes zoomed in on every inch of the ladies' room floor, searching for the envelope.

Bones walked in. "She clipped you?" he asked with a smirk on his face. Brenda rolled her eyes. "That Lorraine is a motha." He chuckled. Bones walked up to Brenda, staring at her ripped blouse and bra that revealed more than she wanted to.

She gasped, grinding her teeth and looked away as he slowly drove his fingers across the top of her breast, stopping to move his fingers down inside her bra. She flinched, but didn't say a word, hoping the free feel would be enough for Bones to replace the cocaine Lorraine had stolen. With the other hand, he reached inside his jacket pocket and pulled out another small brown envelope and pushed it down inside her bra.

Big Ray peeked inside the door, breaking the tense moment.

"Hey Bones, we got to go, man," he said. Relieved, Brenda pulled her blouse together, picked her purse up off the floor, and quickly exited the ladies' room. Her hunger for the drug erased a major thought that would have crept into her mind: *How did I allow myself to get here?*

Two days later, Brenda wrapped more ice cubes in a towel and pressed it against the swollen eye Lorraine had given her. Sober, she finally took time to wonder how her life took such a drastic turn so fast. Frantically, she stormed into her bathroom, and with her back pressed against the wall, she sat on the floor and sobbed.

Her mind traveled back to everything leading up to that day. From the nights of fun and partying with Lorraine, smoking marijuana, to the first night she indulged in cocaine with Bones. She wondered how one night of sampling the white powder caused her to crave and want it so badly. She thought about what Deacon would think and what Bible verses he'd spew at her if he knew she smoked weed and sniffed cocaine. She also thought about Tia and wondered what kind of mother she would be to her if she didn't stop what she was doing.

"I have to stop doing this," she whispered.

CHAPTER TWENTY

*B*renda was glad that Maureen was in a hurry and didn't want to come inside when she dropped Tia off that morning. She shuffled Tia inside the door.

"I have a dentist appointment and Mama's at a meeting at church. I'll be back to get her later," Maureen said.

"OK," Brenda said, looking away. She stood with most of her body behind the door, hoping Maureen didn't notice her drab face and bloodshot eyes.

Tia headed straight for the toys piled in a corner of the living room. Brenda sat watching her play, but all the drinking and drugs she'd done the night before was still in effect, and it wasn't long before she dozed off to sleep.

When Tia got hungry, she pulled and tugged on Brenda. "Mama, wanna eat," Tia said, tugging at Brenda's arm. Brenda was too out of it to respond to Tia. "Mama, eat," Tia cried before walking into the kitchen and climbing up the step stool that rested against the counter. The jar of peanut butter caught her eye. Tia worked the already loose top off and used her fingers to scoop herself a nice hand full. She licked herself full and messy with the peanut butter smeared from her face, hands, and clothes to the counter tops.

A few hours later, Brenda woke up in a panic. "Tia," she yelled, popping up from the sofa. She hurried through the house calling for Tia. She had gone back to the peanut butter for a second helping. "What are you doing?" Brenda pulled her down from the stool. "Look at this mess!"

"I want eat," Tia cried.

Brenda realized it was her fault. "C'mon so I can clean you up." She rushed to clean Tia up and feed her before Maureen came back to pick her up.

***

Brenda dreaded going to pick Tia up from her parents' house. Although she had been having fun partying, the guilt and shame had begun to set in.

She tried to avoid Deacon as much as possible and prayed that Kadie wouldn't zero in with her motherly instincts and figure out something wasn't right.

"Why you wearing sunglasses in the house?" Kadie asked.

"Oh, I got some dust in my eye cleaning yesterday. Made my eyes a lil red and sensitive to light."

"Oh."

She moved quickly, gathering Tia's things, trying to avoid any more questioning. She purposely kept her back toward Kadie as much as possible.

"I'm gonna be getting a dedication award at church next Sunday, and I want you to be there," Kadie said.

Brenda's heart skipped a beat and cart wheeled right up and past the lump in her throat. She hadn't been to church in a good while. With all that she was experiencing in her life, church was the last place she wanted to be. Memories of Sister Abernathy and the deacons confronting the family flashed in her mind. So did the church folks and *their* judgmental ways. She was also afraid that some of the saints would be able to look right into eyes and read her secrets.

"Did you hear me?" Kadie asked.

"I, I'll… be there," Brenda said, shaking herself from daydreaming about the fanatic church folks. She kept moving, picking up Tia's toys and stuffing them into the duffle bag. Tia cried and tried to pull away from Brenda. She ran toward Kadie, and Kadie picked her up.

"You have to go home with your mama, baby," Kadie said.

Tia whined as she hugged Kadie tightly, pressing her little tear-filled face against her chest.

"C'mon Tia," Brenda said, tugging at her. Tia's little hands locked onto Kadie.

"Why don't you let her stay another night, and you can pick her up tomorrow?"

Brenda hesitated to answer. She sighed heavily and left without Tia. She wondered if she could be blamed for Tia's behavior. She thought about the fight with Lorraine and the bruises she still tried to hide. She knew she couldn't miss being at church to see Kadie receive her award.

"How in the world am I gonna do that?" she whispered.

CHAPTER TWENTY-ONE

*A*fter she dropped Tia off with Maureen, Brenda rushed to the bank to cash the hundred and six-dollar welfare check she'd received. After she left the bank, she stopped at the store and bought a pack of Marlboros, three pork chops, some Nestle Quik for Tia, and a loaf of white bread.

Brenda sat at her kitchen table and counted out her money. She had been doing good, putting away $75.00 from each check to cover the $150.00 monthly rent. She rolled up three twenty-dollar bills, a ten and a five together and slid it down into the side pocket of her wallet and walked over to the sink to start dinner.

She turned on the faucet and rinsed the three pork chops under the cold water then laid them on a cutting board. She reached in the cupboard for the seasonings and noticed a bottle of Vodka she and Lorraine had left from a night of partying, stashed in the inside corner. She tried to ignore it, but as she dashed the seasoning salt and black pepper onto the meat, that bottle kept getting her attention.

"I promised I was gone stop the drinking," she whispered. The promises she made to herself to stop the drinking and getting high rolled around in her head, but the temptation was so great. The half full, seven ounce bottle seemed to stare right at her until she could no longer resist it. She pulled it out, twisted off the top, and took a quick sip.

"That's all I wanted."

She heated cooking oil in the large iron skillet Lois bought her as a house warming present and sat down at the kitchen table with her feet up in the chair on the opposite side of the table. She poured the rest of the Vodka into her glass and lit a cigarette. She blew rings of smoke into the air the same way she had once seen her uncle Pap's sister-in-law Earleen do.

As the skillet heated, Brenda's smile illuminated as visions of Tia danced through her mind, but the more she drank the more the visions of Tia faded. She paused and squinted as images of cocaine ripped through her thoughts. She'd felt urges before, but never this strong. Her body jolted. She tried to shake the ugly thoughts away, but the urge became more intense. She put the glass to her mouth, dropped her head back, and drained the glass of the last drop before slamming it on the table.

Jittery, she smoked and puffed her cigarette, desperately trying to fight the urges. Without any more hesitations, she grabbed her keys and purse from the table and headed toward the door. She remembered the stove and turned back to turn it off. She looked at the pork chops and shoved the whole cutting board with the raw meat on it into the refrigerator.

She rushed down the staircase and out the door to the second car she'd borrowed from Deacon. Brenda drove to the Poppa's Pad Club where Bones worked. "Damn!" she said seeing no lights on in the building and no cars in the parking lot. The club had closed hours earlier.

She drove down Saginaw Street to Holbrook Street where Bones lived.

"I hope I can remember the house," Brenda whispered. She'd only been to it once when Bones stopped there when he gave her a ride home from the club. When she pulled up, the house was dark. The big dogs barking out back made her nervous. The lawn was cut low, but the hedges and shrubbery surrounding the house were uneven and shabby.

161

The paint was worn on the wooden steps that leaned to one side, probably from all the heavy body weight Bones carried up and down them.

Brenda noticed a man's head peeking from the side of the curtains as she ran up to the door. He opened the door just as she raised her hand to knock.

"Is Bones here?" she asked.

"Bones not here." The man seemed to be young, in his early twenties and had a deep southern accent. Brenda sighed, pursing her lips with disappointment as she stepped down over a broken step. "I'm Bones' business partner," the guy said. "If you're looking for *something*, I can help you."

Brenda paused in her tracks. She figured that the *something* he mentioned was probably what she wanted. She turned around and walked back up the stairs.

"I'm Henry, Bones' cousin from Mississippi," he said, still chewing meat from the chicken leg he had in his hand.

"You got some white girl?" Brenda asked.

"White girl?" Henry asked. Being from the south and new to the drug business, he wasn't familiar with all the drug terminology people used up north.

"Coke," Brenda explained.

"Wait here," he said and left the door slightly ajar as he dipped back into the house to get what she wanted. She stood on the porch, pulling her coat collar together as the cool night air swirled around her.

Henry returned with a small brown envelope. He tapped the envelope on Brenda's open hand and pulled it back, rubbing his fingers together on the other hand, indicating he wanted cash first. She hadn't anticipated having to pay for it since Bones had been giving it to her on credit or a few times, for *honey*. She remembered the rent money she had tucked away in her wallet. Quickly, she pulled it out, unfolded one of the crisp twenty-dollar bills, and exchanged it for the envelope.

Hastily, she backed out of the driveway, nearly smashing into the passenger side of a passing car. Too anxious to wait until she got home, she stopped at the stop sign and opened the envelope. With her index finger, she scooped out and sniffed a small amount of the bright white powder. She sighed heavily and laid her head back against the seat as it seemed to soothe her. She glanced at herself in the rearview mirror and wiped off the powdery residue she noticed around her nostrils.

Back at her apartment, she pulled out one of her album covers and poured the rest of the cocaine out on it. With The Four Tops song, "Still Waters" playing in the background, Brenda parted the cocaine into four straight lines and sniffed them in order through a cut off end of a drinking straw.

She sang along to the music and danced around the room. As she undressed, she leaned over the cocaine, stopping to sniff more when she felt like it. Before the night was over, she had returned to Bones' house three times, finally giving Henry all the money she had left for the rent and lastly, getting some on good faith credit because she promised she would return to pay him back, but she didn't.

Brenda got so high that she hadn't realized the sun had come up and gone down three times during her cocaine binge. There were knocks at the door. The telephone rang several times, but she was so out of it she never heard a thing.

She lay in the center of her small living room floor. An ashtray full of cigarette butts and ashes sat beside her. The record, scratched from being set on replay, kept skipping.

A stale odor wrapped around the room and the bright lights from the two lamps on the end tables glared against the sunlight coming through the windows. She woke up suddenly, wiped the dry crust from around her mouth and the sleep crumbs from her eyes.

"Oh no," she shouted. She got up from the floor and looked at the wall clock. "Mama's dedication at the church is today." She staggered to her feet and rushed into her bedroom, recklessly ripping clothes out of the closet, searching for something modest to wear to the event. She'd promised her mother she would attend even though she didn't want to.

She turned both the hot and cold knobs on the bathtub to set the water temperature.

"Oh God," she whispered, shocked at the face she saw staring back at her in the mirror. Her light skin was pale, her eyes dark and sunken. She trembled as she pulled out her face cream. She slapped some of it on her face then splashed it with water.

She soaked her body deep into the full tub of hot water, pulling her knees up to her chest. "God, please help me," she prayed out loud. "I don't know what is happening to me. I got to stop doing this. Please help me."

Brenda pulled over to park on a side street near the church and took a second look at her hair and touched up her lipstick in the rearview mirror. As she walked toward the church, she kept pulling and tugging at her clothes trying to press out the wrinkles. She patted her hair that she'd brushed down out of the afro she'd been wearing. Two ladies were on their knees planting flowers in front of the church when Brenda walked up the church steps.

"Hello, young lady," one of the ladies said. "Those doors are locked now. If you want to see the pastor, you'll have to go around to the side door."

"I came for the service," Brenda said.

"Well, Monday morning prayer was over a few hours ago." The lady glanced at her watch.

Brenda looked confused, unsure she'd heard her correctly.

"Monday morn…" she muttered.

"Yes, Monday morning prayer starts at eight-thirty. It's eleven forty-five. Aren't you Sister Wilson's daughter?" the woman asked, recognizing Brenda

"Yeah."

"Oh, the Missionary Society gave her a beautiful award yesterday."

Brenda felt sick to her stomach. She couldn't believe she had gotten so high that she had lost track of the days. She gagged, nearly vomiting right in front of the ladies.

"Are you all right?"

"Uh huh," Brenda mumbled, shaking her head. Brenda walked away, stopping on the side of the church to release the vomit that her nerves had stirred up inside her. With shaky hands, she pushed back the hair back that swung out of place and into her face, and blinked away the tears that formed in her eyes. Weak and barely able to stand, she slipped off the pale pink pumps and walked barefoot the few steps back to the car. Like a baby, she wept as she gripped the steering wheel, pressing her face against it. On the way home, she drove right past her parents' street, too afraid and ashamed to see them.

She returned home, took off her dress, threw it to the side, and plopped down on her bed. Her mind wandered as she thought about what excuse she would tell her mother to

165

explain why she hadn't made it to the church service. She lay in that same spot for hours, praying and crying out to the Lord until she fell asleep.

A forceful knock on the door startled her. Quickly, she put on her bathrobe and went to the door.

"Who is it?" she yelled.

"It's Maureen." Brenda stalled."Open the door, girl. Open the door!" She removed the chain and slightly opened the door. Maureen didn't hesitate to help her open it and walk right in. Immediately, she smelled the stale odor and took notice of the messy house."You need to open up some windows in here," Maureen said, twisting her face and turning up her nose.

"I haven't been feeling good," Brenda said.

"What happened to you yesterday?"

"I told you I wasn't feeling good."

"You ain't looking good either," Maureen added, looking her up and down. "Maybe you need a good bowel movement." Maureen smirked.

Brenda rolled her eyes and folded her arms across her chest.

"Your apartment is a mess!" Brenda ignored her, knowing she was right. "And when was the last time you washed dishes?"

"Would you please ... I told you I don't feel good," Brenda replied.

"You still could have called Mama and told her something. She does have your child, remember ... Tia?"

"Look, Maureen, I told you I don't feel good, and I don't want to hear all this. I'm gonna pick up Tia today."

"You don't have to get antsy with me. I just came to check on you and to let you know ... you're gonna be an auntie."

"What?" Maureen nodded proudly, rubbing her hands across her belly. "You're … pregnant?" Brenda asked.

"Yep."

"You told Mama?"

"Of course."

"Daddy?"

"Uh, yeah."

"What did he say?"

"He said what he's supposed to say … congratulations. I am twenty-two and married, remember?" Maureen dangled her left hand to show her wedding ring.

"Well … congratulations," Brenda said as she unfolded her arms to hug Maureen.

Maureen walked into the living room and pushed a pile of clothes to the side to make room on the sofa. She noticed Brenda's dark eyes and pale skin, but didn't think anything more. She believed Brenda when she said she'd been ill.

"Have you heard from Karl lately?" she asked. "Has he even tried to see Tia?"

"Haven't seen him. I guess he's still up in college at Wayne State. I really don't think about him much anymore. I took Tia to visit his mother and sister a few times."

"Oh, you got a new man." Maureen smiled.

"No, I'm just not thinking about Karl anymore. So what do you want, a girl or boy?" Brenda said, reversing the subject.

"Daniel wants a boy, I want a girl, but we will have to see what the Lord will bring us."

"It will be nice for Tia to have a little cousin to play with." Brenda chuckled.

Maureen noticed the ashtray sitting under the coffee table that Brenda tried to hide before she answered the door.

"That's probably why you're sick … smoking those nasty cigarettes."

"You never quit, do you?" Brenda asked.

"Look, girl, I'm gonna go. I just came to check on you and tell you the news. You are grown, and I can't tell you what to do."

Brenda sighed as Maureen stepped over clothes and other items sprawled on the floor as she headed for the door.

Maureen wasn't sure what she felt, but once she got into her car, she replayed the whole scene in her head. Her gut told her something just wasn't right with Brenda.

CHAPTER TWENTY-TWO

*L*eon worked in the same automotive plant with Marshall, Lois' husband. Brenda had met him at Lois' house years earlier. They ran into each other at the grocery store. It was good for Brenda to spend time with Leon since he didn't do drugs and only drank occasionally. Brenda was a bit apprehensive at first because of her drug and alcohol issues, but she also wanted to be loved. She took to Leon quickly and never revealed any of her discrepancies.

It didn't make her uncomfortable with him being ten years older. He was attractive, tall, and slim, and he wore a short-cut afro and a full beard and mustache. She loved the fact that he was sweet and gentle and that he made her feel good. After meeting him, she wanted to stop using drugs and alcohol. He spoke kind words and encouraged her to do something good with her life and most of all she liked the way he treated Tia.

After tucking Tia into her bed, Brenda snuggled up next to Leon on the sofa.

Leon dozed off, but Brenda couldn't sleep. She went back and forth from the bathroom to the refrigerator to changing the channel on the television. Her mind wandered to the places she'd tried so hard to avoid. She became jittery and riddled with anxiety. She wanted to get high. She looked at Leon as he slept peacefully, letting out a quiet snore.

She whispered to Leon, "I need some aspirin. I'm going to the store." He didn't budge or hear anything she said.

"I'll be right back. He won't even know I'm gone," she muttered.

She slipped on bright green pants and a yellow blouse, grabbed her purse, and tiptoed out the door. She drove across town to the pharmacy that stayed open late. That urge for cocaine tempted her, but she'd told herself over and over she was not addicted to it and had successfully stayed away from it for three weeks. On the way, she drove past Poppa's Pad. The urge got stronger. She turned around and pulled into the club's parking lot and watched people go in and out the club. She hoped she'd see Bones at the door. When she didn't, she sat in the car contemplating whether or not she was going to go inside until finally she parked the car and went inside.

A tall light-skinned man with a curly red afro guarded the door. "I'm a friend of Bones, and he lets me in for free," she explained. He nodded and let her in.

She walked through the club, scanning the dark corners where Bones usually stood. Charlie, one of Bones' flunkies, noticed her looking around.

"Hey there, mama."

Brenda was not in the mood for any flirtatious men. She was there for one thing.

"Hi," Brenda spoke in a "don't bother me" tone, disturbed by his flamboyant attire, an orange polyester suit and a large brown brim hat with an orange feather sprouting from it sat perched atop his head. The first three buttons of his psychedelic shirt were unbuttoned, revealing the tightly curled hairs on his chest. Brenda continued to look around the club.

"You looking for somebody?"

"Yeah ... Bones. You seen him?"

"He left. He's not coming back tonight. But I'm Charlie. You need *something*?"His question immediately got Brenda's attention. She knew exactly what he meant

"Yeah," she responded. She whispered in his ear.

"I can take care of that," he replied, moving the unlit cigar in and out of his mouth as she spoke. He walked toward the door, and Brenda quickly followed him outside to a dark area in the parking lot.

"I'm kind of in a hurry," Brenda said.

"All right, mama, get in, we can go pick it up."

"What?"

"I don't carry it on me. I have a place a few blocks from here."

Brenda hesitated. "I thought you had..."

He sharply cut into her words. "Look, do you want it or not? I have to go get it for you. I'm not gone hurt you or nothing. Do I look like I would hurt you?" He smiled, standing up between the open car door with one elbow on the roof of his car and the other on the opened car door. The feather in his hat fluttered against the wind.

Brenda's first thought was not to go with him, but she was feeling too anxious and desperate to listen to those thoughts. "I'll follow you in my car."

Charlie nodded and smirked as he got into his car, started the engine, and pulled off. Brenda trailed out behind him.

When he pulled into the driveway of his house, he got out the car and walked up the steps to the front door. Brenda parked on the street in front of the house and waited in the car. He waved his hand, signaling her to come inside. Brenda was still skeptical, but anxious to get what she came for, so she went inside.

While Charlie was in the other room, she glanced at his furnishings. Big orange velvet pillows decorated his caramel colored leather sofa. A shaggy orange rug covered the floor area under the fancy glass coffee table that was

donned with a statue of a naked black woman. A large
velvet painting of a naked black couple hung on the wall
over the fireplace.

He entered the room with lines of cocaine already
divided up on a square mirror.

"Go ahead," he said as he sat it down on the table.

"I'm really in a hurry ... I ... ah, I wanted to take it
with me."

"Relax," he said nodding his head, pulling out the chair
at the table for her to sit down. The cocaine was enticing as
it glistened under the bright light of the chandelier above
the dining room table, too inviting for her to reject. She
quickly sat down in the chair and snorted a line. And then
another line, and then another. Several hours had passed
before she realized it.

"I've got to get out of here," she said dazed, hyper, and
fidgety.

"You all right, mama?" Charlie said as he gently
helped her up from the chair. He forcefully pulled her close
to him. She struggled to pull away. "Oh, don't do me like
that," he said.

"I have to go!" she shouted.

"I thought you wanted to have a little fun," Charlie
said as he hugged her body tightly, pressing his wet lips to
hers. "You a fine young thang."

She broke away, wiping her lips. He grabbed her
again. She wiggled loose and ran toward the door."I'm not
done with you," he said gritting his teeth, yanking her back
by her hair. He locked her head back on his shoulder with
his hand and squeezed her breasts with the other. She
broke free when she jabbed him in his groin with the back
of her foot, a self-defense tip that her wise grandmother
shared with her years ago.

Charlie screamed, let her go, and reached for his testicles. She barged toward the door while he stood there shouting obscenities. She made a mad dash to her car. She backed into the three tin garbage cans lined against the curb in front of his house leaving a flood of trash as she sped away.

***

Leon was in the kitchen, sifting through the refrigerator. He had been up since the early morning hours, angry and confused as to why Brenda left him and Tia for hours in the middle of the night. It was a good thing Tia was still asleep and didn't know that Brenda had left. He hadn't realized he'd left the door open when he'd been checking back and forth for Brenda until he heard footsteps leading up to the door. The door swung open.

"Brenda," a male voice spoke.

Leon looked up to see a gray-haired man come into the kitchen.

"Hel -lo," Leon said as he raised his head far enough for Deacon to see his face. Deacon was startled. He only imagined what the barefoot, shirtless man had on behind that refrigerator door. "I'm Leon," he said.

Deacon was stunned and speechless. Tia broke the silence as she walked in rubbing her sleepy eyes.

"Paa paa," she said.

"Hi, little girl. Where's your mama?"

Brenda pulled into the driveway. Her heart dropped to the pit of her stomach when she noticed Deacon's car parked in front of her house.

"Oh Lord," she whispered. She hoped nothing happened to Tia. She dashed up the staircase, tripping up a few steps as she rushed into the apartment. Stepping into the kitchen, she could see that Tia was fine, standing against the kitchen chair in her pink nightgown, holding her baby-that-a-way doll.

Brenda looked at Deacon, as he frowned with disappointment. Both Leon and Deacon were too angry to speak, and Brenda didn't know what to say to either of them. She just stood there huffing and puffing, trying to catch her breath.

"Mama," Tia said.

"Go on in your room and play. Gone," Brenda said, still gasping, giving Tia a little shove.

Deacon cocked his eyes at her, looked at Tia, and then again down at Leon's big feet, and shook his head in disgust. He could only imagine what the man had on as he hid himself behind the opened refrigerator door. Without any words, he took a deep breath and went out the door, closing it behind him.

Brenda felt crushed, shaking her own head in disgust. Leon pushed the refrigerator door closed, revealing the plaid boxer shorts that he was too embarrassed to be seen in by Deacon Wilson.

"What did he say?" Brenda asked when Deacon left.

"Nothing, I said hello and he said ... nothing!"

"Nothing?"

"Yeah, nothing. Why don't you stop questioning me and tell me where the hell you've been. I've been up since four a.m. waiting on you."

"I, ah, I went out ... to get me some aspirin. I didn't want to wake you. Then I got a flat tire..."

"A flat tire?"

"Yeah."

"You're a liar," Leon said calmly.

174

"I'm not lying. That's what happened," Brenda said, tossing dirty dishes into the sink.

Leon walked back into the living room, picked up his pants and shirt and slipped them on fast.

"Do you really expect me to believe that?" he asked. "What kind of fool do you think I am?"

"I'm not lying."

"I don't even know why I even got involved with some lil young girl like you anyway." Leon buttoned his shirt.

"Don't leave," Brenda said, grabbing his arm.

"You go ahead and go back to whoever you were with."

"I wasn't with nobody," she cried.

He noticed a small scratch on her face. "Looks like he was a bit rough with you."

"I was attacked."

"Wait, first you said you had a flat tire, now you were attacked? Dracula right?" he said sarcastically.

"I was attacked." Brenda continued trying to explain, jamming her lies up even more. "I mean, I did get a flat tire. I, I stopped at a friend's house, too, and there was a guy who tried to … Ah, Leon I'm sorry. I won't let it happen again."

"Let what happen? I haven't got the truth yet. And you know what, I don't want to know." He grabbed his keys from the coffee table and stepped toward the door.

"Leon!" Brenda followed him to the door. He walked out and slammed it behind him. Feelings of shame and worthlessness swept over Brenda like a brush fire. She felt abandoned by yet another man. And worse, by Deacon too. She wondered what Deacon thought and what he'd gone home to tell Kadie.

Brenda slid to the floor in a crying heap.

"Mama, why you cry?" Tia asked as she walked back into the kitchen.

"Go in your room," she snapped. Tia ran away, crying.

"Why, why, why me?" Brenda screamed before lowering her head onto her knees.

CHAPTER TWENTY-THREE

*S*everal weeks passed without Brenda seeing Leon. She missed him and longed for his encouraging talks and craved the feelings of security and love she believed she'd found in him. She regretted going out that night, but felt she could never tell him the truth about what really happened. She just wanted to see him, talk to him, and apologize again. Since Leon always came to visit *her,* she didn't know where he lived. And she didn't know that the phone number she had for him was his brother's house and that number was disconnected. She really didn't want Lois to know that she had been seeing Leon since he was her husband's co-worker, so she dared not ask her for any information about him. But her inquisitive aunt seemed to be the information center for gossip from the church to the community.

Brenda drove around to the few places she knew Leon hung out playing cards. She asked around, but no one could give her any information. It was as if he had disappeared.

Depression was an understatement. Keeping her hair combed back into a ponytail revealed the dark cast on Brenda's light complexion. The dark circles around her eyes were even drabber. Brenda had successfully avoided Deacon after his introduction to Leon at her apartment. She deliberately came around when she thought he was working or on Wednesday nights when she knew he was teaching Bible classes which is why she was surprised to see Deacon sitting at the dining room table, eating fried catfish on a Wednesday night.

"Hi, Daddy," Brenda said, trying to walk past him quickly, carrying Tia on her hip and Tia's overnight luggage over her shoulder.

"Hi, Brenda," Deacon replied in a sharp dry tone. "Hi little baby," he said to Tia.

"Hi, Paa paa."

Brenda exhaled the deep breath she had taken in when she entered the house. She relieved her shoulder, dropping Tia's heavy bag down on the living room floor and sat Tia down next to it. She gasped when she heard the ice cubes in his glass of ice tea shift as he moved the glass away from his mouth back down on the table.

Kadie walked in the room, breaking the tense moment.

"Hi, Baby," Kadie said to Tia, swooping her up in her arms and tickling her. Tia giggled. "Your aunt Lois has been trying to reach you," she directed toward Brenda. "She says she's been calling you all week."

"Guess you been too busy shackin' up," Deacon added sarcastically.

"Daddy, I'm not shacking up."

"No, you just have naked men hanging around looking in your refrigerator?"

"No, Daddy…and he was not naked."

"Humph."

Brenda was ready to get out of there quickly. She kissed Tia on her forehead and headed toward the back door.

"You ain't got to run off. I want you to hear what I got to say."

"John, don't start that loud talking in front of the baby," Kadie said.

Deacon rose from his seat. "I'm still waiting on you to act like we raised you with good sense. You better start making better choices in your life. You hear me, girl!"

Brenda sighed and hung her head, her hand touching the doorknob. She was ready to run. "You need to get yourself back in the church," Deacon affirmed. He rambled on and on as always. Brenda stood there in silence, allowing her mind to drift elsewhere as she stood there taking his scolding.

"You call your aunt Lois," Kadie said quickly while Deacon composed himself.

"I will," Brenda said as she rushed out the door.

Brenda wondered what Lois wanted to speak to her about. Instead of calling her, she went to her house. Lois' oldest daughter Dawn sat in the lawn chair on the front porch.

"Mama's mad," Dawn said.

"She's mad at you?" Brenda asked.

"Nope."

"At me?" Brenda asked

"Ion't know."

Brenda walked into the kitchen where Lois sat at the kitchen table with her chair against the wall. Her face exhibited the expressions of a frustrated woman. Her left hand rested on her thigh as the fingers on the other hand clutched a Kool Milds cigarette. An ashtray full of cigarette butts and ashes sat beside her as if it was a plate of food. Brenda knew Lois only smoked like that when something was seriously bothering her.

"What's wrong?" Brenda asked, wondering if she had anything to do with the reason Lois was so mad.

Just then, Marshall stumbled past the kitchen toward the bathroom. He was obviously very drunk, gripping the counter and kitchen table to keep his balance.

"He's what's wrong," Lois replied. "I'm sick of him. He's been staying out all night, coming in here filthy drunk and smelling like some nasty woman." Brenda didn't know what to say. She always thought Lois and Marshall had a great marriage. "Never mind that fool, I'll deal with him. I need to talk to you," Lois said firmly as she blew smoke up toward the ceiling.

Brenda sat down in a chair across from her.

"Wha'd I do?" Brenda asked.

"I know what you've been doing, Brenda."

"Huh?"

"So you're getting high now."

"Who told you that?"

"Don't worry about who told me. Is it true?" Brenda sighed and looked away. "You don't have to answer. I can look at you and see something is wrong with you." Brenda wanted to deny it, but the words wouldn't come out. She knew if she lied, Lois would see right through her Lois was already upset with Marshall and his lies, and saying anything outside the truth might cause her to explode.

"Well!" Lois yelled.

Brenda shrugged and pursed her lips. "Well … what do you want me to tell you?"

"The truth!"

"Ok, yeah, I've been drinking a little … I smoked a few joints." Lois dropped the lit cigarette in the ashtray and nearly flew across the table into Brenda's face.

"You know darn well you're doing more than that. You're snorting cocaine." Brenda wondered how she'd

180

found out. "Mrs. Lilly's daughter, Minnie, saw you get it from some fat man in the club."

Brenda sighed. Mrs. Lilly lived across the street from Lois. Her two daughters knew Brenda from school. Brenda did remember seeing them at the clubs a few times.

"So you believe her!"

"Brenda!"

"Ok, so, I partied a few times. It was nothing."

"Nothing? Look at you. You look a mess! You got bags under your eyes ... and you're losing weight."

"I'm still losing baby weight. I'm tired and I haven't been getting much sleep."

"I wonder why."

"Aunt Lois, I'm no addict."

"Brenda, you're a grown woman now. I've always been there for you. I just don't want to see you mess up your life. Kadie would have a heart attack if she knew what you were doing. You keep it up, she will find out."

Brenda was terrified. He stomach curled in knots. The last thing she wanted was for Deacon and Kadie to find out about her alcohol and drug use.

"You gone tell her?" Brenda asked nervously.

"No, you are ...without opening your mouth. Just like she was suspicious when you got pregnant. You keep it up, she is going to figure you out."

"I know better. I shouldn't have done it, and I won't do it no more," Brenda said, wishing her words could be true.

"I hope you mean that. I don't want you getting strung out. Poor Lee Ann, the young girl down the street. She couldn't be more then twenty-four, twenty-five years old and so strung out on heroin that the state took her two kids. You need to think about Tia."

"I promise I won't do it no more. I'm not gonna get strung out. It was nothing. I certainly wouldn't do heroin."

"OK," Lois said, taking another puff of her cigarette.

Marshall stumbled out of the bathroom and walked back into to his bedroom.

"Oh yeah, about Leon Jones, you need to stay away from him."

"I haven't seen him. How did you know…"

"Don't worry about how I know," Lois said, cutting off Brenda's words.

"I don't see him no more," Brenda said sadly.

"Good."

"Why, because you think he's too old for me?"

"Because he's *too* married for you!"

"Married?"

"Oh, you didn't know?"

"No, I didn't know he was married. I guess that's why he never told me where he lived."

Brenda was visibly crushed. She really cared for Leon. Finding out he was married was just as devastating as the scolding she'd just received from Lois. Once again she felt betrayed by another man.

"There's a box of your things in the girls' closet." Lois walked back to the girls' room and brought the box out and handed it to Brenda.

"You remember what I told you," Lois said as she watched Brenda walk out the front door carrying the box.

"I promise," Brenda replied.

Brenda thought about the conversation she had with Lois for the rest of the day. She knew everything her aunt had said was right and that the last thing she needed was for Deacon and Kadie to find what was really going on with her.

***

Brenda successfully made it through three months without using any drugs or drinking. She avoided contact with the group of friends she'd normally hang out with. She even thought about going to church. Deacon always made comments about when kids that were raised up in the church strayed away they always came back at some point in their life, often after experiencing a plethora of hell.

Spending a lot more time with Tia was good for Brenda, but she still felt lonely and desired the affections of a man. Victor Simmons had recently started calling her since they had ran into each other a few times at Poppa's Pad. She'd known him from high school and liked him back then, but since he was a few grades ahead of her they never got the chance to get to know one another before he graduated. Plus, at that time she was head over heels in love with Karl.

Victor was a slim, brown skinned, average height man, who was a magnet for wild women, but he liked Brenda because he never knew her to be wild and because the saying was true, bad boys often found their way into the hearts of good girls.

Brenda didn't exactly still have her good girl status, but she was very soft-hearted and naïve when it came to men. Victor worked in the Buick automotive plant and could afford to wear expensive clothes and shoes. His hair was always neat and styled with a process, much like members of the group The Temptations.

One quiet afternoon while Tia was at her grandparents' house, the honking of a car horn outside her apartment window, startled Brenda. She giggled when she saw that it was Victor sitting on the hood of his new Lincoln

Continental. She clicked open the window latch and slid the window up.

"Is this what I have to do to get your attention?" Victor yelled up at her as she hung her head out the window.

"Shush. You better cut out all that noise." Brenda chuckled.

"Well, you gone let me in or what?" Victor said, posing with his arms extended out.

"I guess so, or else you're gonna wake the neighbors." Brenda opened the door and watched Victor trot up the stairs to her apartment.

They spent much of the evening laughing and talking. Victor fell asleep on her sofa asleep while Brenda lay awake. Her mind pondered thoughts of love, hate, and the feelings of betrayal and abandonment she had experienced from past relationships. She liked Victor, but was apprehensive about what would become of them. She desperately desired a loving relationship.

Victor wasn't the man she dreamed of. He was just the opposite, but she liked his lively personality and the attentiveness he showed her, especially since it was embedded in her mind that no man would be serious about her.

For the last three months, she'd made promises to herself, vowing to refrain from drugs and sex in hopes of getting her life on track. She'd done well staying away from the drugs, but the affections of a man were her weakness.

After a few weeks of spending time together, Victor introduced Brenda to some of his friends and relatives at a gathering at his cousin Skeet's house. The small house was wall-to-wall packed with people standing around in every room drinking and smoking. Brenda was surprised to see a plate of cocaine sitting openly on the dining room table where a group sat playing cards. They passed the plate around as if it was a bowl of mashed potatoes at the dinner table. It went from person to person so that everyone could get a nice helping. She watched as each player paused to take a sniff.

Brenda had been around Uncle Pap during poker games at his house and at the gambling joints where they drank and smoke cigarettes and cigars, but she'd never seen cocaine being passed around in the open.

Victor mingled with the guests, mostly the females, as Brenda sat in a lawn chair they used for extra seating near the dining room. Brenda eyed him, wondering if they were females relatives or women he was flirting with or maybe he'd been with them at one time. It didn't seem like too much of the family gathering that Victor said it was.

Brenda turned her attention to the game. Quietly, she sat observing the players. It was obvious that the alcohol and drugs were affecting their personalities as several outbursts, obscenities, and angry hands waving in the air erupted at the table.

"You want to get in the game?" Skeet asked Brenda as one player got up from the table and staggered off.

Brenda smiled as she took the available seat. She was confident playing poker since she'd learned so much about card games from Uncle Pap. Skeet shuffled the cards and dealt everyone a new hand. As time passed, she became even more comfortable with the atmosphere and the people in it.

She knew Victor liked to party and get high. They had admitted each other's faults, but never had they indulged in anything together other than a few drinks of alcohol.

Brenda was trying to stay clean as she promised herself and Lois.

The plate of cocaine was passed around once again. Brenda tried not to look as the players sniffed it, keeping her attention on the card game. She thought about the vows she'd made to herself. She caught a glimpse of Victor standing near the door sampling the cocaine. When the plate was passed her way again, she hesitated for a few seconds, but fell in line to do what Victor and most of the others were doing. She didn't want to look like an oddball plus the "Get high" was free. She sniffed and flicked her finger under her nose continuously as the white powder swirled up into her sinuses. Skeet's wife handed her a glass of homemade liquor. She coughed and nearly choked. Her throat burned from the quick swallow.

"Oh honey, you got to sip on that pot liquor or it will tear a hole in your gut," a female card player said. She laughed at the sour expression on Brenda's face.

Victor and Brenda were two of the last to leave the party. Brenda felt a little hazy yet agitated as her high wore off. She drove slowly the few miles back to her apartment while Victor lay intoxicated on the passenger seat.

With all her strength, she pulled Victor from the car, wrapped his arm around her neck, and helped him up the stairs to the apartment. He passed out on the sofa as Brenda slipped off his brown leather earth shoes and tossed them to the side.

"Ugh," she said as the stench of liquor roared on his breath. He lay as still as a dead man. His loud snoring was disturbing.

"No mistaken ... he's alive," Brenda whispered.

It was the early hours of the morning and Brenda couldn't sleep. She paced around her apartment, her mind flooded with guilt for once again going back on her promise. A smelly, drunk, drugged man lay halfway off her sofa, his left leg and arm slumped down against the wooden floor, her nose still burning from the cocaine she sniffed.

The next morning Victor seemed to be back to normal. Brenda was fine, too. She hadn't sniffed a lot of the cocaine. She was still a little apprehensive about him being there, but she was just glad to have a man in the house.

CHAPTER TWENTY-FOUR

*L*ess than a month after Brenda's *family* outing with Victor, she found him living in her apartment. He moved his things in, giving up his room at his grandfather's house. Brenda felt happy and liberated even though she'd totally defied every ounce of her upbringing. All those biblical scriptures drummed into her head while she'd grown up got pushed to the back of her mind.

"I am grown," she said firmly during a conversation with Maureen.

"You just playin' house."

She didn't care that she was *living in sin* or *shackin' up*, as Deacon put it. She just wanted the feeling of having a man in the house even if they weren't married and even if he wasn't the best candidate for marriage.

Brenda enjoyed cooking for Victor and doing things wives did. Tia liked him, too.

Brenda loved curling up with Victor in bed even though several of those nights she curled up alone. Victor claimed he had to work double shifts at the plant, but Brenda got suspicious when his double shift duties began to happen too regularly.

One evening while Victor was supposedly working, Brenda got a phone call from her cousin, Shon. Shon told her that she had seen Victor a few times at a woman's house who lived on her street.

"What's the address?" Brenda screamed into the phone.

After writing the address down on a note pad, Brenda slammed the phone down, grabbed her keys and her coat,

188

and rushed out the door. Thankfully, Tia was with Kadie, so she didn't have to worry about her.

Brenda pulled up to the address. Her high beam headlights glared at Victor who stood in the driveway embracing a skinny, dark skinned woman. Brenda barely put the car in park before she jumped out screaming at him.

"What do you want!" The woman got up in Brenda's face and began cursing her. Victor caught Brenda's hands as she launched toward the woman. She slapped at his face, pulled his hair, and called him every obscene name she could think of. He scooped her up in his arms and carried her to her car as she kicked and screamed.

"I hate you," she screamed. "You lying, no good bastard."

"Get in the car," Victor yelled as he struggled to push her into the driver's seat and shut the car door.

She revved the engine, put the car in drive, and slammed head-on right into the rear end of Victor's Lincoln parked in the driveway. Victor had to jump out of the way when Brenda quickly switched the car from reverse to drive and started toward him. The woman ran up on her porch, cursing at Brenda before she ran into the house. Brenda swerved, skidded, and burnt rubber in the street as she angrily drove away from the scene.

Once again, Brenda felt betrayed. Enraged, her flesh trembled as she stamped through the house, yanking Victor's clothes from the closet and dresser drawers, throwing every item belonging to him into a pile on the living room floor.

She fussed and cussed to the top of her voice about how no-good he was, and how ugly and skinny the dark skinned woman was. She grabbed a book of matches from the coffee table, but thought twice about burning his clothes. She didn't want to burn down her whole apartment. Instead, she headed for the kitchen to search the cabinet under the sink for the chlorine bleach. She figured if she couldn't burn them black, she'd bleach them white.

"Damn it," she shouted, shaking the near empty bleach jug. She slammed the bottle on the floor.

The steak knife lying on the counter caught her eye. Angrily, she used it to stab holes into his shirts. In her mind, she was stabbing Victor—him and every other man, including Karl, she felt deceived her.

She heard Victor speed into the driveway behind Deacon's car. She opened the window and began stuffing his clothes outside the window. An array of colorful items floated down and scattered onto the ground.

"Gone back to that ugly woman!"she screamed.

Victor ran zigzag across the lawn, gathering up his slacks, shirts, and belts. His arms were full as he reached for two of his expensive knit sweaters that clung to the sticker bush in front of the house.

"Damn it," he yelled when he noticed the slices in his shirts.

All the commotion prompted the neighbors to come outside and watch as he ducked and dodged his shoes that Brenda tossed from the window. She pushed the last of his things out of the window, slammed it shut, and pulled the curtains.

Victor gathered all his things and threw them in the back seat of his car.

Brenda gritted her teeth when she noticed one of Victor's shirts that she'd dropped from the pile. She rushed across the room and picked it up. She glanced at the window with the thought of throwing it out, but she decided to ball it up and toss it in the trash can in the kitchen. She plopped down on the sofa and searched through her brown leather purse for her cigarettes and matches.

One after another, she smoked four cigarettes before she got up and searched behind the books on the bookshelf where Victor stashed his liquor. There was nothing there. On the way into the kitchen, she tripped over one of Victor's dress shoes that she'd dropped. Angrily, she slammed it into the trash with a few items she'd missed throwing out the window.

With both hands, she swung open every cabinet door in the kitchen searching for any drop of alcohol she could find.

"Nothing!" she shouted.

Once again, Brenda had managed to stay clean for a few weeks even though she saw Victor indulging in cocaine. She was once again promising to stay clean, but at that moment all that promising didn't mean anything. She wanted to be as drunk and as high as she could get. She didn't want to think about anything or anybody. Her mind wandered with thoughts of each of the men who she felt betrayed her. She wondered who was at fault and if she could have done anything to prevent the pain she felt. She wondered what she could have done to change things.

She hadn't seen Bones in a good while, but she knew if she could find him, she could get whatever she wanted. She glanced over at the wall clock and figured Bones would be working at the club. She changed her clothes and threw herself together quickly. She gathered her purse and keys and headed out the door to the car.

CHAPTER TWENTY-FIVE

*B*renda got high most of the week while Tia stayed
with Kadie and Deacon. Kadie never got tired of keeping
Tia, and since Brenda claimed to have the flu, she
definitely didn't want Tia catching it.

Brenda was awakened by a knock at the door as she
slept on the sofa. Startled, she pulled herself up and
staggered to the door. She hoped it wasn't Bones since the
last time she saw him they got into a big argument and she
ran off with his drugs.

"Who is it?" she yelled.

"It's me," a familiar male's voice responded.

She kept the chain on the door as she opened it far
enough to see it was Victor.

"Can I come in?" he asked.

"For what?"

"I just want to talk to you."

Brenda hesitated a moment then unlocked the chain,
opened the door, and walked back to the living room and
sat on the sofa. The light was dim, so she patted around the
table for the matches to light her cigarette. Victor pulled
out his lighter and lit it for her.

"Thanks," she said, inhaling the smoke.

"Guess you heard about my cousin, Skeet," Victor
said.

"No, I didn't," Brenda said. She leaned back and
stared at Victor. "What happened?"

"He was shot yesterday."

"What, who …."

"His wife," he said, cutting in to her words. "He's
gonna be OK, might be paralyzed though."

"Why she do that?"

"Caught him with another woman."

"Humph." Brenda frowned. "Must run in your family," she added, pursing her lips and rolling her eyes.

Victor ignored her comments. "Look, I didn't come over here to argue. You never gave me a chance to explain."

"What was there to explain? You were *supposed* to be *working*, and you were out all hugged up with some ugly tramp."

"She was just a friend. Her father died, and I was just consoling her."

"Yeah right. You expect me to believe that one, too, huh?"

"I'm not gone beg you to believe me. I don't want that woman. I only want you."

Brenda stared into his face to see if she could see some truth in him, to see if his eyes could reveal what was really in his heart. She wasn't sure. She just knew his words sounded nice. Like the words she dreamed a good man would say to her. She thought about playing hard to get or be big and bad and spew out some of the curse words that she had shouted at the walls about him and make him believe she was a strong woman who didn't need him. None of those words came out.

"I don't know, Victor," she said. "I'm not gone put up with you foolin' round with other women," she said, puffing on her cigarette as she waited on his response.

He gently took the cigarette from her hand, put it out in the ashtray, grabbed her hand, and pulled her up from the sofa to him.

"Like I said, I don't want nobody but you." His sweet words rolled off his lips and Brenda melted in his embrace.

Right then and there, everything wrong that Victor had done was wiped clean off his slate. He was, to her, the only man that would love her.

Brenda went to the kitchen to make them dinner while Victor ran up and down the steps, bringing in his clothes from the car. Brenda ignored the little voice in her head telling her not to take Victor back because he was not a good man and that she would only regret it.

After they ate dinner, they talked and laughed as if nothing had happened.

"To Vic and Brenda," Victor said as they toasted their glasses of wine Victor brought in with his belongings.

"Forever," Brenda replied and kissed him.

***

Brenda rolled over in bed and found Victor's side empty. She heard the sound of music playing softly on the record player out in the living room. She rubbed her eyes, squinting trying to focus on what Victor was doing. He knew she was standing there, but he was too involved in what he was doing to acknowledge her presence. He sat on the sofa, flicking a lighter under a spoon as he heated a white liquid substance then picked up a syringe and drew the heated liquid into it. He tightened a leather belt just below his left bicep. He then tapped his fingers around the area of skin near his inner elbow, searching for a bulging vein to poke with the needle. Within seconds of injecting himself, his body relaxed. He dropped his head and his eyes rolled back into head. He removed the belt from his arm and laid the needle on the table.

Brenda was stunned. She had heard about people shooting drugs in their veins, but she'd never seen anyone do it and she certainly didn't know Victor did it.

Telishia Berry

"What are you doing?" she asked.
"It's smack," he replied with a cold expression on his face.
"Smack?"
"It's heroin. Come here," he said, motioning his hand. Slowly, she walked toward him and sat down beside him. He took a second needle he had, filled the syringe, and flicked the barrel end with his fingers a few times, attempting to release the air bubbles. Wordless, Brenda allowed him to tighten the belt around her arm as if she were in a trance. "I promise, this is gone make you feel good," he said.

Brenda stared into his glassy eyes. She watched as he patted her veins, rubbing his fingers around her arm in search of a good one. For a second, she hesitated, pulling her arm back. Victor gripped it tighter.

"Don't," he whispered. "I promise. It won't hurt." Words she'd heard before. "It's better than coke," he added. "You said you love me … then trust me."

Like a naïve little girl, she nodded her head, relaxed her arm, and watched him pierce her skin with the bevel of the needle and slowly inject the heroin. Immediately, she felt it flow through her veins. Her head bobbed as her body swayed like she was grooving to a popular love song. She felt the room spinning as if she was on a merry-go-round. Her mouth drew open as she sighed with satisfaction. Victor removed the band from her arm. In slow motion, Brenda rubbed at the injection area on her arm as undecipherable words drizzled from her mouth.

The two kissed, embraced, and fell asleep in each other's arms.

195

CHAPTER TWENTY-SIX

*M*aureen brushed and twisted the last section of hair she parted on Tia's head, added white hair balls and bright red barrettes, and then put the cap back on the ultra-sheen hair oil.

"Mama, I know you love Tia being here with you all the time," Maureen said, "but Brenda's getting too comfortable with it. She should be spending more time with her own child."

Kadie ignored Maureen and continued bouncing Maureen's five-month-old daughter Vanessa on her knee.

"She's just the fattest little baby I've ever seen," Kadie said, chuckling.

"They're both gonna look so cute," Maureen said as she dressed Tia in the identical red and white checkered sundress she'd bought for the girls to take pictures in.

"I am so glad they discharged Daniel from the service. He needed to be here to see his baby girl," Kadie said.

"Mama, I know you're ignoring what I'm saying. I just don't want her to take advantage of you while she rips and run the streets."

"How you figure she's taking advantage of me? I'd rather Tia be here with me than over there with Brenda and her men friends. That certainly is not good for her."

Maureen put the second white bobby sock on Tia's foot and slipped her black patent leather shoes on her feet.

"These shoes fittin' her a little snug," Maureen said.

"I'll get her some new ones," Kadie replied.

Maureen smirked, shook her head, and finished getting Tia ready. "Mama, I ain't tryin' to talk down about Brenda. Truth is, I'm worried about her. I heard some things about

Victor. Well, Danny has heard some things about him.
People say he's on drugs. And Brenda, lately she's been
acting strange and looking strange, too. She's always
saying she don't feel good and the apartment is always a
mess."

"You know Brenda always been a little messy. That
ain't nothin' new."

"No, Mama. It's more than the messy house.
Something ain't right with Brenda."

Kadie glanced at Maureen while she wasn't looking
then turned her attention back to the baby on her knee.

"Patty cake, patty cake, baker's man," Kadie sang with
Vanessa, gripping her little hands and patting them together
as she sang.

Kadie heard everything Maureen said, or tried to say.
The last thing she wanted to hear was that her baby girl was
using drugs.

Maureen and Kadie paused when they heard the back
door open and shut, and then saw Brenda as she walked in.

"Hi Mama," she said.

"Hey Brenda," Kadie replied.

"Boy, is she plump. What y'all feeding her?" Maureen
ignored her. Brenda bent down and picked Tia up. "Don't
you look pretty," she said then looked back at Vanessa.
"Where are they going all dressed up?"

"I told you I was taking them to get their pictures
taken. Don't you *remember*?" Maureen asked, shifting her
eyes toward Kadie.

"Ok. I forgot."

"You've been forgetting a lot lately. Forgot you got a
child, too?" Maureen asked.

"You always got something to say," Brenda said,
raising her voice. "You need to mind your business."

"All right now," Kadie jumped in. "I don't want to hear you two arguing."

Brenda rolled her eyes and plopped down in the dining room chair.

"We need to get out of here before we miss the photo appointment," Maureen said glancing at her watch. She lifted Vanessa up from Kadie's lap and held her close.

"C'mon Tia," Maureen said, grabbing Tia's hand.

"Bye Mama," Tia said, waving.

"Bye baby." Brenda smiled at Tia and rolled her eyes at Maureen.

When Maureen and the girls were out the house, Brenda turned to Kadie. "Mama, I've been fixing on Tia's bedroom. It's real pretty, too. I bought her a new bed spread. It's white with pink flowers and lace trim. It looks really pretty on her bed. They did have matching curtains, but I didn't have enough to buy them. You think you can loan me the money so I can get them while they're on sale?"

Although Kadie didn't hesitate to reach across the table for her black leather purse, something about the look on Brenda's face made her a bit uneasy. She wondered if the money was really for curtains or something else.

"How much do they cost, Brenda?"

"They're about fifty dollars."

"Fifty dollars?"

"Yeah, for the two windows in her room."

Kadie pulled out her wallet, opened it, and handed Brenda a crisp 50-dollar bill.

"Here, you better go to Stride Rite and get Tia a new pair of shoes, too." Kadie handed her an extra twenty-dollar bill.

Kadie couldn't help but think about the things Maureen said about Brenda. She studied Brenda's face. Tired lines scattered across her light complexion. The white in her eyes, tarnished and marbled with redness. Brenda noticed the questioning look on Kadie's face and looked away.

***

Just as Maureen put Vanessa in the car, Johnny walked up.

"Hey, lil sister."

"Hi, Johnny," Maureen answered, frustrated.

"What's wrong with you?"

"Your *other* sister."

"What about her?"

"I'm trying to figure that out now. I don't know, Johnny. I think she's getting high on some kind of drugs."

"What?" Johnny waved to the girls before taking Maureen by the hand and moving a few steps away from the car. "Why do you think that?"

"She's been acting really strange and hostile, and she's not taking care of her child. Tia's always here with Mama."

"Brenda always went with the beat of her own drum. And besides, Mama loves to keep her grandbabies."

"Yeah. OK, but I think it's more to it than that."

"I'll have to look into this," Johnny said.

"She's in the house with Mama."

"Don't worry yourself about it. I'll find out." He hugged her.

"OK," Maureen said, sighing against Johnny's shoulder.

Johnny wondered what he would do or say to his baby sister if what Maureen was saying was true. Maureen had a tendency to think the worst about things. It's probably not drugs at all, but what if it were true. He stopped at the back door before going inside and waved at Maureen as she backed out the driveway.

He walked in and went straight to Kadie.

"Hi Mama," Johnny said before kissing Kadie on her cheek.

"I made you a sweet potato pie. It's in there on the kitchen counter."

"Hey Brenda," he said, stealing a chance to observe her.

"Hey," she responded softly then looked away.

He studied her appearance from the way she wore her hair to the shoes she had on. To him, she looked like she always did except her demeanor was a little off, and she never looked at him the whole time he was there.

"What you been doing, Brenda?" he asked. "I haven't seen you in at least a month."

"Nothin' much." Even when he asked her a question, she looked down at the placemat or at the plastic fruit in a bowl in the center of the table. He took notice to her fidgeting as her fingers fumbled with the corners of the placemat in front of her. He looked a little deeper into her face and noticed the dark rings around her eyes as they darted around in her eye sockets.

"Where did Maureen find those pretty dresses?" Brenda said, looking out the window, trying to change the subject. She was uncomfortable with Johnny's questions, and she felt he was staring at her. She wasn't conscious of her sloppy hair style and she didn't wear much make-up unless she was going out on the town or to church and she hadn't done either lately. It was the guilt she felt inside that was telling on her.

"Maureen got the dresses at Smith Bridgeman's downtown," Kadie said

She moved the placemat squarely in front of her and smoothed it out with her hands before she picked up her purse.

"Bye Mama." She hugged Kadie.

Johnny extended his arms to embrace Brenda. With hesitation, she grabbed her big brother around his waist and gave him a nonchalant hug, then stepped back. Johnny felt something was wrong. He watched as she walked quickly out the back door.

"Is she OK?" he asked Kadie as soon as Brenda was outside the door

"You been talkin' to Maureen, huh?"

"She told me what she suspects, that's all."

"I don't think there's anything to worry about," Kadie said, not admitting her doubt.

"All right Mama," Johnny replied, knowing that he was going to look into Brenda's situation anyway.

"I hope that pie is not too sweet," Kadie said.

"Ah Mama. You always say that. It won't be too sweet for me." After giving her a hug and kiss, he said, "Tell Daddy I said hi." With a wave, he was gone.

Kadie walked through the house picking up Tia's toys and dusting things with the cloth she had tucked in her apron. She stopped to stare at the shelf display of family photos. A sweet smile spread across her face as she reminisced about all of her children. With the cloth, she dusted off Al's Army photo, hugged it, and then sat it back on the shelf. She dusted Brenda's photo and stared at it. The things Maureen said wavered in her mind, but she quickly dismissed them.

"Ah, Brenda wouldn't do nothin' like that," she whispered.

CHAPTER TWENTY-SEVEN

*V*ictor had a lot of time on his hands since he'd lost his job at the plant due to too many absences. Most days he hung around the apartment drinking and entertaining his friends.

Brenda heard several male voices as she came in through the back door into the kitchen, her arms full with brown paper bags of groceries. Victor and his two friends, Saxton and Josh, crowded the small living room. Brenda didn't care much for Saxton and Josh. She'd met them at the friends and family gathering Victor took her to weeks earlier. She told Victor they acted like criminals.

"Hey Brenda," Victor greeted.

"Hi," Brenda said, rolling her eyes at him.

"Hello," Josh spoke, too.

Brenda noticed the drugs and paraphernalia spread out on the coffee table.

"So she's the *hit woman*," Saxton said sarcastically.

"Huh," Brenda replied, frowning.

"I told them you were good at hitting … veins," Victor said, pointing to his forearm. Hearing that statement from Victor and the fact that he would tell his friends bothered her. Brenda never gave much thought to how easy hitting the right veins had gotten for her. Victor made jokes about it.

"You should be a nurse."

"Well, I ain't good at it," Josh said. "Will you help me out?"

Brenda looked at Victor. He nodded, giving her the OK.

The Baptist Junkie

Josh handed her the needle he already had filled with heroin. She popped the tip with her finger to get one last air bubble out. He tied his own belt around his forearm and pulled it tight with his teeth. Brenda kneeled down in front of him and patted at the veins in the center of his forearm. Carefully, she poked the needle into the raised vein in his arm.

"Oow," Josh said, feeling the exhilaration move through his body. She released the belt. Both Victor and Saxton held their arms out next like they were both little boys waiting to get shots at the doctor's office.

"C'mon, hit woman." Victor smiled. She kneeled down next to Victor first then used the same needle to inject Saxton. The room was silent as all three men sat dazed. Victor sat slumped over in a chair he had pulled from the kitchen. Saxton occupied the sofa, his kinky afro sloped forward as the back of his head pressed against the sofa. Josh's six-foot plus body sat deep in the side chair. His head bobbed, and his eyes rolled as he wiped the saliva that trickled from the corner of his opened mouth, revealing gums and several missing teeth.

Brenda was still a little shy about shooting heroin in front of people other than Victor, so she took the packet of heroin that Victor handed her into the bathroom. She pulled open a bathroom drawer where she kept her own stuff, including a brand new bag of syringes. She pulled the lid of the toilet seat down and sat on it. With a lighter, she heated the heroin on a small piece of aluminum foil and filled the needle with it. Constantly, she wiped the perspiration that drew on her forehead back into her hairline. Her tiny veins became more visible under her light skin when she used her teeth to tighten the belt she took off one of her dresses. She pushed the plunger of the syringe up, allowing some to

204

squirt into the air before she injected herself. Her heart pounded rapidly as she snatched the belt off her arm and leaned back against the back of the toilet. Her mind raced with thoughts of fun and good times with Tia and how much she wanted to spend more time with her. Then as fast as she thought good thoughts, stressful thoughts of how rapid it seemed her life was going down and how disappointed Kadie and Deacon would be if they could see what she was doing at that very moment. Tears slowly drizzled down her cheeks as she rubbed the sore spot on her arm. She nodded on and off for about twenty minutes until Victor knocked at the door.

"Hey Bren. You all right in there?" he asked.

Startled, Brenda pulled herself up. "I'm fine," she replied, wiping her eyes. She cracked the door open, revealing the black lace bra she was wearing. "I'll be out in a minute." She took a few more moments to put away her stuff and button her blouse. After letting the faucet water run cold, she splashed a hand full in her mouth, trying to eliminate the bitter taste that settled on her tongue.

Victor was standing at the door when she came out of bathroom.

"Josh and Sax need a ride home," Victor said, dangling the keys to Deacon's car.

"I'll take them," Brenda said quickly. She knew better than to allow Victor to drive Deacon's car. She still felt Victor was not truthful about what really happened to his Lincoln Continental.

The sound of big sluggish feet trailed down the staircase behind her as she walked outside to the car. Josh and Saxton crowded their long legs into the backseat while Victor sat in the passenger seat.

"We going to Foss Street," Josh said as he laid his head back on the seat. Josh and Saxton whispered to each other as Brenda drove into the area.

"It's the green house on the corner," Saxton said. Brenda pulled up in front of the dull looking green house that had bed sheets up to the window and an old tireless car in the driveway.

"Pull over there," Josh instructed.

"I thought I was dropping them off," Brenda said to Victor.

"Josh needed to get a few dollars from his sister. Just pull over there," Victor responded. "They'll be right out."

Brenda rolled her eyes as she pulled the car over on the side of the street near the corner. She didn't like what she was feeling. Something wasn't right about Josh and Saxton, and she knew it.

"The next time you invite folks over to my apartment at least let me know," Brenda muttered.

Victor didn't respond, he just stared at the house, waiting for Josh and Saxton. Within minutes, Josh was tapping forcefully at the passenger window. From her rearview mirror, Brenda noticed Saxton running toward the car. Victor pulled his seat up as the two men jumped in quickly.

"Drive, drive!" Saxton yelled.

"What's going on?" Brenda yelled back.

Saxton and Josh began to laugh and brag about how they had just robbed the dope man. "Man that was easy as hell," Josh bragged.

"That was better than getting high," Saxton added.

"You just robbed somebody?" Brenda asked. The two men ignored her and kept laughing.

"It's not like that, baby," Victor said.

"I can't believe you got me into something like this."

"I said it's not like that."

"Hey, can you can pull over right there and drop us off?" Josh said.

Brenda hurried to pull over to let the two men out. Josh handed Victor some money before they quickly pulled off.

"I can't believe you got me involved in some mess like this," Brenda said.

"It was nothing. Here." Victor handed her a hand full of money.

She took a few seconds to count it. "Fifty dollars! You had me involved in a robbery for fifty funky dollars! Getting high is one thing, but robbing folks?" She sighed and flung her hands in the air in disgust. Brenda was extremely angry, gritting her teeth as she pulled her chest toward the steering wheel, gripping it firmly. She sped through the streets, rainwater puddles splashed against the car. She thought about the sad direction her life was going and turned her thoughts to getting a hit of heroin to soothe the anger.

CHAPTER TWENTY-EIGHT

*B*renda felt Maureen was suspicious of her, and she knew it wouldn't be long before she'd convince Kadie or Deacon to be suspicious, too. Brenda made an effort to keep Tia home with her a lot more even though most of the time she was in no condition to properly care for her.

"Mama, Mama," Tia yelled, yanking and tugging at Brenda.

After trying unsuccessfully to wake Brenda, Tia took it upon her three-year-old self to make herself some water. She climbed up the step stool that was sitting in front of the sink and with all her little strength, turned on the water faucet. She picked up a dirty cup from the sink and filled it with water, spilling most of it on the front of her pink nightgown when she tried to drink it. She left the water running, reached for the bread bag, and worked vigorously to open it. She'd watched Brenda and Kadie use the Toaster many times so she figured she'd give it a try on her own. She dropped a slice of bread in and pushed the lever down, but the toast wouldn't stay down. As she kept trying, the cup of water fell over, sending the water all over the counter and dripping on to the floor.

"Hungry," Tia said as she stared at the toaster. She noticed the cord to the toaster lying on the side of it. She'd watched Brenda plug it in each time she used it. With her hands dripping wet, she stretched her little body across the counter, trying to insert the cord into the wall socket behind the toaster. A forceful knock at the door startled her and she knocked her cup onto the floor.

"Hey Brenda, open the door. It's me Johnny. I hear you in there," Johnny said. "You might as well open the door."

Brenda flinched as Johnny knocked harder. Finally, she rose from the sofa. She heard sounds coming from the kitchen and went in.

"Oh my God, Tia," she said, snatching the toaster cord from Tia's hand. She lifted her down off the stool and turned off the water faucet. "You're gonna electrocute yourself."

"Open the door, Brenda!"

As Brenda unlatched the chain, Johnny pushed the door open.

"What is wrong with you?" Brenda yelled.

"No, what is wrong with you?" Johnny said. He stormed through each room, Brenda racing behind him.

"Who do you think you are running up in my apartment like this?" Brenda screamed.

"Well I've only been knocking for ten minutes." Johnny marched into the kitchen.

"I was sleep."

"It's three o'clock in the afternoon. I heard noises, and I wasn't leaving until you opened the door."

Tia stood, peeking from behind a kitchen chair.

"Hi pretty baby," Johnny said, lifting her into his arms. "She is soaking wet... and you were sleep!"

He sat Tia down in her high chair and used the dishtowel to wipe her hands while Brenda stood there with her arms folded and her mouth twisted.

"What's going on, Brenda?" Johnny spoke in a firm tone.

"What do you mean?" she replied, twisting the tie back on the bread bag.

"Don't play dumb with me, girl."

"I don't know what you're talking about." Brenda bent down to pick up the cup.

"Where's your low-life boyfriend?" Johnny asked.

Brenda tied the belt on her robe and leaned against the counter with her hands resting on her hips. Johnny took a moment to examine Brenda's appearance.

"You been getting high?" Johnny said, staring into her eyes.

"What!" Brenda exclaimed, walking away. Johnny pulled her back by her arm. "Let go of me," she yelled, snatching her arm from his grip. "I smoke a lil weed every now and then, so what. I'm grown."

"Girl, you know you're doing more than that. Look at you. Look at your house. You're laying up in here sleep, and your baby's walking around getting into things. You can't tell me weed is all you're doing."

"Why you all in my business anyway?"

"You know you're gone always be the same. Just think you can do whatever the hell you want to do no matter who you hurt. I hope you don't get yourself all messed up foolin' around with that low-life you shackin' up with."

Brenda didn't say a word, just rolled her eyes and took what he dished out to her. Her judgment might have been a bit vague at that time, her religious upbringing suppressed, but she wasn't crazy. She knew there was some truth to what he was saying. Her life was spinning out of control, but she really didn't realize how far out she'd gone. Johnny shook his head in disgust as he eyed Brenda from head to toe then smiled as he glanced over at Tia. "You need to get yourself together 'cause you ain't the same. And you're right, you are a grown woman. I can't whip on you. I just hope you use the good sense God gave you and get your life in order. And take these wet clothes off of her!" He kissed Tia on her cheek and exited out the door.

Brenda slammed dishes into the sink and grabbed the dish towel and vigorously wiped the rest of the water that spilled all over the counter.

"Who does he think he is? I'm grown. This is my house, my child, my life." She glanced over at Tia standing nearby looking up at her. They stared at each other for a moment before Brenda pulled the wet nightgown up over Tia's head.

"Mama, you mad?" Tia said softly.

Brenda didn't respond. She went into Tia's room, pulled a dry nightgown from the drawer and tossed the wet one in a basket of dirty clothes. She put the clean nightgown on Tia and collapsed in the kitchen chair and lit a cigarette. She thought about the state of her life and the many things she was doing to cause the dysfunction in it. With every bad thought, she took another puff of the cigarette and another. And another.

CHAPTER TWENTY-NINE

*B*renda sat the half banana she'd just sliced on the tray of Tia's highchair. She walked through her house picking up clothes and trash that lay around the room then went into her bathroom to dump the pile into the hamper before turning on the water to make a bath for Tia.

Tia splashed around giggling and playing in the bathtub. "Play, Mommy, play," Tia said with the toy stethoscope plugged into her ears. "Ouch, "she yelled as she pretended to give herself a shot with the toy syringe. Tia's actions startled Brenda. She wondered if Tia somehow witnessed her injecting heroin. "Play, Mommy, play." Tia put the toy syringe on Brenda's arm. She gasped, startled by Tia's innocence pretending to give herself a shot. Suddenly, she looked toward the drawer where she stored her works and rushed to open it. With her back toward Tia, she picked up the black satin purse she kept her needles in just to make sure it was there. She knew she didn't have any heroin, but she frantically searched through the drawer as she might find some. She snapped out of it when she heard the loud knock at the door.

"What does he want now?" Brenda said, assuming it was Johnny back to scold her more. She slammed the drawer closed and made her way to the door.

Through the peep hole she saw her mother. She patted her hair and face, pulled her robe close tight, and opened the door.

"Hi Mama," Brenda said and walked away.

"Where's Tia?"

"She's in the tub."

"You left her in there alone?" Kadie replied, rushing into the bathroom.

Brenda rushed in behind her to make sure she'd pushed the drawer closed tight. Tia grinned when she saw Kadie's face. Kadie grabbed a towel from the towel rack, wrapped it around Tia, and lifted her out of the bath tub.

"You know better than to leave this baby in the tub by herself. It only takes a minute for a child to drown," Kadie fussed.

Brenda didn't respond; she just handed her Tia's panties and socks.

"Look what Grandma bought for you," Kadie said. Kadie pulled out a yellow dress from the bag. Tia giggled as Kadie held the dress up in front of her. "This is for you." Kadie handed Brenda a second bag.

Brenda pulled out a blue skirt and white blouse. "This is for me?"

"Yes, it was on sale at Smith Bridgeman's. I want you to come to church tomorrow."

"Mama, I'm not feeling so good today," Brenda began her lie. "I don't know if I will feel well enough to go to church tomorrow." Brenda was fidgety, rubbing her hand back and forth over her elbow, and barely looking at Kadie as she spoke.

Kadie examined Brenda's demeanor closely, looking for any signs of what Maureen and Johnny said about her.

"Is everything all right with you?" she asked.

"Yeah, everything's fine, Mama."

"You need to come on to church tomorrow. It'll lift your spirits."

"I'm gone try, Mama."

"You sure you all right?"

213

"What, you've been talking to Johnny and Maureen about me?" Brenda said, frustrated. Kadie just stared at her. "Well, I wish everybody would stop asking me that. I'm fine. Just a little tired. I don't feel well. That's' all."

"Maybe you need a good bowel movement."

"Mama."

"Well."

"You ain't smoking none of those funny cigarettes?"

"No, Mama." Brenda smirked, shaking her head.

"We just concerned, Brenda. I lost one child. I just don't want to see nothing wrong going on with none of my others, and I don't say nothing."

"OK, Mama, but I'm Fine, OK."

Kadie grabbed her purse and took a few steps toward the door. She didn't believe Brenda. She didn't know much about drugs to know the signs, or that all that rubbing and scratching that Brenda was doing was a junkie itch, but she knew something serious was going on with Brenda.

"Try to make it to church tomorrow," Kadie said, staring into Brenda's eyes, her hand resting on Brenda's left shoulder. Deep down, Kadie wanted to scream at Brenda and demand she make it to church, but she knew how rebellious Brenda could get.

"OK, Mama, I will be there," Brenda replied.

"Good."

"Aren't you gonna take Tia with you?"

"No, I want you to bring your own daughter to church tomorrow."

It was 11:55. Church started at 11:00. Tia was still running around playing in her pink nightgown, and Brenda was laid out on the sofa. She knew Kadie would be upset at her for not making it to church, but she was willing to deal with that. She lay on the sofa wondering where Victor was.

He hadn't been there in two days. She knew when he did come home he'd have some new lie as to where he'd been. The drug urges always seemed to follow her angry thoughts, but something inside her told her that she needed to work on getting clean for real this time.

Brenda squirmed, tossed, rubbed, and scratched as the desire for heroin got stronger. From her head to her feet, perspiration seeped through her pores. She gagged, her body jolted. She grit her teeth and whispered in prayer.

Tia zipped around the room pulling the little red wagon Deacon had bought her. Her baby dolls piled inside.

"Look Mommy, my car," Tia said.

Brenda ignored her.

"Look Mommy," Tia said again.

Tia pulled the wagon over by the stereo and turned the knobs on it.

"Leave that alone, Tia," Brenda's voice trembled. Brenda fought hard as the perspiration increased. She rocked. Tia kept messing with the stereo until the Sunday morning spirituals were playing on it.

"Tia!" she rose and yelled.

Tia pulled her wagon away. Brenda paused, listening to the song playing on the radio. She looked over at Tia wondering was her playing with the buttons on the stereo, turning on the spiritual music a sign from God.

If I won't go to church, I guess church is coming to me, she thought.

Brenda rocked to the rhythm of the soothing music. "Blessed Assurance," a soft female voice sang. Tears flowed from her eyes as the lyrics she'd known since a child came into her remembrance. She sang softly as the words penetrated her soul.

The Baptist Junkie

Blessed Assurance, Jesus is mine
Oh, what a foretaste of glory divine
Heir of salvation, purchase of God,

Born of His Spirit, washed in His blood.

This is my story, this is my song,
Praising my Savior, all the day long;
This is my story, this is my song,
Praising my Savior, all the day long.

As the tears flowed from her eyes, she knew it was
time to stop struggling with trying to get clean and sober
for good— and just do it.

CHAPTER THIRTY

*A*fter dropping Tia off with Maureen, Brenda grabbed a few items from the corner store and rushed back home. She huffed and sighed as she walked up the steps to her apartment carrying two chicken pot pies in a brown paper bag, her mind in deep thought. As she put the bag on the kitchen table, she noticed two silver wheel looking objects on the floor propped up against the wall. She knew immediately Victor was home. As she moved closer, she could see that silver objects were hubcaps. Victor was sitting in the center of the living room floor with a bottle of cleaner and an old cloth polishing more hubcaps. She started right in on him.

"Where have you been?"

"I went on a business trip."

"A business trip?" She rolled her eyes and pursed her lips. "What is all this?"

"It's hub caps."

"I can see that. I mean what are you doing with so many?"

"Well, I'm doing a lil business."

"Business? Did you steal these?"

"I wouldn't call it that. I got a few buyers who are looking for hubcaps."

"So ... you take them from other people's cars?"

"Well."

"You're crazy, and I don't want this stuff in my apartment!"

Victor went back to polishing the hubcaps.

"Did you hear what I said? Get this stuff out here now."

Victor stopped, pulled himself up off the floor, and walked to Brenda. He pulled her hands gently."Ah c'mon baby," he said, "we gone make a good lick with these."

"No, I don't want nothing to do with this. I don't want to go jail. Just get 'em out of here!" she screamed, breaking away from him.

Victor advanced toward her again. "C'mon Bren, We could use the dough."

"No! If you hadn't got fired from your job, we'd have *the dough*. I think it is time for you to go. Why don't you go stay at your brother's house?"

Victor frowned at her at first then softened his expression as he reached into his shirt pocket and pulled out a small brown envelope. Brenda knew what came packaged in those little envelopes.

"I don't want it," she said. "I don't want no more! I'm cleaning up my life."

Victor smirked. "Cleaning up your life?" he snarled. "You been watching that slick-haired TV preacher again?"

"No, I've been thinking and praying. It's just time for me to get my life in order. Maybe you ought to try getting better yourself."

"So you done gone and got religious on me. Well praise the Lord!" he shouted sarcastically.

"I mean it, Victor. Get this stuff out of here."

"You know it ain't that easy," he said, gritting his teeth in her face as he gripped her arms.

"I can't do it no more," she said, struggling to break free, but his grip was too tight.

"You don't want it no more?" He laughed, dangling the packet in front of her. Her eyes followed his hand movements. "You know you want this, don't you?"

"No!"She snatched her hand from his and walked away.

"You sure?" he growled, lunging toward her from behind. With one arm, he gripped her tightly with her back against his chest. He opened the envelope, pulled some out on his index finger, and spread it across her lips. She spat it out and struggled to break free.

"I said, I don't want it," she cried.

"You still a dope fiend!" he yelled.

With fury in her eyes, she turned around like an angry bull and charged toward him. "Get out, get out!" she yelled, shoving him with all her strength.

He shoved her back into the wall. She regained her balance and charged at him again, swinging her arms and slapping at his face and chest. After stumbling over one of the hubcaps, she picked it up and threw it toward him. He ducked and ran out the door, slipping and falling on his way down the stairs. Quickly, she stepped back into the living room, grabbed each hubcap one by one, and threw them down the staircase. She didn't care about the noise and clatter the hubcaps made as they toppled down the wooden stars. She slammed the door and bolted the three locks and chain.

"No good bastard ..." she yelled. She snatched her bag of pot pies from the counter and tossed one of them into the freezer and cooked the other one in the oven. She grabbed a handful of napkins from the napkin holder in the center of the table to wipe her tear-soaked face and runny nose. She continued mumbling about Victor as she kicked her flat leather slippers off near the door and stepped back into the living room.

She noticed a box of 8-track tapes she'd recently took from her parents' house and sifted through them. The only two gospel tapes she had were Reverend James Cleveland and The Hawkins family. They were Deacon's tapes that had gotten mixed in with hers. She remembered listening to them a lot.

She dusted them off and put the James Cleveland tape in first and turned it up loud, attempting to clear her mind of Victor, the anger she was feeling, and the drug urge that was riding up her back. Like a baby, she curled up on the sofa listening to the spiritually moving voice of Reverend Cleveland singing "Peace Be Still." Before the songs ended, she had fallen into a deep sleep.

In the dream, she had awakened in a flower garden to colors she had never seen before, scents she'd never smelled before, and soothing sounds she had never heard before. She walked through the garden barefoot until she walked into a foggy mist. A man reached out to her, his face hidden in the fog, his voice strong and clear. She felt his hand.

"I am with you, come unto me," the voice said to her. She stood there as the hand disappeared and the voice and fog faded away. She stepped forward, looked around, but saw nothing.

"Wait," she yelled and woke from the dream.

The house was peaceful other than the clicking sound the 8-track player made when the taped ended, and the smell of burned food in the oven. A little disoriented, she stared at her hand, remembering the hand she'd felt in the dream. She smelled the potpie in the oven, popped up off the sofa, and headed for the kitchen. She wiped her eyes to clear her vision then she swung open the oven door. Smoke blew out of the oven into the air as the potpie, burned black and crisp, sizzled. She grabbed the two pot-holders and pulled the pan out of the oven.

She flipped open the lid of the trash can and tilted the
baking sheet down, allowing the charred food to slide into
the trash can. Her mind whirled in deep thought. The
words the voice spoke played over and over in her mind.
She turned off the stereo and sat quietly on the sofa. Her
thoughts shifted to the fight she'd had with Victor then to
the drugs he dangled in her face. The urges to get high were
getting stronger as she rocked faster. Her body began to
tingle and twitch. She tried to fight the feelings. The vision
she saw in her dream as well as the songs played over in
her mind. She moaned and cried with each sharp feeling
and tingle she felt move through her body. She wiped away
the sweat that raced down her forehead.

Her humming of "Peace Be Still" faded into silence.

CHAPTER THIRTY-ONE

Brenda sifted through her things for any dollars and coins she could come up with and counted out one dollar and forty-six cents.

"Ugh," she growled, slamming her hands down on the steering wheel. She sat there thinking about how she was going to get the money to get some dope. She did try to get that monkey off her back, but she just couldn't. Seemed like every time she attempted to quit using and didn't stick it out, things got harder.

Brenda drove around pondering the situation until she came near the north side of town near Pap's street. The car jerked as she pumped the breaks trying to stop before she rammed Uncle Pap's white Cadillac parked way back in his driveway. She noticed someone peek out the window when her breaks squeaked loudly. It was late, but she knew Uncle Pap always had a house full of gamblers at all hours of the night.

A big dude stood at the entrance of the house.

"Who are you?" Brenda asked. "What's going on? Where's my uncle?"

"I think I should be asking who you are," the guy responded.

"I'm Brenda, Pap's niece."

"Pap's place was robbed recently, and I help him out, making sure everything stays cool around here. Go on in."

Brenda entered and found Uncle Pap resting in the corner rocking chair while a group of older men played poker at the table in the dining room. His silver and black thirty-seven Smith & Wesson pistol set on his lap with his hand on it, ready to shoot if he needed to.

"Hey Uncle Pap," Brenda spoke and lowered her body down to hug him.

He opened up his arms to embrace her. "Hey there, baby girl. What you know good?"

"Nothing."

"I ain't seen you in a good while."

"Yeah, I've been all right." Brenda fidgeted with the straps on her purse.

Pap glanced up at the Roman-numbered clock mounted on the wall.

"What you doing out at this hour?"

"I just come from a friend's house. I'm on my way home and ... I'm almost out of gas and um..."

"You need some money?" he said, cutting her off.

She nodded. Pap sat the gun on the end table next to his chair and stood, but limped on one leg to dig into his pants pocket for his roll of money.

Brenda's eyes bulged as he flipped through the thick wad of money. He pulled out a fifty-dollar bill and handed it to her.

"Here, spend this on that baby," he said handing her a second fifty-dollar bill.

"Thank you," she replied, smiling, slipping the money from his hand to hers. Pap was getting old, but he wasn't stupid. He knew she wanted the money for more than gas. He could see she wasn't keeping herself up liked she used to. He rocked in his chair and stared at Brenda from head to toe, holding the unlit cigar in his mouth.

Brenda rolled the two fifty dollar bills in her hand since she'd left her purse in the car.

"Thank you, Uncle Pap."

"Don't worry about it. You gone and take care of yourself and that baby."

"OK," she said moving toward the door.

The guy at the door opened it for Brenda. She walked off the porch quickly and on down the driveway toward the car, not noticing the man walking toward her until she bumped right into him. The money she had in her hand dropped on the ground. They both reached for it, but the man grabbed it first.

"Give me that," she yelled, reaching for it.

"Here you go, Miss Lady." the attractive man said. He smiled as he handed it to her. His voice and face were familiar, but she wasn't sure who he was. She stood a moment longer and then quickly took the money and walked away. Almost to her car, there was something about the encounter that made her turn back. The man was still standing there, smiling at her.

"Take care, pretty girl," he said in his smooth tone.

When he said that, she remembered exactly who he was. It was Jake. She had seen him at Pap's house a few times over the years and at the nightclub. She remembered how attractive and smooth he was, but she was too anxious to get high to give him any more thought. She got in the car, pushed the money down in the inside pocket of the purse, and drove off.

Brenda thought hard on where she could get some heroin. She didn't know many people to buy from since the only dealers she really knew were Bones and his flunkies, and she'd burned those bridges.

It was 1:30 a.m. and the liquor store's lights lit up the corner of Wood Street, the area of town known for drugs. She slowed down and pulled into a parking spot between two cars both occupied with passengers. She glanced at the people in each car and at the people going in and out of the store. She watched a short, stocky man wearing a full-length mink coat strut into the store. He looked familiar to Brenda.

A woman was standing near the door smoking a cigarette as she got out the car and headed for the door. The woman dropped her cigarette on the ground and smashed it with her foot. As Brenda got closer to the woman, they both looked at each other.

"Darlene?" Brenda asked, stunned.

"Brenda?" The woman asked.

Brenda was shocked to see Pastor Pearson's daughter standing outside a liquor store at that hour dressed in fish net stockings, high heel shoes, and a quarter length fur coat.

"What are you doing out here?" Brenda asked.

"I'm just waiting on my friend," Darlene said nervously, pulling her coat closed to hide her cleavage that was telling her business. Abruptly, a light-skinned man with long straight hair walked up between them, grabbed Darlene by her arm, and pulled her toward his car.

"See ya later," Brenda said softly.

Darlene never said a word.

Brenda stood there curious as to who the man was to Darlene. Because if he were her boyfriend, he sure seemed rather cold and rough, definitely, not someone she would imagine on the arm of the pastor's daughter. Seconds later a short stocky guy came out of the store carrying a bag with two bottles full of whiskey that clinked in the bag as he walked.

"Hey, sexy mama," he said, walking fast and pulling his collar up around his neck.

"Don't I know you?" Brenda asked. She'd seen him at the clubs around town.

"Maybe, I be's around. I'm Tiny. You looking for somebody?" he asked in a smooth gangster tone.

"No, I'm looking for some ... some."

"Some what?" he asked.

"Some smack," she said.

"Follow me." Brenda stopped short and thought back to another time she was with a man who promised her drugs. That encounter had ended badly. "It's cool. You want it, don't you?"

Brenda hesitated a few seconds. She was secure knowing she had a switchblade in her purse. She jumped into the passenger seat of Tiny's car. He was familiar, and he didn't seem like the type that would try to harm her, but most of all he was a small man and that, to her, made him a little less threatening.

They pulled up the long driveway in his Lincoln Continental to a beautiful brick house surrounded by tall green shrubbery that was neatly manicured. Three black Cadillacs were parked in the cemented backyard. A tall muscular man wearing a waist-length black leather jacket guarded the door. He didn't ask any questions, just held the door open as Brenda followed behind Tiny.

Immediately, the large, immaculate kitchen impressed Brenda with the shiny aluminum toaster centered on the counter and the red tiled floors that sparkled under the fluorescent light fixture on the ceiling. She followed him into the living room where three young girls dressed in skimpy lingerie sat on the sofa polishing their fingernails quietly, never looking up to acknowledge their presence.

A heavy-set woman walked into the room. "This is Betty Lou," Tiny said.

Brenda's eyes zoomed in on the large black mole mounted on the side of the woman's nostril before she noticed her ruby red earrings that glistened, accenting her sculptured up-do.

"Just call me Miss B," the woman snarled as she sashayed across the room toward the built–in bar wearing a red satin lounging coat. She pulled two glasses from behind the bar and poured cognac in each. "Well, don't just stand there, girl," Miss B said, holding up her drink. Brenda walked over to the bar and sat on the stool. Miss B slid a drink across to her. Brenda looked back and noticed Tiny had disappeared.

"You working?"

"No", Brenda replied.

"Pretty yellow girl like you ain't married?" Miss B asked.

"No." Brenda smirked.

Miss B. mumbled as she sipped on her drink

"I do have a daughter."

Tiny came back into the room, interrupting their conversation, nodding his head at Miss B, gesturing for her to come in the hallway with him. Brenda heard them whispering, but couldn't make out what they said. She didn't think much of it. She took a moment to look around at the nice furnishings and at the three girls still quietly polishing their nails.

"You like chicken and dumplings?" Miss B. asked as she walked back into the room.

"No, thank you. I won't be here that long," Brenda replied, looking at her watch.

Miss B grinned.

"You ready?" Tiny said as he walked up behind Brenda, tapping her shoulder. She got up and followed him through the house. Brenda didn't know that Miss B. was a madame and her house was a whorehouse. Miss B stared at Brenda's backside as she walked away. She tilted her glass to her lips, drinking the last drop of her cognac, thinking how much trick money she could get for her.

Brenda got nervous and suspicious as she followed Tiny down a long hallway into the last bedroom on the left. He pushed the door open and walked toward the dresser where he had some drug paraphernalia already laid out. Brenda marveled over the beautifully decorated bedroom with red velvet bedspread and matching drapes, both trimmed in gold. Tiny pulled up an antique cherry wood chair padded with a red seat cushion.

"Oh, I can't stay," Brenda said. "I'll take it with me. How much I owe you?"

Tiny pulled his brown polyester suit jacket off and laid it across the bed.

"Oh this one's on me. The least you could do is stay and enjoy it with me."

Brenda sighed, twisting her lips. Getting high with him was not her intention, but the "free" offer sounded enticing. She unbuttoned her white blouse and wiggled her left arm out of her sleeve. Tiny pulled his shirt off and threw it on the bed. He slid his belt off, handed it to her, and watched her wrap and tighten it around her forearm. His eyes trailed the seams of her white lacy bra that revealed a peek at her honey-colored breasts. He licked his lips, flickering the lighter, heating the heroin on a spoon. Carefully, he drew it up into a syringe.

"I'll do it," Brenda said taking it from Tiny. Skillfully, she pushed up the plunger and flicked the barrel to release the air bubbles through the bevel of the needle then injected it into her arm.

Brenda sighed, feeling the juice swirl through her veins, her eyes rolling back into their sockets. Tiny watched her moan as he took the syringe from her hand and the belt off her arm, and laid them on the dresser. He walked around behind her chair and put his hands on her shoulders, massaging her neck. His hands crept down from her shoulders, down her chest, stopping to caress her breasts.

"No, don't do that," Brenda said drowsy, pushing his hands away.

Tiny ignored her, rubbing her breasts again firmly, driving his fingers inside her bra.

"I said, don't do that!" She jumped from the chair.

"What do you mean, don't do that. I gave you what you wanted, now you're gonna give me what I want."

Brenda snapped herself sober enough to realize that the free get high session was over and the situation could turn ugly if she didn't leave quickly.

As she made a move toward the door, he grabbed her, locking both his hands around her throat.

"Ain't nothin' in this world free," he yelled with rage in his voice.

She cringed as speckles of his spit sprinkled into her eyes. She felt weak, coughing and gagging as he squeezed tighter. Barely able to scream, she scratched at his hands that held her life. He gripped her tightly, her face inches from his rough, scarred face and decaying teeth. Her eyes watered when he licked her lips and she felt his tongue, hot and nasty, against her flesh. He kissed her face hard then slammed her down on the bed, slapping his wild, straight hair back into place. Still hazy, Brenda coughed and gagged, swinging and kicking at him.

He laughed and threw his body on top of hers, straddled her, backhanding her to the right and slapping her back to the left. She continued to fight and managed to break loose, crawling across the bed. He snatched her legs, pulling her back toward him as he fumbled to unzip his pants. He ripped his pants and underwear down to his ankles. With one hand, he gripped a fistful of her hair on the top of her head and pushed her head down toward his groin.

Her screams seemed to turn him on. She wondered how once again she found herself in yet another vulnerable position, how Deacon's baby girl had fallen so low. She worried if this was it this time, and if her death would follow this violent encounter.

"You in Daddy's house," Tiny yelled.

"Go to hell," she shouted.

"C'mon baby, *please* your Daddy!"

"No," she cried, grinding her teeth together.

"Open your mouth before I kill you!"

That statement frightened her. She reached for her purse, but it was on the bed, too far for her to reach. With tears streaming down her face, she opened her mouth and slowly moved toward his manhood.

"Yeah, that's it," he mumbled, plunging himself into her mouth.

Suddenly, he gasped, his eyes bucked as her teeth latched on deep, cutting into his male organ. His loud howl followed a piercing scream. With the thought of saving her life, she bit harder, forcing him down on the floor into a fetal position. Helplessly, he lay on the floor, whining with his feet tangled in his pants.

"I'ma kill you!" he yelled. His voice cracked.

Quickly, she got up, grabbed her purse and coat from the chair and ran out the door with her blouse dangling on one arm. She looked to the left then to the right of the narrow hallway. A woman who had heard the commotion was peeking out from one of the other bedroom doors.

"Brenda," the woman whispered. Her shoe heels clicked against the hardwood floor as she ran down the hallway and into the woman's dimly lit bedroom.

"Darlene?" Brenda asked, surprised.

"Quick, hide in here."Darlene helped Brenda into the fancy cedar closet behind the door.

Tiny regained himself enough to stumble out of the room and down the hallway, and back to the kitchen.

"He's gone," Darlene whispered, pulling the closet doors open.

Brenda stepped out. "Thank you," she said. Tears clung to her eyelids.

"What are you doing here?" Darlene asked.

"What are *you* doing here?" Brenda replied.

"I know you're still in here!" Tiny yelled as he went up the hallway, searching every room. Darlene cracked the door to peek at him.

"You got to get out of here," she whispered as she moved quickly toward her window and pushed it open. She peeked out to look first and saw the door guard standing at a distance not paying attention to the window. "C'mon girl. This is your only way out."

Brenda pulled her blouse on and buttoned only one button, put her coat on, and climbed out the window. She dropped down in the dirt behind a row of neatly trimmed bushes and crawled around near the front of the house, keeping an eye on the doorman walking up and down the driveway. When he walked back toward the back of the house, she made a run for it.

"Run girl, don't let that fool catch you," Darlene said. "He's crazy."

She shut the window and slammed the drapes together just as Tiny pushed her door open. She gasped."What happened?" Darlene asked.

"You didn't see that whore run through this hallway?" Tiny asked, scanning her room.

"No."

He looked at her with a sharp eye and backed out of the room. She shut the door behind him grinning, satisfied that she had helped her childhood friend get away.

Brenda ran as fast as she could down the sidewalk, huffing and puffing, looking over her shoulders. The sun was coming up and neighbors were scraping the light frost off their car windows or taking their trash to the curb.

Out of breath, Brenda stopped in the parking lot of the liquor store where she'd met Tiny and left her car. The store was closed and Brenda's car was gone.

"I know I left the car here," Brenda said, gasping for air. She sat down on the ledge of a cement wall to gather herself, button up the remaining buttons on her blouse, and fasten her coat. "How am I gonna explain this one?" Brenda whispered as she began to walk down the street. She screamed when she felt hands clench the back of her neck. A hand covered her mouth.

"I'ma kill you!"

Brenda recognized the voice and the smell of his breath. She wondered how Tiny had found her so fast; she didn't see or hear him coming. He was crazy. She knew she was going to die. He pulled and tugged her toward his car as she kicked and screamed.

A shiny black car slowed down in front of them. A man got out and ran toward them.

"Hey man, why don't you leave the lady alone?" the man said.

"You ain't got nothin' to do with this," Tiny yelled.

Brenda managed to wiggle herself from his grip and run away.

"Hey!" the man shouted, pulling Tiny back.

"She owes me," Tiny said, yanking his arm back.

"Look man, will this take care of it?" the gentleman asked. He took a wad of money from his pocket and rolled out three, hundred-dollar bills. Tiny hesitated for a second then took the money. "Damn good Samaritan," Tiny said. He pulled up his collar and strutted back to his car.

Brenda walked with one barefoot on the cold sidewalk, carrying her shoe with the heel broken in her hand. She was grateful for the man who'd helped her and possibly saved her life although she didn't see what he looked like.

The shiny black car drove alongside her. The driver stopped and rolled down the passenger window. "Hey miss lady, can I offer you a ride?" the driver asked through the passenger side window.

"Thanks, but no thanks," Brenda replied. The last thing she wanted to do is fall for another man's scam.

"You shouldn't be walking out here alone and ... barefoot."

"I'm fine," she replied, walking with her head down.

"I'm not the bad guy, you know."

Brenda kept walking. The man stopped the car, got out, and stood in front of the driver's side door. "You know your uncle Pap wouldn't want you out here walking like this, so c'mon, pretty girl. Get in."

Brenda paused when she heard her uncle's name and suddenly recognized the voice. Looking up at the man, she realized it was Jake.

"And I'm sure he wouldn't mind if I gave you a ride home."

233

Jake walked around to the passenger side and opened the car door. She stood there hesitantly for a few seconds, looking down at her sore bare foot then walked over to the car, got in, and rolled up the window.

"You remember me, don't you?" he asked.

"Vaguely," she lied, gazing out the window, her mind still cloudy from the drugs and the incident she'd just had with Tiny. "Somebody took my car."

"From where?" he asked.

"From the liquor store on that corner. I left it there a few hours ago."

Jake looked puzzled, but didn't ask questions.

Brenda noticed her father's mustang on the side of an old mechanic's station as they drove past it. "That's my car! Brenda yelled.

Jake slowed down and pulled into the parking lot.

"Wait here."

Brenda saw that all four tires were missing "My God. What happened to the car?"

Jake got out and walked up to an older gray-haired man wearing dirty blue denim overalls. Brenda couldn't make out what they were saying, but she could see from both their body movements and hand gestures that the conversation was heated. Jake got back into his the car and started the engine.

"What happen? Where's the tires? Can't I get my car?" Jake pulled off as she continued yelling about the car. "Wait, that's my Daddy's car," Brenda cried.

Jake stopped the car abruptly.

"Calm down. You're gonna get your car."

Brenda calmed down and stayed quiet. She cringed at his loudness. She couldn't stand to hear another male voice yelling at her or another incident like with Tiny.

"They found the car with the tires missing this morning. Why did you leave your car anyway? Are you working the streets?"

"Hell no," Brenda shouted.

"That pimp back there didn't hesitate to take my money," Jake said.

Brenda looked puzzled. "You gave him money?"

Jake nodded. "You think I'm a whore? Let me out of this car!" Brenda yelled, fumbling with the door latch.

"Wait a minute. I'm not looking for no whore. I'm just trying to help you get your car back."

"I ain't no whore!" Brenda yelled.

"That guy's a pimp and he said you owed him."

"I only owed him twenty dollars, and I didn't know he was pimp. I met him through a friend," Brenda lied.

"Well, I'm just trying to help you."

"How much you give him?"

"Doesn't matter," Jake replied, continuing to drive. He drove through a nice, quiet neighborhood and pulled into the driveway of a small white house with green windowpanes. "This is my house," Jake said, getting out of the car. "Well, aren't you gonna get out?"

"For what?" Brenda asked, rolling her eyes.

Jake walked up to the side door and went inside the house. At this point, Brenda was skeptical of any man, especially if she had to follow him into a house. Twice already that route had proven too hazardous. She gave it some thought. She knew that anyone who was friends with Uncle Pap knew better than to harm anyone in his family, so she got out the car and went inside.

"Have a seat," Jake said, tossing his keys on the kitchen table.

Brenda took a seat at the small round table. "Look, I just need to get my car," Brenda said.

"Don't worry about the car."

"What do you mean, don't worry? My father's car is sitting at some old mechanic's shop on bricks."

"I'm going to take care of it."

Brenda folded her arms across her chest, shaking her head in disbelief that all this was happening to her. She knew she had tried hard to refrain from drug use, and each time she went back to it, something bad happened.

"You want something to eat?" he asked.

"No," she said, twisting her lips irritably.

Jake pulled out a foil cover pan and pushed it into the oven, and then took the orange juice jug and poured two glasses half full.

"Here you go," he said, handing her a glass then sitting down in a chair across from her. He didn't say anything. He just stared at her.

"Why are you looking at me like that?" Brenda asked.

"No reason."

"I told you I ain't no WHORE!"

"I know that. I know a whore when I see one." He grinned. He could see from her appearance that life was taking her through some challenging times, but her beauty was still there hidden under her pain. "You're still as pretty as the day I first saw you."

Brenda sighed, rolling her eyes, annoyed by his comment because after all the hell she had been going through, the last thing she felt was pretty. "I remember when I first saw you at your uncle Pap's house. I was there when he gave you your first poker lesson. What were you, about seventeen?"

"I was sixteen."

"Oh, so you do remember me?"

"I remember my first poker lesson."

"I've run into you a few times," Jake said.

"Literally," Brenda mumbled. Jake stood and took the food from the oven. He made two plates and sat them on the table.

"I said 'no'. I'm not hungry," Brenda complained.

"C'mon. I promise you'll like it." Brenda pulled off her coat and laid it across the back of the chair. "I know you like chicken," Jake said, pointing to the plates he made displaying the chicken casserole he'd cooked the night before.

"You can cook?" Brenda asked.

"What, I don't look like I can cook?"

"I just don't know any men that can. Humph, maybe your mama's in the back sleep, or maybe your wife's at work."

"My mother has passed on, and I don't have a wife. You think I would have you here if I had a wife?"

Brenda shrugged as she forked up a small amount and tasted it quietly.

"I am the oldest of four boys. When my father died, I had to learn how to cook and take care of my brothers while my mama worked."

"I'm the youngest of four," Brenda said.

"I can tell."

"What do you mean, you can tell?"

"I can tell you're the baby just by the way you say '*My Daddy's car*'," he imitated her voice.

After they ate, Jake drank down the last drop of his orange juice then scraped the scraps from his plate into the garbage. Brenda attempted to get up with her plate, but Jake took it for her.

"I have to make a run," Jake said, glancing at his watch. Brenda began to put on her coat. "No, you can stay here," Jake said.

"Stay here?"

"I won't be long."

"What about the car?"

"I told you not to worry. I'm gonna take care of it. Just relax ... make yourself at home."

Brenda walked over to the sofa and sat down. She rummaged through her purse and pulled out a pack of cigarettes and a lighter as Jake watched.

"What?" Brenda said. "I can't smoke?"

"Go ahead. I said make yourself at home."

Jake pulled a glass ashtray from a shelf in his living room and sat it on the coffee table.

"It was good," Brenda said sheepishly. "The casserole...it was good."

"I'm glad you liked it." He smiled and grabbed his coat from the coat rack in the kitchen and rushed out the door. With his key, he locked the door from the outside. Brenda cringed from the sound of the dead bolt latching together. She puffed her cigarette, glancing around at the black art fixtures around the room. She was impressed by his neatly kept home and the casserole he had cooked. She snuggled back into the sofa and covered herself with her coat.

CHAPTER THIRTY-TWO

*I*t was daylight the next day when Brenda woke up on Jake's sofa. He had spent most of the night watching her sleep.

"What time is it?" Brenda asked, stretching, looking down at the blanket he had covered her with.

"It's a little after eight," Jake answered, sitting in a chair across the room.

"In the morning?"

"Yep," he replied.

"I have to get out of here." Brenda stood.

"You hungry?"

"No," she said as she rambled through her purse. She pulled out her wallet and other things, searching for a cigarette. "I really have to go. She put the cigarette in her mouth and lit it with a book of matches she found in her purse.

"Don't you know cigarettes are bad for you?"

"So you gone start preachin' to me?"

"No."

"I really need to get my car and go."

Jake stood and walked toward her, extending his hand.

"C'mon."Brenda hesitated for a moment, and then took his hand.

He led her toward the window and pulled back the sheer curtain. Brenda was surprised and relieved to see her father's car sparkling clean with four new tires out front of the house.

"How did you..."

"You left your keys on the table," he said, handing her the keys.

239

"No, I mean how did you get the car?"

"Don't worry about that. You have the car back. That's all that matters, right?"

"How much do I owe..."

"You don't owe me anything. Just don't get yourself in that situation again."

For a moment, they stopped and stared into each other's eyes. She noticed his attractive facial features that had only changed slightly over the years. His skin was still smooth and blemish free, but his face was fuller. His dimple still showed when he smiled, and his sideburns and goatee were smooth and nicely trimmed.

"I don't want to see nothing happen to you out here," Jake said.

Speechless, Brenda was startled by his sincerity.

"I have to go ... thank you." She grabbed her purse and headed out the door.

CHAPTER THIRTY-THREE

*B*ack in her apartment, Brenda sat on her sofa drinking an herbal tea she'd heard would help reduce drug cravings. She'd bought it a while back during one of her periods of serenity when she vowed to stop using.

"I have got to change my life," she whispered, shaking her head.

As she walked past the mirror mounted on the living room wall, she stopped to look at herself. For the first time, she noticed her dark sunken eyes. Her olive green bathrobe hung open. She looked closer to examine the redness in her pupils. The knock at the door startled her.

"Hey girl!" a female voice yelled from the other side of the door. She looked around at the messy kitchen and living room and thought twice about opening the door. "I know you're here. Open the door. It's Cheryl. It's cold out here."

Brenda finally opened the door after tying the belt on her bathrobe. "Hey girl," Cheryl yelled. She hugged Brenda.

"Well, well, well," Brenda said, obviously unexcited to see Cheryl.

Cheryl walked in and noticed the messy house. "I came home for my aunt's funeral. I spoke to your mama. She told me where you lived. Where's Tia?"

"She's with Maureen for Halloween weekend. She made her a cute bunny rabbit costume."

"Tabya's with my brother and sister in-law. She's gonna hang out with their kids for Halloween. So what's up, girl? How have you been?"

"Good," Brenda lied.

"I heard Big Steve is having a Halloween costume party. Why don't we whip us up some costumes and go?"

"I don't want to go to any parties, and I definitely don't feel like dressing up."

"Girl, remember when we used to dress up for Halloween? Remember that time when you dressed like a witch, and I was a ghost and went trick-or-treating, and your daddy come driving down the street saying, 'Y'all shouldn't be wearing those demonic costumes. Ya just giving the devil a foothold'? All the kids in the neighborhood were cracking up. I think they mimicked your daddy's words for years after that."

Brenda slightly chuckled. Her mind was far from anything Cheryl was talking about, and it was obvious to Cheryl.

"Girl, I am so happy to see you," Cheryl said.

"I'm happy to see you, too."

"So tell me what's been going on with you. You and Karl ever get back together?"

"Humph, I haven't seen him, and I don't care to."

"I heard that. I told you we'd be all right without them fools. I ain't thinkin' 'bout William either. I'm still in college, working on my degree in psychology. I heard they have good jobs in Seattle. Tabya and I are gonna move there when I graduate. Me and *my* baby gonna be just fine."

"Congratulations. I'm happy for you."

"You working?"

"No, but I'm planning to go back to school, too ... ah ... beauty school," Brenda lied.

"That's good, girl. Maybe you and Tia could move to Seattle with us."

"Maybe so."

Cheryl chuckled, strutting around the room, patting her hair and clothes.

"I'm gonna need somebody to do my hair. I'm gonna have to wear fancy business suits and high heels. And, I am gonna marry me a doctor or lawyer. William can kiss my butt." They both laughed. They sat for hours talking about old times.

"Remember when you stole that joint from your neighbor Meekos?" Brenda asked.

"Yep, that was funny," Cheryl said.

"You still do that?" Brenda asked, wondering if Cheryl had kept up some of the things they did as teenagers.

"What, smoke weed? Nah, girl. I can't do that anymore. I have to keep my head together if I'm going to finish school." Cheryl was sure something was different about Brenda. "I have to get going, but we have to get together later, let the girls play together."

Someone knocked at the door just as they were walking toward it. Brenda opened the door, surprised to see Jake standing there.

"Hmm." Cheryl grinned. She walked past Jake and behind his back, gave Brenda the OK sign and a wink.

"I'll call you later," Cheryl yelled as she trotted down the staircase.

"What are you doing here?" Brenda asked.

"You left this," Jack replied, pulling her wallet from his inside jacket pocket. "I looked at your driver's license to find your address."

"Thanks. I didn't realize I left it."

"Nice kitchen," He said as he looked into the tiny kitchen that was the only entrance into the apartment.

"I guess you want to come in."

"Not if you don't want me to." He smiled, wetting his lips with a quick swipe of his tongue. His smooth tone of voice flowed like music. Brenda paused. She knew her house was a mess and really didn't want to let him in. "Really, I can't stay," Jake said. "I just wanted to bring you your wallet."

"OK," Brenda said, relieved.

"Maybe another time." He gently brushed the back of his hand down her cheekbone. Instantly, Brenda felt a warm sensation flush through her body as she dropped her head bashfully. Jake pulled an ink pen and note pad from his inside pocket and wrote down his phone number. She stood there in a trance until the sound of the paper ripping from the pad shook her from it. Without words, he backed away and walked back down the staircase. Her eyes followed his trim physique. She wanted to yell, "Wait, come back," but the words wouldn't come out. She shut the door and dashed toward the window to peek at him from behind the curtains. Intrigued by his whole demeanor, she watched him get in his car and drive off. He wasn't like any other man she'd dated. He was kind, had a gentle spirit, and was extremely attractive-- the kind of attractive man she'd always heard would only break her heart. She'd had enough heartache.

CHAPTER THIRTY-FOUR

"*W*e wore those girls out ripping and running today," Cheryl said, chuckling. Brenda and Cheryl spent the day together, hanging out with their daughters.

"Yep, they are knocked out," Brenda replied, looking at Tia and Tabya sleeping on both ends of the sofa.

"Sometimes, I sit and watch Tabya sleep and pray that I can give her a great life."

"Same with me and Tia," Brenda replied.

"You haven't forgotten about the pack we made in the hospital after we delivered them, have you?"

Brenda thought about it. "About the orange juice? Oh, I haven't forgotten." She chuckled.

"As soon as Tabya reaches womanhood, I'm going to slip birth control pills in her orange juice to be sure of no slip ups!" Cheryl smirked.

Brenda was silent. She couldn't help but to think and be worried about her future with Tia. Would she turn her life around and be a good mother to her daughter?

"You all right?" Cheryl asked.

"Yeah, I'm fine," Brenda replied, frowning. "I don't want Tia slippin' up either."

Cheryl sensed that there was something wrong with Brenda, her appearance a little drab, and her fun-spirited demeanor absent, but she accepted her "*I'm fine*" responses each time she asked Brenda if she were all right.

Brenda struggled to pull herself up off the floor and headed toward the bathroom.

"That chicken and dressing was a bit much for me," she said.

Cheryl flipped through the *Jet* magazine she bought at the supermarket. She drank the rest of root beer from her glass and poured the rest of the bottle into the glass. She glanced at her watch and at the two sleeping girls, wondering what was taking Brenda so long in the bathroom.She got up and walked toward the bathroom. "What are you doing in there?" she asked. "You're gonna overflow the river!" Cheryl chuckled.

"I'm coming right out," Brenda yelled.

Cheryl stood by the door for a few minutes before saying, "Well, I'm gonna have to get going." She gathered her purse and Tabya's bag and sat them on the coffee table.

"You hear me?" Cheryl called out. "I'm leaving."Cheryl walked back to the bathroom door. "I'll see ya tomorrow," she said. Brenda still didn't respond.

Scared, Cheryl gripped the doorknob and opened the door. She was shocked to see Brenda injecting herself with heroin. She watched Brenda's eyes roll and her head bob from one side to the other. She gasped and backed away from the door, gripping her chest. The shock drew tears to Cheryl's eyes. She covered her mouth and backed up against the wall in the hallway.

Cheryl felt like bursting into the bathroom and slapping some sense into Brenda, but the shock kept her from moving. Just as she got nerve and was about rush into the bathroom, she was startled by the knock she heard at Brenda's front door.

"Brenda, it's me, Maureen." The knocking continued until Cheryl went to open the door.

"Hey, Cheryl." Maureen and Cheryl hugged. "I heard you were in town. How have you been? Where's your daughter?"

"Been fine. Tabya's on the sofa asleep. Brenda's ... in the bathroom."

Cheryl turned away from Maureen. She couldn't bear
to look at her or anyone for that matter.

"She's so big," Maureen said as she looked at Tabya.

Cheryl wanted to tell Maureen what she'd just
witnessed, but she couldn't find the right words.

"You all right?" Maureen asked, noticing Cheryl's
expression

"I have to go," Cheryl said. "Just tell Brenda that I'll
talk to her later."

Cheryl picked Tabya up off the sofa and slung her
body up over her chest.

Maureen could see that Cheryl was bothered. She
walked Cheryl to the door and closed it behind her.

"Did you forget that I was coming back to get Tia
tonight?" Maureen yelled, walking toward the bathroom.
"What in the world are you doing in there?" Maureen
pushed the door open. Startled, Brenda dropped her stash
she was attempting to push into its drawer. "What in the
world ... what are you doing with that?" Maureen covered
her mouth and stared at Brenda. Tears rolled down
Maureen's cheeks. Brenda hung her head shamefully.
"What are you doing to yourself, Brenda?" Maureen asked.
Brenda gathered her stash, stuffed it in a drawer, and
stormed past Maureen. "Don't you walk away from me,"
Maureen screamed. "I'm talking to you." She yanked
Brenda's shoulders back toward her. "What is that stuff,
Brenda?"

"Would you leave me alone?" Brenda yelled.

Maureen forcefully pushed Brenda against the wall.
Brenda was still dazed from the drugs, but managed to push
her back and they started wrestling each other.

"Why are you doing this to yourself?" Maureen
screamed, breaking away from Brenda. "Are you crazy? I

knew you were doing drugs. I knew it. Johnny and I both knew it. How could you do this to yourself, to Tia ... to me?"

"To you! I'm not doing anything to you!"

"You are, to the whole family, to Mama, to Daddy."

Brenda shook her head and wiped at the tears that poured from her eyes.

"You have no idea how I feel or what I've gone through," Brenda said.

"Girl, don't you dare give me no cry-baby excuses. You haven't been through nothing that would make you shoot dope up your arm," Maureen yelled.

"See, that's what I mean. You don't understand."

"Well, why didn't you just talk to me?"

"Talk to you?"

"Yes."

"Talk to you? Miss Perfect, got it all together, wife, mother, good Christian girl? Everything Mama and Daddy wanted you to be. But me, pregnant at sixteen, no husband. Humph, my baby's father dropped me like I was nothing! What did Daddy always say? *She's ruined, ain't no man gone want you now.*"

Maureen shook her head.

"I know doing drugs ain't right. It ain't no good for me," Brenda said, "but it numbs my pain." Brenda staggered, still woozy from the drugs.

Maureen embraced Brenda tightly.

"You can't let the things Daddy said to you in the past still hurt you like this, make you want to do drugs. That ain't gone solve nothing. It ain't gonna do nothing but kill you."

"Maybe that's what I deserve."

"Brenda, you're talking crazy now, girl. Think about Tia."

"I do. I've tried to stop, over and over. And I have stopped, but something happens to me and I go right back to it."

"I know there are some places you can go for help."

"I'm gonna be all right. Just go ahead and take Tia."

"Why don't you come home with me, too?"

"No, take Tia. I'm gonna be fine. Please don't tell Mama and Daddy." Maureen ignored her and continued getting Tia ready to go. "Did you hear me?" Brenda asked.

"I heard you."

"There you go being just like you always been. Miss Goody Two-Shoes. For once, can you be a real sister to me and not run and tell every damn thing?"

Maureen stared at her, a herd of fury raced up her spine. "First of all, if you want to call me Miss Goody Two-shoes because I don't do drugs, never slept around, and wasn't a teenage mother, then you go right ahead! Daddy only wanted the best for *all* of us, wanted us to be good people and not whores, alcoholics, or *drug addicts*. Maybe he was a bit too strict at times, shooting scriptures at us *all the time* and barring us from doing certain things, but that's all he knew to do."

"Humph," Brenda snarled.

Maureen's expression was evidence that Brenda's attitude was making her even angrier. Maureen tightened her lips and moved her face in close to Brenda's. Her hot tempered breath swept against Brenda's face. "If I told anything on you, it was because you were doing wrong and you knew better. And doing drugs Brenda, you know better than this!" Brenda hung her head. She had never seen

Maureen so angry with her. "Right now, Brenda, you need your ass whipped!"

Brenda paused, visibly stunned by Maureen's show of anger and the curse word she'd added in, a word she'd never heard come from Maureen's mouth ever before or any other word like it. By the tone of her voice, a word of prayer didn't sound like it would come next as an alternate solution either. Brenda wasn't sure if she should duck and run or break down crying because Maureen was right.

"I'm gonna stop."

Maureen sighed heavily, staring right into Brenda's eyes. She wanted to believe everything Brenda said. She hoped she would because she really didn't know what else to do for her sister other than *tell*.

"All right, but you better do what you say or..."

"I promise," Brenda said quickly.

Brenda picked Tia's sleepy body up into her arms, kissed her forehead, and handed her to Maureen. "I promise," Brenda whispered as tears flowed down her cheeks.

With Tia secured in her arms and her overnight bag draped on her shoulder, Maureen turned toward Brenda.

"You promised," Maureen said with tears rolling down her cheeks.

Brenda nodded. Maureen closed the door behind her.

CHAPTER THIRTY-FIVE

A few weeks had gone by, and Brenda still hadn't made good on her promise to Maureen. She didn't even show up at the first appointment she made at Forsyght Rehabilitation Clinic. She thought she could kick the habit on her own. She felt all she needed was some happiness in her life and at the moment spending time with Jake was keeping her spirits up. He'd been coming by her apartment sitting, talking, and they'd been getting to know one another. The thought of the age difference crossed her mind. She thought about Leon. He was a several years older than she was, and Jake was even older. But the good conversations and the warm spirit he had made her care less about their ages. She loved the security she felt with him. She continued to struggle to free herself from her addiction. She felt that continuing to laugh and have good times with Jake would help her to recover. She only hoped her feelings about him were not proven to be faulty and he wasn't really like any of the other men she'd fallen for.

Brenda chuckled, sitting at her kitchen table when Jake handed her two Coney dogs he brought in from her favorite restaurant. She had told him how much she loved their Coney dogs since she was a kid.

When Jake excused himself to the restroom, the telephone rang. It was the intake worker from the Forsyght Rehabilitation Clinic. The lady was very pleasant on the phone and not angry that Brenda hadn't shown up for her appointment, but encouraged her to make another appointment and keep it.

"Remember, we are here to help you achieve and maintain your sobriety," the lady said.

251

Brenda knew that *maintaining* her sobriety was the key
to being a stable person and mother. She knew she had to
eventually make good on that promise she'd made to
Maureen so that she wouldn't tell Deacon and Kadie and
she definitely didn't want Jake to find out either.

"I know, and I'll be there Wednesday at two o'clock,"
Brenda said.

Just before Brenda hung up the phone, Jake heard the
last sentence as he was walking from the bathroom.

"Is everything OK?" Jake asked.

"Yes." Brenda finished up her lunch and took a seat
on the sofa next to Jake. "Thanks for the Coney dogs."

"I'm gonna take you to Mr. P's tomorrow," Jake said
as Brenda sat down next to him.

"Mr. P's?" Brenda questioned.

"It's a nice restaurant in Pontiac. An old Jewish friend
of mine owns it."

"Why we have to go all the way to Pontiac to eat? You
afraid one of your women might see us?" Brenda asked
sarcastically.

"I told you I don't have a woman. Why do you always
think so negative? Do you think every man is up to no
good?" Brenda shrugged. Jake shook his head. "Well, I'm
not out to hurt you," he said. "The only woman I'm
interested in right now is you."

Brenda smiled at the sweet words, but in many ways
she was still reluctant to believe him since no other man
had treated her like he did. Leon was kind, but not as kind
as Jake.

"A woman, is that really what you think of me?"

"What you mean by that?" Jake looked puzzled.

"You're much older than I am. To you, I may be just a
young girl."

Jake grinned, revealing his deep dimples. He leaned toward Brenda, and her eyes zoomed in on his rose-colored lips. "No, you're a woman," he said. He pecked her neck gently then pulled her close to him. Just as he released her from his embrace, one of her cuffed, elbow length sleeves was pushed back to reveal the needle track scars in the inner crease of her elbow.

Jake took a double take and immediately zoomed in on the scattered needle tracks on her arm. "What is this?" he asked. "Do you..."

Brenda yanked her arm back and quickly pulled herself up off the sofa. Jake got up and followed behind her. He twirled her around and gripped her elbows in both his hands to get a second look.

"Stop it," Brenda yelled, pulling away from him.

"What's going on with you?" he yelled reaching for her. She turned her back, covering her face with her hands. "I'm not gonna hit you," Jake said. He backed away and threw his hands up in defense. Brenda collapsed to the floor crying. Jake stood, shocked. He knelt down on the floor beside her.

"What do you want me to say, huh?" Brenda cried out. "Yes, I'm a junkie, a heroin junkie."

Jake was at a loss for words. He continued to stare into her face. He noticed the dark lines on her face that were hiding the depth of her beauty. He saw the red lines in her eyes that he hadn't noticed until that moment. He swiped her hair back away from her face. Jake was very streetwise. He'd known something was going on with Brenda. She had revealed to him that she used cocaine, but was no longer doing it. He'd felt like she was still doing some kind of drugs, but didn't know it was heroine.

"You ain't no junkie unless you want to be," he said.

"You think I want to do dope, well, I don't. I keep trying to quit. I have been doing better since you've been around," she added.

Jake wiped her tears with his fingertips. "I'll be right back," he said. He pulled himself and Brenda up off the floor and left. Brenda didn't believe he would come back.

An hour had past, and Brenda was feeling depressed and lonely. Tears rolled down her cheeks as she managed a chuckle, watching Flip Wilson play Geraldine on her black and white TV. Brenda heard the footsteps rush up the stairs, and then the door open.

Brenda sat, staring at him, her eyes wide, still swollen from crying. "I didn't think you were coming back," she whispered.

"Is that why you left the door unlocked?" When Brenda didn't respond, Jake added, "I told you I would be back. I want to help you. I don't want to see you mess your life up."

Brenda desperately wanted help. She was exhausted from all the failed attempts she'd made. She wanted Jake not only to help her, but to love her even though she didn't think she was worthy of a good man's love.

Jake walked into the kitchen with a small brown bag tucked in his arms. He pulled out a medicine bottle of cough syrup from the bag.

"Here, drink a few swigs of this," he said. He handed the bottle to Brenda.

"What is it?"

"It's Amanel with codeine. It will help ease the heroin cravings and help wean you off of it." Brenda hesitated, staring up at him as he stood over her. "If you want me to help you," Jake said, "you're gonna have to trust me."

254

Brenda slowly tilted the bottle to her lips and drank it. "I'm gonna get you some Methadone."

"What's that?" Brenda questioned.

"It'll help you get off that stuff. I know someone that works at a drug clinic." Jake looked at his watch. Brenda took one more sip. "Just promise me you won't leave your apartment."

"OK.

"I won't be long."

"Why are you doing this for me?" she asked.

"Because I care about you, but I told you that already." He stared at Brenda. "I think you are a beautiful woman..."

"Why do you always say that?"

"Say what?"

"That I'm..."

"That you're beautiful?" Brenda nodded. "Because you are."

Brenda's eyes glistened. Jake smiled and took the syrup from her hand and sat it on the counter. "I'll be back," he said.

"I wonder what my uncle Pap would say if he knew that you were here with me."

"Oh, he knows."

"He does?"

"Yes, but he also knows I'm a good man." Jake smiled as he exited out the door.

Jake pulled into the garage at Big J's Auto Repairs where he had a small office. He had been a gambler and a numbers runner for many years. Everyone in the neighborhood knew that he owned the repair shop and the barbershop next door to it. The back room of the barbershop was a gambling house, where only the big spenders could gamble twenty-four hours a day. Most of the neighbors knew about the gambling at the repair shop, but no one ever gave him any problem. Once a year he sponsored a big block party for the Baker Street residents and often purchased ice cream for all the kids on the block during the summer and gave them gifts at Christmas. Although Jake had a good job building trucks for General Motors for years, he never quit his first job, running numbers. It had always been a part of his life.

Jake walked through the opened garage door and waved at the three men working on cars parked inside the garage. He headed for his office that was clean and neat, minus the smell of motor oil. His black leather chair sat behind the large oak wood desk that took up one whole side of the room. Landscape paintings of mountains and green pastures covered one wall. The opposite wall had shelves that displayed his bowling trophies.

He sat down at his desk and flipped through the pages of his telephone book to call his friend that worked at the drug clinic. A loud noise and voices yelling alerted Jake that something was wrong. He got up fast to see what the commotion was. He reached toward the secret compartment on the side of his desk for his gun, but before he could get to it, his office door flew open. With their guns drawn, four white police officers yelled at him.

"Put your hands up!"

Jake calmly surrendered, raising his hands up in the air.

"Jacob Harris?" the short chubby officer asked.

Jake nodded.

The tallest officer grabbed him, slammed him down on the desk, and handcuffed him while the bald-headed officer read him his rights.

Jake remained calm, and he barely flinched when the officer tightened the cuffs and pushed him into the back of the police car.

"We got you now, you slick-haired nigga."

Jake twisted his lips and sucked his teeth, trying hard to ignore the racist cops. The repairmen working in the garage, the men working in the barbershop next door, and the men that were gambling in the back were all lined up outside. One by one, the officers helped them into the two white paddy wagons that were parked at the curb.

"Hey man, don't forget me," one man yelled at the police car, believing Jake would use his money and power to get himself and his friends out of jail. Jake didn't say a word. He sat there quietly, uncomfortable with his hands behind his back and his head resting on the back of the Paddy wagon wall.

Hours later, Brenda felt the first pains of withdrawal. Her body was wet from perspiration. She sat waiting, watching the clock. As time passed, her body twitched and shook. Her teeth chattered, and she trembled as cold chills ravaged her body. She picked up the bottle of Amanel and took a few sips. She sat back on the sofa, pulled her knees up to her chest, and rocked back and forth. She cried as her body trembled uncontrollably. Her eyes darted from the TV set to the wall clock.

"Where is he?" she growled.

Numerous thoughts raced through her mind. She wanted to jump up and run out to get drugs as she always did when she felt like this, but she promised she wouldn't leave

At the police station, Jake stayed cool, cooperating with the hostile police officer as he released him from the handcuffs to fingerprint him.

"I need to call my lawyer," Jake said.

The police officer ignored him. A few minutes later, Jake asked him again and received the same response.

"All right, turn to your left," the officer yelled as he snapped the mug shots.

Jake continued to cooperate, gritting his teeth. The officer escorted Jake to the telephone. After Jake made his call to his lawyer, the officer walked him to an empty cell. The officer snarled, chewing his gum on his front teeth.

"I hate uppity niggas," the officer whispered.

Jake smirked and grinned. He took a seat on the bench and rested his back on the cold cement wall. His hands clasped together, resting on his lap. He had only been arrested a few times and was confident that his lawyer would work things out. Most of all, he wondered about Brenda and how she was doing. He knew the Amanel would help with the pain and effects of heroin withdrawal, but it would not totally stop the cravings. Brenda would still have to be strong and go through it. He wondered if she could.

Brenda paced the floor, rushing toward the window whenever she heard a car drive by.

"Where is he?" she said with fury in her voice. She was getting aggravated. Her body jerked as she felt the need to throw up. She shivered, biting her lips and grinding her teeth. She gagged as saliva swirled around in her mouth. Both her arms were red from rubbing them so much. She looked down at her trembling hands then wiped the dripping sweat from her forehead and the moisture from around her mouth. Her eyes were red and puffy.

These were the worst withdrawal symptoms she'd experienced. Jake didn't warn her that the cravings would get worse before she got better. Jake's last words, "Don't leave" played over and over in her mind as she kept watching the clock. Brenda shook more profusely with each passing minute. Suddenly, she jumped up and rushed into the bathroom to vomit. She gagged, until the Coney dogs she ate earlier came up. She turned on the sink faucet and splashed water on her face and inside her mouth.

"I can't do this!" she screamed, crying loudly, her body twitching.

She pulled open the drawer where she stashed her needles. She had one, but no drugs. Tensely, she went back into the living room and plopped back down on the sofa. She ripped the zipper back to open her purse and searched for her cigarettes. The pack was empty. In a frantic fit, she crumbled the empty pack and tossed it across the room.

She paced the floor, walking from room to room. She stopped and stared at her jewelry box and pulled out the tiny box inside that held the pearl earrings that her grandmother Wiletta had given her before she died. Visions of her grandmother flashed in her head as she held the earrings in her hand, but the frustration and withdrawal pains she was feeling quickly erased the visions. Still gripping the earrings, she paced her way back to the kitchen. Barely dressed and wearing only a pink blouse and pajama bottoms, Brenda paused staring at the note on the table that she'd written the clinic appointment date and time on. With a deep sigh, she grabbed her coat, keys, and hurried out the door. She couldn't take it anymore.

CHAPTER THIRTY-SIX

*B*renda promised herself that she would not go into the drug-infested neighborhood of Wood Street again after the incident with Tiny at the whorehouse. At least that's what she said after making it out of there. But that was then. Now, she was desperate and broke. She pulled out the pearl earrings her grandmother had given her in her hand; she was willing to pawn them for a hit.

She crept slowly up the street toward the party store where most of the drug dealers, pimps, and prostitutes frequented and only the next block over from where her car was stolen. At this moment it didn't matter that this was one of the most dangerous neighborhoods, as well as the same neighborhood where Tiny lived.

Instead of pulling into the parking lot, she parked on the street near the corner and turned the car off. Anxious, she squirmed in the driver's seat, surveying everyone that went in and came out of the store, hoping she could quickly pick out the right dealer that would take the earrings for a fix.

A large man got out of a green Cadillac. She looked closer. It was Bones. Nervously, she ducked down past the steering wheel. Bones was the last person she wanted to run into considering their last encounter when she ran off with his drugs.

She watched Bones go into the store. When he came out, a woman got out of his car on the passenger side. They stood there arguing. Bones slapped the woman. They argued louder. He slapped her several more times, shoved her back inside the car, and walked back around to the driver's side. As he was wiggling, maneuvering his fat body into the driver's seat, the woman jumped out and ran. The woman, wearing high-heeled black leather boots and a short rabbit fur ran fast.

"Oh my God," Brenda whispered as the woman ran toward her car. "That's Darlene." When Darlene passed, Brenda started the engine, flashed her headlights, and pulled up to Darlene. The last thing Brenda wanted to do was get involved with anything that had something to do with Bones, but she remembered when Darlene helped her get out the whorehouse with Tiny. Brenda blew the horn, and Darlene turned around.

"Unlock the door," Darlene yelled as she pounded on the passenger side window. Brenda quickly reached over and unlocked it. "Drive, fast," Darlene said after slamming the door shut. Brenda pressed the gas pedal down to the floor. "He's gone kill me," Darlene cried.

"What did you do?"

"Just drive!"

Frantically, Darlene looked through the back window for any signs of Bones and his Cadillac. Brenda didn't see any cars in the rearview mirror when she pulled into the alley behind Greenly's Furniture Store and stopped.

"You got a light?" Darlene asked, digging through her purse for her cigarettes. Nervous, she held the unlit cigarette in her hand.

The pair looked around, scanning the alley for any signs of Bones.

"I don't think he saw us drive in here," Brenda said.

Suddenly, they both gasped as a car drove past the alley.

"It's not him." Brenda sighed.

"We have to get out of here," Darlene said.

"No, let's wait to make sure he's gone."

"I need a light," Darlene insisted. Brenda searched her purse for a lighter. A loud bang on the passenger side window made both Darlene and Brenda scream. Bone's large face loomed on the other side of the window. "Drive!" Darlene shouted.

Before she could turn the ignition Bones was standing in front of the car. His body was nearly as wide as the car's front end. His long black leather coat blew back, fluttering against the wind as if he was going to fly right through the front windshield.

"Hit him!" Darlene growled as Brenda fumbled, trying to turn the key ignition.

"Lock the door!" Darlene hollered as she watched Bones walk over to the driver's side door. Frantically, Brenda fumbled to press the lock down as Bones wrestled the car door open.

Brenda and Darlene trampled each other trying to escape through the passenger door, falling to the ground outside the door. They quickly pulled themselves up and ran fast, splashing through puddles, their purses swinging from their arms. Brenda nearly fell when her slippers came off, but she kept running without them. They ran until they found an unlocked door and ran inside an abandoned building. In the dark, they ran up three flights of stairs to the top floor of the building. Brenda held on to Darlene's arm as they felt their way through an opened door.

"His fat tail won't find us in here ... too many stairs to climb," Darlene said.

Brenda was too exhausted to respond. Trembling and wet, they sat on the cold dirty floor. The light from the adjoining building shined through the window on the other side of the room. Brenda flicked on the lighter she pulled from her purse. Their faces glowed in the light of the small flame.

"That damn Bones made me drop my cigarette," Darlene said, pulling another one from her purse.

"Gimme one," Brenda said. Darlene popped out her last two cigarettes and handed one to Brenda. "Why is Bones so mad at you?"

"'Cause I won't do what he say do ... and 'cause I took this." Darlene smirked, holding up a tiny packet of heroin. "Yeah, I know what you thinking," Darlene said, her voice laced with attitude. What is the pastor's daughter doing out here on the street, getting high? I want to ask you the same thing. I guess we'd better admit the truth since we can't seem to stop running into each other."

"Well, how did you..."

"How did I end up a whore, and a drug addict? Humph, you know how it is, Brenda, being a preacher's daughter. Having a strict, Bible-toting daddy. Can't do this, can't do that, can't go there, don't hang around with them, my dad would say." Darlene shrugged. "Being rebellious, I guess I just got caught up in it." Brenda was silent.

"Sound familiar, huh?" Darlene asked.

"Yep, and look what we've become," Brenda blurted sarcastically.

Darlene pulled a black leather case from her purse then got up and moved closer to the light. She pulled out a baby food jar full of water, a spoon, and a syringe. Brenda watched her heat the heroin on the spoon and draw it up into the syringe, then tie a piece of panty hose she had in her purse around her arm. Brenda's mouth watered, anxious to share it with her. She crawled the few feet toward

Darlene to join in the get high session. They sat across from each other like little girls having a tea party.

As Darlene took her hit first, Brenda slapped at her forearm for a good vein then switched to the other arm, slapping it to see if that arm had more appeasing veins.

As Darlene slipped the panty hose off her arm, Brenda held her hand out to receive it. "I knew that fat, nasty fool wasn't gonna find us in here. It would take him a month to climb those stairs," Darlene said, chuckling.

Brenda laid her head back against the wall under the window seal, enjoying the exhilarating rush that soothed her craving.

"I just don't know why life takes so many twists and turns," Darlene said. "Why we ended up here. I always saw myself being famous like Ruby Dee or Dorothy Dandridge.

"I wonder what those good, sanctified, church folk would say if they saw us right now." Darlene pressed her left hand on her chest and waved the other one hand in the air, doing her imitation of a church member. "The pastor's and the deacon's daughters, shooting heroin," she said in a performance tone.

Brenda chuckled. "Girl, you know you should have been an actress."

"Now you know them holy folk over at Mt. Moriah Missionary Baptist Church would have something to say 'bout that."

"Shush," Brenda said as she bucked her eyes and looked into the darkness of the large room after hearing a noise.

"Girl, Bones is long gone. Listen, you don't hear no cows, do you?" Darlene laughed.

"Come on, Darlene. Please, be quiet." Brenda listened closely. She was sure she heard something.

"Ah, girl, you're paranoid. That's some good dope." She chuckled.

They both sat quietly for a few minutes. "You remember when we were little singing in the choir?" Darlene asked. "I used to get so nervous when my daddy called me out to lead a song."

"Why? You and Sister Huntington and Sister Campbell were the best singers in the church."

"I hate my daddy," Darlene said strongly, changing the subject, the drugs shifting her thoughts, encouraging her to divulge her deep wounds and secrets as if it were truth serum. Brenda was stunned, wondering why she said that and what horrifying family secret was she going to reveal.

"Why you hate him so much?" Brenda asked, edging her to confess.

Darlene tuned up her face and began to cry. "Remember when I went to Georgia for a while to help my grandma when she got sick?" she asked. Brenda nodded. "She wasn't all that sick," Darlene continued. "I was pregnant, and my belly was swelling up fast. When I couldn't hide it no more, my daddy sent me down south to have the baby so I didn't shame myself … and him. It was a girl. She had curly black hair, pretty brown skin, and big bright eyes. No sooner than I kissed her little forehead, they took her away, right out of my arms. I never saw her again."

All Brenda could think about was Tia and how she would feel if what happened to Darlene had happened to her. They both sat crying, tears streaming down their cheeks. Brenda scooted closer to Darlene and put her arm around her. Darlene laid her head on Brenda's shoulder and began to sing the song she used to sing with the choir. They both swayed to the melody.

"Amazing grace how sweet the sound that saved a wretch like me."

Brenda related to her pain. She reminisced on all that she endured and joined her in the song. They both sang it softly. "I once was lost, but now I'm found. Was blind, but now I see." Suddenly, they paused when a loud bang interrupted their moment of sorrow. The door swung open. Crumbles of plaster fell to the floor as the metal doorknob slammed against the wall.

"Bones," Brenda shouted. They both screamed and ran through another door, down a dark hallway and down another flight of stairs guided only by the little light that shined in through the windows from the surrounding buildings.

"This way," Darlene yelled, pulling Brenda's arm.

They ran fast, not realizing they had run in different directions when Darlene let Brenda's arm go.

"In here," Brenda said, pulling the squeaky door to the maintenance closet open.

"Darlene," Brenda whispered, reaching into the darkness for Darlene, but she was gone and Brenda was alone. Brenda stepped inside the closet, pushed the mops and brooms to the side and sat down in the corner on the dirty floor.

Silently, she sat. "Lord, please get me out of here alive," Brenda said. "I promise I'm gonna change my life. Please Lord." Brenda cried, covering her face with her hands.

Darlene made it outside to the alley and ran. As she looked back over her shoulder to see if Brenda was following, she ran straight into Bones. She screamed as he grabbed her by the neck and pushed her up against a brick wall.

"I got you now!" he yelled, gasping, trying to catch his breath.

Darlene gagged and scratched at his hands as he choked her with one hand and held a knife to her face with the other. "Don't you ever steal from me again," Bones growled.

"I won't. I promise I won't," Darlene pleaded, struggling to get the words out, her eyes following the knife in his hand.

"I know you won't," he said, grinding his teeth as he steered the tip of the knife like a painter down from her face, to her breast.

Darlene gasped as Bones shoved the sharp blade into her abdomen then snatched it out, her blood dripping from it. She gurgled as the blood flushed up her throat, spilling from her mouth. Her body fell limp onto the pavement behind a stack of cardboard boxes. Coldly, Bones stepped over her and walked a few steps away panting and breathing hard. He felt weak, staggering, reaching for the brick wall to brace himself. His eyes bulged as he tried harder to breath. He gasped loudly, dropping the knife on the ground. He reached for his heart with his right hand and tried to grip the wall with the other. His large body jolted. He fell back against the brick wall and slid down until his butt hit the ground. He gasped for air again and again. His pupils were dilated, his expression paused.

Brenda pulled herself up off the floor and pressed her ear to the door. She pushed the door open, listening for any sign of Darlene or Bones. Slowly, she peeked out into the darkness then ran out toward the light. She made it to the door that led back to the alley, pushed it open and ran as fast as she could to her car. She slowed down when she noticed Darlene's black boots sticking out from behind a pile of boxes.

"You think Bones won't see those big feet of yours?" she whispered, tipping closer. "Darlene," she called out in a whisper, waiting for her to respond. Brenda pushed the boxes away. "Come on, girl," Brenda said tugging at Darlene's arm. Brenda screamed when she saw the puddle of blood beneath her friend. Brenda quickly covered her mouth with her hand that was smeared with Darlene's blood. In shock, she backed away, tripping and falling over Bones' legs. "Oh my God," she yelled. Terrified, she pulled herself up off Bones' lifeless body and ran. Speckles of mud splashed up her pant legs as she ran barefoot through puddles toward her car. She panicked when the keys were not in the ignition. She remembered she dropped them when she was trying to get away from Bones and hoped he hadn't found them. In the dark, she fumbled through paper and trash items on the front seat and the floor. She exerted a sigh of relief when she found the keys on the floor.

She had to shift the gears from forward to reverse a few times in order to maneuver her car past Bones' Cadillac. The car tugged a bit as Brenda realized that Bones must have sliced some of her tires. She didn't care. She kept driving as fast as she could to get out of there.

CHAPTER THIRTY-SEVEN

*D*azed and crying, Brenda fled the scene and sped through the streets of the Northside with the flat tires flapping loudly. Confused, she didn't know whether to call the police or go into hiding. After a few blocks, the car began to stall, but she was able to pull over on the side of the road before the car completely stopped. Scared and angry with herself and all that was happening, she felt as if she was losing her mind. She gripped her head trying to shake away the pictures of Darlene's and Bones' faces that flashed in her mind.

She wept profusely. Hysterical, she kicked and screamed, slamming her hands on the steering wheel and the driver's side window.

"Oh God!" she yelled.

She got out the car, weak and distraught, keeping her balance by holding on to the car door as she regurgitated. She reached back into the car for her purse and walked away from the car barefoot.

Brenda's clothes were wet and dripping as cold rain poured. With her feet covered in mud, she walked in search of the nearest telephone booth. She felt lost. The dark streets were deserted. Only the light from inside the telephone booth lit up the area near the corner of Iroquois Street. As she closed herself up inside the telephone booth, she thought about calling Deacon and Kadie, but she didn't. She couldn't think of a good enough lie to explain her condition and she didn't want to be ridiculed by Deacon.

She didn't have any money so she dialed the operator to call Jake collect. Frustrated, she slammed the phone down after the operator refused to try a fourth time when the first three calls went unanswered.

She stood inside the telephone booth and closed her eyes. Her childhood splashed on the back of her dark eyelids. She saw herself running and playing as a happy little girl. A frown grew on her face when she thought of her pregnancy and the backlash she received from some of the church members, but pretty visions of Tia smiling cured the angry thoughts. She longed to hug and kiss her baby girl.

She dialed the operator, again and gave her Aunt Lois' phone number. When Lois answered the telephone, all she could hear was Brenda crying on the other end.

"Who is this?" Lois asked. Brenda continued to cry. "Brenda, is that you? "Brenda still couldn't bring herself to speak, but Lois knew it was Brenda. "Brenda, are you ok? Are you hurt? Where are you?

"I don't know what to do," Brenda said, her voice muffled from crying.

"Tell me where you are. I'll come get you." Brenda looked out at the dark streets around her. In her confused state, the streets looked like a faraway jungle that she was lost in. "I don't know," Brenda cried.

"Everybody is worried about you. Maureen and Johnny have been everywhere looking for you."

"Is Tia..."

"Tia is fine. She just wants her mama."

"I know they all hate me."

"No, they don't. They just want you to get ...better."

Brenda dropped the phone as she cried, screamed, and then laughed uncontrollably. The drugs and the traumatic encounter she had just experienced were affecting her mentally. Visions of Darlene's face smeared in blood and

Bones lying dead near her consumed Brenda. She took off running again through the dark neighborhood.

"God help me!" she shouted, collapsing to her knees onto the wet pavement. Soft rain drizzled down her face as her puffy, tear filled eyes stared up at the sky. She hoped God could hear her pleas.

Rain dripped from her hair that had formed into tight ringlet curls around her face. Her wet clothes clung to her skin. The sound of cars passing by startled her. With her mind raging and engulfed with fear, she ran away fast as if the cars were chasing her. As she wiped the rain from her eyes to clear her vision, she was blinded by a pickup truck's headlights that were headed directly in her path. The driver honked his horn and slammed his brakes, skidding to stop. She gasped, her body halted, frozen stiff. The driver jumped out of the truck and ran toward her.

"Are you all right?" the driver yelled. Brenda looked crazed, shielding her eyes from the blinding headlights, standing only five inches from the truck's front bumper. "What's wrong with you, lady? Do you need a doctor?" Without responding, Brenda ran off again.

It had been a few hours since Brenda used heroin with Darlene. The craving was creeping up on her again. The pouring rain slowed and softened to a mist as Brenda came across a dilapidated house. Two young drug dealers stood outside the front gate servicing users as they drove or walked by. They were not the owners of the house, but they used it as a drug den for the addicts.

"Yo Red," one of the young men said. "Check out this chick."

"Dang lady, you soaking wet," Red said. Brenda didn't respond. They assumed she was a junkie in need of a fix. "What you need, lady?" Red asked.

"Man, she don't look like she got no money," the other young man said, eyeing Brenda from head to toe, assessing her ability to pay money for drugs.

"Chill, Duke," Red said.

Brenda unzipped the outside pocket on the purse and pulled out the pearl earrings her great-grandmother gave her.

"I don't want no earrings, lady!" Red yelled.

"They're real," she insisted, shivering. Her voice crumpled.

"They better be." Red shot her an evil look.

Brenda told them what she wanted and exchanged the earrings for the drugs.

"Welcome to my humble hell hole," Red said sarcastically in a deep spooky voice.

"Where all your dreams come true," Duke said, adding to his sarcasm.

Like a gentleman, Duke held the gate open for Brenda. "Go on in," Duke said.

Slowly, Brenda walked up the stairs and into the house, glancing back at the two guys talking before entering the house.

"She looks so familiar. I just can't place her," Red said, jogging his memory.

The house was dark and reeked of odorous people who were lost in their minds from using cocaine, heroin, and any other drugs Red and Duke had available.

In the corner, a man and a woman sat on the dusty hardwood floor, sharing needles under the light of candles.

"What you got, girl?" A frail young woman asked Brenda, her top front teeth missing. Brenda sat down next to the man and woman, to use the light of their candle. She pulled a syringe she had in her purse then heated and fixed the heroin inside a soda pop top and prepared it for injection. The frail woman licked her lips, hoping Brenda would share with her. Brenda used the man's belt to tie around her arm and tighten it with her teeth. Just as she tapped at her veins, she heard many voices swirling around in her head. Deacon, Kadie, Maureen, Johnny, Lois, and Jake. Jake's voice and his words, *"Don't leave"* played over and over in her mind.

Mommy, she heard Tia's voice in her head. Suddenly, a strong, powerful voice startled her, demanding her attention, causing her to snap straight for the moment.

"Come unto me all ye that are heavy laden and I will give you rest," the voice said.

"Ah!" Brenda yelled, waving and punching her fist at the air as if she was fighting the voice. She knew exactly whose voice it was. With all the biblical teachings she'd had all her life, she was sure it was the voice of God. Although she had called out to God many times that night, she never thought he'd respond like that.

"What's wrong with that girl?" the frail women asked, walking toward her, swaying back to dodge Brenda's fist as she performed an emotional fit.

"Them drugs got her mind just like they got your teeth," one man said with a raspy chuckle.

"She's fighting the devil," another man from across the room said.

Suddenly, Brenda jumped up and ran out of the house. The syringe fell onto the floor, the belt still clinging to her arm.

Telishia Berry

"Hey, where you going?" the toothless woman yelled. They all were too high to chase her for their treasured paraphernalia, and Red and Duke were too busy servicing other junkies to care.

"God, where are you?" Brenda screamed. She knew she heard God's voice.

She walked and cried loud, reciting scriptures easily, the same scriptures Deacon had recited over and over for years.

For God so loved the world that he gave his only begotten son. That whosoever believeith in him shall not parish but have everlasting life.

"John three sixteen" Her voice cracked.

"Yea though I walk through the valley of the shadow of death. I will fear no evil for though art with me."

Exhausted and lost in the darkness, she walked until she came upon some cement steps and sat down. She knew God was speaking to her, but she tried to fight it. She heard God calling her, but the devil was calling her, too, laughing, telling her how much she needed that heroin.

"Where are you now, God?" she screamed into the air. "I know you don't love me now. I'm ruined. Don't nobody love me!"

Brenda suddenly took notice of her surroundings, the dark street, quiet and peaceful. She looked down at the stairs where she sat. They were clean and free of debris.

Where am I? Where do these steps lead? she thought. The long staircase and the wide double doors were familiar. She gasped. Her body fell limp and she collapsed across the cement steps and cried out loud.

"God," she cried. "I'm so sorry." Her tumultuous journey had led her to the steps of Mt. Moriah Missionary Baptist Church.

CHAPTER THIRTY-EIGHT

Due to some technicalities and some strings Jake's lawyer was able to pull, Jake was released from jail on bond after only six hours. Jakes cousin that worked at the drug rehabilitation clinic picked him up. He had also had the Methadone Jake wanted for Brenda. When Jake got his car he immediately went to check on Brenda. But she was nowhere to be found.

He drove all over town looking for her, in bars, clubs, and places she'd told him she'd been. He even asked a few drug dealers he knew if they had seen her. From Jake's description of Brenda; Red, the young drug dealer from the drug den was sure she was the one that pawned him the pearl earrings. "I don't know where she went, but she did pawn me these sorry earrings," Red said.

Jake sat at his kitchen table, holding the bottle of Methadone he'd gotten from his cousin, hoping it wasn't too late to help Brenda. He paced the floor of his kitchen then filled the teakettle with water from the faucet, turned on the front burner on the stove, and set the kettle on the fire. He grabbed his favorite cup, set the tea bag in it then sat quietly at the table.

He was concerned about his legal troubles, but more concerned about Brenda. Jake could see his TV from the table in his kitchen. The local news flashed across the TV. A woman and man were found dead. Names were not released pending notification of family. Jake was nervous. He hoped that the woman found was not Brenda.

It was a colder than usual fall season and the rain had started up again, pricking at the house and beading on the window glass. The teakettle whistled. Just as he turned off the fire and began to pour the hot water into the cup, he heard a knock at the door.

Jake walked cautiously to the door, hoping it wasn't the police attempting to haul him back to jail again. When he peeked through the small windowpane on the front door and immediately opened the door.

"Brenda," he said. The rain had drenched her clothes again. She collapsed into his arms.

"Why did you leave me?" she asked, her voice a soft whisper. He held her body close to his.

"I'm sorry," Jake replied. He lifted her into his arms and carried her into the house. He grabbed a blanket that was folded on the sofa and wrapped it around Brenda's cold and shivering body. He held her in his arms as she sobbed like a baby.

"I asked you not leave," he said, pushing her hair back from her face. He got up and got her a clean pair of his pajamas and handed them to her.

Brenda went into the bathroom and turned on the shower allowing it to run as she sat on the floor. "This must be rock bottom," she whispered to herself. She felt she had reached the end of the line, and if she didn't stop and get some serious help, she was going to die.

After she showered and got dressed she stepped out of the bathroom and Jake handed her a cup of hot tea.

"Here drink this," he said. "It'll warm you up."

Brenda looked at him with questioning eyes as she took the cup into her hands.

"It's just tea," he added.

With her cup in one hand, Jake took her other hand and led Brenda to his bedroom where he fluffed two pillows up against the headboard. Brenda took a few sips of the warm tea then sat back against the pillow.

"Thank you," she said, her voice cracking, hoarse from being in the cold and rain. Jake sat down on the foot of the bed and told her how he had been arrested and why he didn't come back that night. He told her that he knew she was at the dope house and she didn't deny it.

"I am ready to straighten my life out," she said. She went on to explain to him what happened to her that night. She didn't tell him that she was with Darlene or had been chased by Bones or that she saw them both dead. She was too afraid to talk about it.

"Did you get the m...met..." Brenda began. "Methadone?" Jake finished for her sentence. Brenda nodded.

"I have it." Jake went into the kitchen to get the bottle of pills he'd left on the table. "You know this is still not going to be easy," Jake said.

Brenda looked up at him with sadness in her eyes. She knew that kicking the habit would not be easy since she'd made several attempts to quit and couldn't. But this time she was determined. "Ain't nothin' been easy for me," she said.

Jake's cousin who'd given him the Methadone told him how much of the liquid Methadone he usually told his patients to take. Jake followed his instructions. Brenda took the bottle from Jake, took two swallows and washed it down with a sip of the hot tea, then scooted her body down under the covers. Within minutes, she was fast asleep from exhaustion.

As Brenda slept, Jake walked in the bedroom occasionally to check on her. With her body drenched from sweat, Brenda tossed, turned, and moaned like she was in pain. Jake pulled the quilt back over her every time she kicked it off. He figured she was just experiencing withdrawal symptoms until she frantically woke up screaming. He rushed over to the bed and wrapped his arms around her. "You're having a bad dream," Jake said.

She trembled and cried as Jack held her.

"He killed her, he killed her!" she yelled.

"It was just a dream."

"No, Bones, he killed Darlene. I was there."

"What are you talking about?" he asked, releasing her from his arms so that he could see her face. Brenda told him everything that happened the night Darlene was killed. Jake was astonished but believed her. He thought back to the news coverage he saw earlier. "You're safe now."

"I need to go home."

"No, you need to stay right here and let me help you." Jake didn't want her to get into any more mischief that night. He knew he needed to keep her calm. He flipped off the ceiling light and turned on the soft lamp on the night stand then turned on the black and white TV that was sitting on top of the chest of drawers. The late news was airing. The identities of the two people that had been found dead in the alley had been confirmed.

"Darlene Pearson, the daughter of Pastor Pearson of Mt. Moriah Missionary Baptist Church, a well-known pastor in the community, and Benjamin Bonner, known on the street as *Bones,* were found dead at the scene. The exact causes of deaths have not yet been determined; however, foul play appears to be a factor," the newscaster stated.

Brenda erupted, crying hysterically. "I can't stop thinking about Darlene," Brenda said, sniffling. "I keep seeing her face. That could have been me."

"Yeah," Jake said, nodding. "You're blessed."

Brenda looked at him as if he had cursed. "Huh, if I'm so *blessed* then why is my life so messed up?" Brenda asked. "Can you tell me that?"

"You're blessed because your life was spared, that's why. It really could have been you they're talking about on the news."

"What do you know about being blessed?"

"'Cause I know. Sometimes you got to go through the horrors of life and come out OK to realize just how blessed you are."

She sat up straight. "Who am I? I ain't nobody. I was ruined a long time ago," she said. "Look at me, Deacon Wilson's baby girl, a junkie, I'm a damn junkie!" She cried. Brenda frowned and scooted back down into the covers. Jake didn't say a word. Brenda closed her eyes and within minutes fell back asleep. Restless, she woke up every hour, complaining about the Methadone. "That Metha... didn't work!" she yelled after several hours. Once again, the cravings crept up her spine and danced around her flesh.

"Well you've only taken a little of the Methadone and it's only been a few hours since I gave it to you. Did you really think it was gonna work that fast? I said this was not going to be easy. It's definitely not going to help you in a day. It may be weeks, months before you're better."

"What!" Brenda rolled her eyes.

Jake sat on the side of the bed. "Methadone," he began, "is a...."

"Look, I have to go," Brenda said, yanking the covers off her legs.

"I told you it would not be easy. You have to go through it."

Brenda stared at Jake, her face hard. "I can't do it."

"Yes, you can."

Brenda spun her legs out the bed. "Where are my shoes?" she asked, looking around the room.

"You didn't have on any shoes when you came." Brenda squinted her eyes and looked down at her feet. "Brenda, I'm not gonna let you go. You gonna have to weather the storm." Brenda sighed heavily, glaring at him. "Hey," Jake said in a comforting tone as he pulled her toward him. "I'm only trying to help you."

Brenda sat up straight. "You wanna help me?" she asked in a doubtful tone.

"Yes, I do."

"Then go get me what I need!" Jake snickered. "What the hell are you laughing at?" Brenda asked, looking at him squarely, wrinkles drawn in her forehead.

"You're trying to make this hard for me, but I'm not going anywhere. And I'm definitely not buying you no dope."

Brenda's eyes watered as she begged him, "Please. I need it. I can't do this."

"Do you want to live or do you want to die?" Jake asked.

"Right now, I feel like I'm gonna die. I'm hurting. Please, just one more hit!"

Jake sighed and shook his head. He couldn't believe that she was the same beautiful young girl he had met a few years earlier. To him, she was still a very nice looking young woman, but he could see that her true beauty was hiding beneath the surface of her pain and the evil that plagued her life.

"I don't want you to hurt anymore," Jake said, taking her hands into his.

"Then let me go get it," Brenda said.

"I'm not letting you go."

Brenda broke away from him, screaming, pounding her fists on his chest. "Who do you think you are? You can't make me stay here. I'm calling my uncle!" Jake pulled the telephone off the nightstand and handed it to her. Brenda took the phone, hesitated to dial, and then threw the phone to the floor. He held her as she sobbed in his arms. She really did want his help, but those demons kept calling her.

Maybe God sent him to help me, she thought.

"Jake," Brenda whispered against his shoulder.

"Yeah."

"I don't want to die."

"You're not going to die." Brenda coughed and gagged, then jumped up and rushed to the bathroom across the room.

"I can't do this," she moaned as waves of vomit rushed out of her.

"Yes, you can," Jake said, rubbing her back as she bent over the commode.

"I got to go home to see about my baby," she lied. She knew Tia was being well taken care of by her mother. She just said anything possible to try to convince him that she was gonna leave and do the right thing, but he didn't buy it.

Jake stood, blocking the bathroom door. Brenda rammed her body into his. He locked his arms around her waist. She wiggled, trying to break free.

"I can't do this," she cried repeatedly.

"Yes, you can!"

"Just let me go home. I promise I won't do nothing."

"Is that what you really want? You want to continue your life like this?"

Brenda fell over on the bed crying. "Oh, God please."

Jake sat down on the bed beside her. "You're gonna be OK," he said, cradling her in his arms. Slowly, her body sunk into his. She felt safe in his embrace, and she wrapped her arms around him.

"The Lord is your help and your shield," Jake said.

Brenda paused, stunned at his words. "That sounds like something out of the Bible."

"It is, maybe not the exact way it was written, but it's in there."

"I don't want to hear nothin' about no Bible. I know I'm not living right. I know that."Brenda was still shaking, but Jake tried to comfort her. He made her a cup of hot tea to help calm her. "I don't want anything," Brenda said, pushing the cup away.

"It will help you," Jake insisted. He handed her the bottle of Amanel.

"Take a few sips of this first." Brenda took the Amanel and turned the bottle up to her mouth then chased the syrup with the hot tea. Hours went by. She drank more tea, she suffered the agony of the heroin withdrawal and slept off and on, and when she was awake, they talked. They shared family stories. Brenda told him about how strict Deacon was and how she felt about getting pregnant out of wedlock.

"I grew up just like you did. My daddy was a preacher."

"Did your daddy try to ram the Bible down your throat?"

"Yeah, but he died when I was fourteen. So of course you know me and my brothers and sister slacked off a bit. When he died, the church helped us for a while then they stopped. Mama had to work cleaning white folks' homes to take care of five kids. Since I was the oldest, I had to do whatever I could to help my mother. My uncle ran a juke joint, and I ran numbers and bets for him. He died when I was seventeen. My dad, my uncle, and your uncle Pap were good friends. I guess you could say I took over the family business. Uncle Pap showed me the ropes.

"Your mama didn't mind?"

"What could she say? Scrubbing floors was barely enough to feed five kids."

"Were you mad at the church?"

"Yeah ... I was bitter for a long time. And I know you're bitter and angry right now, but you will get over it. You will be OK. Now, how about you lie back down and get some sleep, pretty girl?"

Brenda couldn't understand why Jake would say that. As much as she was going through and as terrible and sick as she felt, the last thing she thought she was, was pretty.

"Why do you keep saying that?" Brenda asked.

"What? Get some sleep?"

"No, you know ... what you keep calling me."

"Pretty girl?"

"Yeah. I'm not. Especially like this."

"Yes, you are. You just need somebody to tell you that." He kissed her forehead and turned out the light and the TV.

Brenda tossed and turned, fighting the drug cravings. Her body twitched as she fidgeted with the sheets and bedspread. The room was dark, but the light in the bathroom glowed across the room just enough for her to see her way through the living room.

After Jake fell asleep on the sofa, Brenda quietly tipped past him as he lay snoring. His car keys hung on a small hook on the wall near the back door. With a glance back at Jake, Brenda snatched the keys and bolted toward the door, still wearing the pajamas he'd given her to put on.

His voice stopped her in her tracks. "Where do you think you're going wearing my pajamas and without these?"

He pulled the car keys from his pocket and dangled them in his hand.

Brenda sighed heavily looking at the keys in her hands. "Did you think I would leave the keys lying around?"

"You can't make me stay here. This is kidnapping."

"Kidnapping? You came to me, remember? I'm not trying to make you do anything." Jake stood up. "I'm just trying to help you."Brenda sat on the sofa, her arms folded. Jake groaned. "Some man has hurt you so bad that you can't see that I sincerely want to help you."

"Humph, you just want to be my daddy," Brenda said.

Jake snarled. "You know what, if you really feel like that, then you are welcome to walk right out that door. I won't try to stop you."

Brenda didn't say a word. She rolled her eyes and looked away. Although she didn't say it, she believed he was only trying to help her. "I know my family is worried about me," Brenda said.

"I spoke to Pap."

"What! He knows...?"

"Did you think you would be able to continue what you were doing without your family figuring you out?" Brenda hung her head. The thought of her secrets being disclosed to her family frightened her. "I promised him I'd take good care of you."

"So why'd you say I could leave if I wanted to?"

"Because I knew you wouldn't." Brenda batted away a tear that slipped from her eye.

"I don't think I can do this," she whispered in a trembling voice.

"You will," Jake said. He pulled her toward him. "And I will help you every step of the way. Brenda closed her eyes and tried to block out the gnawing she felt in her belly. Her cravings were hard-hitting, but she believed Jake could help her and finally she would be drug free.

CHAPTER THIRTY-NINE

*B*renda and Jake sat in his car across the street from the cemetery during Darlene's burial service. "There's my sister," Brenda said, noticing Maureen and other familiar faces among the crowd of mourners.

"They planned this funeral pretty quick. It was just a few days ago that her body was found," Jake said snacking on the peanuts he held in his hand.

"Pastor Pearson is one of the most well-known preachers in the city. He probably wanted to put her to rest quickly." Brenda sat quietly for a moment as she watched the crowd of mourners pluck roses from the spread of white roses that adorned Darlene's casket.

"This could have been me," Brenda said, tears streaming down her cheeks. "Please, let's go."

Jake started the engine and drove off.

***

"Are you sure you're ready to do this?" Jake asked as he pulled into Brenda's driveway. Brenda smiled when she noticed her car sitting in the driveway. Jake had found it parked on the street where'd she left it. No one had harmed it, but he did have to replace the tires and rims since Bones slit the tires. She was grateful for all the things Jake had done to help her.

"Are you sure you're ready?" he repeated.

"It's been four days. I can't stay with you forever. I'm going to have to face my family. I feel like I'm going to be OK." Brenda opened the passenger door. Just before she got out of the car, Jake grabbed her hand and kissed it.

Brenda smiled. "Thank you," she whispered. "For everything."

"Wait, I have something for you." Jake reached into his pocket, pulled out a tiny jewelry box, and handed it to her. Brenda gasped when she opened it.

"My grandmother's earrings," Brenda said. Her eyes watered. "How did you…" She stopped mid-sentence as Jake shook his head. She knew not to question him any further. He had gotten the earrings from the drug dealer she'd pawned them to. Brenda hugged Jake and thanked him again.

Jake watched as Brenda left the car and made her way inside her apartment. He hoped she would be OK.

The house was still messy like Brenda left it. "Ugh," she said, smelling the dirty dishes piled in the sink. Today is the day I change my life, she thought. She got down on her knees in front of her bed and bowed her head to pray. "Lord," Brenda began, "I know I keep coming to you, asking you to help with the same ole thing. I know I'm not worthy of anything so special, but Lord, you said all have sinned and come short of your glory. I just ask you to strengthen me and help me get my life back."

Brenda was so exhausted from the week's events that she fell asleep in her praying position. The next morning, she felt refreshed. She pulled the curtains open, and a ray of sun shined across the living room.

"This is the day I change my life," she spoke. She got dressed in her nice pink suit that Kadie bought her a few years earlier. Dressed, she picked up the phone again and dialed Jake.

"I'm ready," she said into the telephone. After she hung up, Brenda walked into the kitchen and made herself a cup of tea and took a dose of the Methadone Jake had given her. She had been doing OK for the last few days. Her cravings were not completely gone; in fact, she had moments that the Methadone kind of made her feel high and sometimes sick, but she knew she would eventually kick the heroin habit. She took less of the Amanel. When she felt pain or discomfort, she whispered prayers. She knew that was the only way to make it through. She knew she was not yet at her best but she was going to get there.

Brenda prepared herself for church. She felt getting back to church was a major step in correcting her life. A smile spread across her face as many of the scriptures Deacon quoted when she was growing up rolled around in her mind.

"Train up a child in the way that he should go and when he is old he will not depart from it," Brenda said softly.

At that moment, she felt a sincere appreciation for Deacon even though she still felt his child-rearing tactics were often too stern. She couldn't stand the way he'd recited the same scriptures over and over for years. But now she understood the words of God through scriptures were being imparted in her soul, and much of it was coming back to her remembrance. She shook her head at the thought of all the hell she had been through and realized that if she didn't believe anybody else loved her, she knew God did. She hummed the lyrics to "Yes, Jesus Loves Me" as she took a quick final look at her hair, grabbed her purse, and headed out the door.

She primped and pressed on her clothes and hair as she walked toward the sidewalk in front of her apartment. She noticed Jake coming up the street toward her and two police cars coming from the other direction. The police cars made it to her first and stopped. Four police officers, three white and one black emerged from both cars.

"Are you Brenda Wilson?" the chubby white officer asked.

"Yeah," Brenda said hesitantly.

"You are under arrest for the murder of Darlene Pearson and George Bonner," one of the other white officers said. By this time Jake pulled up and got out the car with concern.

"What?" Brenda cried out. "I didn't kill nobody!"

"You can explain it when you get to the station," the black officer said as he proceeded to read her, her rights.

"But I didn't..." Brenda began to pull away. The black officer and a white officer grabbed her arms.

"Cuff her," the chubby officer said.

"I didn't do nothing," Brenda yelled. Her heart raced inside her chest. Tears spilled down her cheeks. The chubby white officer put Brenda into the back seat of the police car.

"What happened?" Jake asked.

"She's under arrest in a double homicide," the black officer said. The black officer's white partner shot him a look as if he wasn't supposed to disclose any information. The chubby officer smirked and shook his head as if he was saying, *Damn rookie.* Jake remembered two of the white officers were the same officers that arrested him. They all eyed each other, but neither mentioned that arrest.

Stunned, Jake looked at Brenda sitting in the back of the police car. Brenda's eyes revealed her fear.

"Don't worry," Jake mouthed. Brenda read his lips. Jake knew what Brenda told him about what happened that night with Darlene and Bones and believed she had nothing to do with any murders. Jumping in his car, Jake raced to

his attorney's office. He couldn't let her go down for
something he believed she didn't do.

Brenda read the name Boch on the chubby white
officer's name tag as he helped her out of the police car and
escorted her into the police station proudly as if he was the
hunter showing off his catch. He walked her right to the
fingerprinting area to Officer Benelli, a female officer who
had no fears about showing how she felt about black
people, especially high-yellow females. She curled her top
lip and turned up her nose at Brenda as if she was
something nasty and dirty. Brenda eyed her back,
wondering how she had the nerve to look at her like that
when her pale white skin was speckled with ugly, red zits
and her limp, dingy blonde hair looked like it was past due
for a shampoo.

"Spell your name," Officer Benelli said as she typed
up the report. Brenda cringed as the stench of Officer
Benelli's smelly breath went up her nostrils. After Brenda
mumbled out the letters in her first, middle, and last names,
Officer Benelli snatched the paper from the typewriter and
slapped it on a pile of others.

Benelli walked her small frame around the counter and
gripped Brenda's fingers, forcefully pressing them into the
black ink and rolling them onto a fingerprint card. Brenda
felt a combination of shame and humiliation as she stood in
front of camera.

"Turn to your left, now to your right," were the only
other words Officer Benelli said while taking Brenda's
police photos. Just as she finished the photos, Officer Boch
returned to escort Brenda to a holding cell.

Brenda paused, frozen at the sight of the dirty, dull jail cell with one bench lined against the dark wall. "Go on," the officer said with a nudge, releasing the grip he had on Brenda's arm. "You'll be in this holding cell until you've been questioned."

Brenda slowly stepped into the cell. A cold chill ravaged her body and the taste of vomit drew a lump in her throat. She stood there in the center of the cell, panning the nine-by-nine-foot cell that to her looked like a hellhole. The concrete floors looked rough and sticky. The windows were on the other side of the room away from the cell. Brenda glanced back at the officer, and her body jolted from the sound of the bars slamming shut and the arrogant smirk the officer projected.

She sat in the center of the bench, gripping her biceps, hugging herself tightly. A flood of tears soaked her face, smearing the pressed powder she'd just put on for church.

She couldn't believe she was sitting in a jail cell. *What evidence do they have?* she thought. Her mind traveled back to that night she and Darlene was running from Bones. She wondered had she been so high or disillusioned that night that maybe things didn't happen the way she thought they did. *Maybe ... I did kill Bones.* She fought hard, jogging her memory trying to recount every detail of that night. She wondered how of all days, the one day she truly decided to change her life had such a turn of events.

"Lord, is this my punishment?" she whispered, rocking her body back and forth.

"God, help me, please. I didn't do it."

The harsh conversations she heard among the officers, the constant slamming of office doors and the time waiting in the cell brought on the agitation that progressed into pains from heroin withdrawal. She thought about the

Telishia Berry

Methadone that was at the apartment, but the thought of heroin satisfying those urges were even more intrusive. She flinched as perspiration damped her skin and the drug cravings ripped at her flesh. She closed her eyes tightly and prayed. All she could think about was one of Deacon's favorite words, *Repentance,* one he often shouted at her along with a Bible verse he could easily recite from memory. She continued praying, the only thing she knew to do when there was nothing and no one else.

God please, I know I have done so much wrong, but I am sorry. I'm so sorry for all of it. I don't want to be a drug addict. I don't want to go to jail. Lord, if you give me one more chance, I promise I will live right. Please Lord.

The four hours she sat in the cell, to her, seemed like an eternity. She prayed, cried then prayed again. She felt like her prayers were being answered as the cravings lightened, and she began to think a little clearer. The last thing she wanted was for Deacon and Kadie to find out she was in jail, but she knew that the situation was very serious and that it was time to call them. Even if Deacon was going to yell and ridicule her, she knew she needed her parents' support.

"Officer," she yelled, "can I please make a phone call?" *Don't I get at least one phone call,* she thought as she recalled jail scenes from many police TV shows she'd watched.

The officer sitting at the desk across the room took his time walking over to the cell after she interrupted his telephone call that was actually another officer telling him to move her to a room to talk to the detectives. The large ring of keys attached to his belt slapped loudly against his waist as he walked toward the cell.

"Can I please use the telephone?" she repeated.

The officer took his time responding, chewing his gum with his front teeth, using a key from the key ring to unlock the cell.

Brenda followed the officer down a hallway past several closed office doors to a small room. She hesitated before stepping into the dim room. *There's no phone in here,* she thought.

"Have a seat. The detectives will be in to see you."

Brenda sat quietly in the dull cold room and waited.

***

"I am Detective Sharp," a baldheaded white man said as he stepped into the room. His wide belly bulged between the navy blue suspenders that held up his Khaki-colored trousers. Detective Sharp was an interrogation expert. He reviewed the case as well as Brenda's file. She had no police record, not even a parking ticket. He could see she was nervous, and with the right questions, he could get her to disclose some pertinent information or perhaps a confession of murder. The room was cold and silent as Detective Sharp sat in the chair across from her flipping through papers he had in a manila envelope. Brenda squirmed in her seat as the silence pricked her nerves.

"I didn't kill anybody," Brenda blurted.

"Well," he said, moving his eyes from the papers to Brenda, "can you tell me why your fingerprints were at the scene of the crime and why a witness saw you there?"

"A witness? There was no one else…" She stopped mid-sentence.

"So you were there." Detective Sharp leaned back in the chair and crossed his arms, appeased by how quickly his tactics revealed she was at the scene of the crime.

"No … I mean I…" Brenda struggled with her words.

294

Another officer walked in carrying a large plastic bag and handed it to Officer Sharp. "Is this yours?" the officer asked, lifting the bag that held Brenda's change purse that she kept inside her handbag. It had a few family pictures inside of it.

Brenda hesitated. Her eyes bulged, shocked to see her small change purse bagged at the police station."Yeah," she said softly.

"Lady, you're going to prison for the rest of your life," Detective Sharp said. He knew her change purse being at the scene didn't automatically mean she killed anyone, but if he could get into her mind, Sharp thought she might crack and confess.

"No," she cried. "I didn't do it." Brenda went on to explain what she remembered happened that night, how she picked up Darlene on the street as she was running from Bones then how Bones chased her and Darlene and how they got separated when they hid in the abandoned building.

"I don't know how they died. I ran out of the building, and they were there." She choked. "Dead. Darlene was my friend. I could never kill her or anybody." She dug deep into her memory for any other details she hadn't mentioned. She squinted her eyes tightly, pressing her hand against her forehead as the stress brought tears.

Without warning, a tall, brown skinned man wearing an attractive navy-blue suit walked into the room.

"I'm Brenda's attorney," he said, interrupting the interrogation. "I need to have a word with my client. Alone." Brenda displayed a look of confusion.

Detective Sharp wiggled his way out of his chair and left the room, huffing. The officer followed.

"Who are you?" Brenda asked.

The attorney slapped his briefcase down on the table. "Attorney Harold Johnson. Jake sent me." He held out his hand.

"Oh," Brenda said, cautiously shaking his hand.

He sat down across from her, popped open his briefcase and pulled out his pen and note pad. "Now, tell me what happened."

Brenda explained to him exactly what she'd told the detective and what she told Jake the way she remembered and believed it happened.

"What have I done?" Brenda mumbled, dropping her face into her hands.

As they talked, the detective came back in the room.

"The coroner's report just came in."

Brenda took a deep breath, swallowed hard, and listened carefully to what Sharp had to say. "George Bonner, aka Bones died of a heart attack," the detective began. "Though it took a while for testing to be completed, we found Bonner's fingerprints on the knife found at the scene used to kill Darlene Pearson. Apparently, Bonner killed Pearson then suffered a heart attack."

Brenda's forehead touched the table as sobs ripped from her throat. "Thank you, Jesus," she said under her breath.

"You need to sign the release papers then you are free to go," Detective Sharp added. "We may need to talk to you later."

Brenda nodded. She was too relieved and choked up to speak. After signing all the paper work, Attorney Johnson escorted her outside the building where Jake was standing in front of his car. She rushed into his arms.

"That devil is working, ain't he?" Jake said, chuckling.

"But God is good," she said, wiping the remaining tears from her cheeks. "The devil is a liar." She paused. She'd heard Deacon say that numerous times. and Pastor Pearson during one of his huffing sermons. "Today is still the day I change my life," she continued.

"Thank you," Jake said, shaking Harold's hand before he got into his own car and drove away.

Jake looked at his watch and said, "We'll try to make it to church next Sunday."

"We?" She assumed Jake was going to drop her off at church and be on his way.

"Yep, what, you don't dig my suit?" Jake stepped back and spun around, showing off his three-piece duds.

"Yeah, you do clean up well." Brenda smiled. She loved Jake's well-groomed appearance.

"Let me get you home. Thank God that's over." Jake slid into the driver's seat.

Brenda got into the passenger seat. "Yes, thank you, Jesus, thank you."

CHAPTER FORTY

*K*adie sat across from Deacon at the dining room table; a pitcher of tea and Deacon's full glass sat near him. Brenda had been the topic of most of their conversations for the past week. Both were overwhelmed with emotions ranging from anger to worry to questioning who was to blame for their youngest child's unfavorable life decisions.

Kadie didn't agree or disagree with Deacon as he ranted on about why he thought Brenda turned to drugs. She hung her head, tears streaming down her face, and rocked back and forth as Deacon went on and on.

"Brenda's been rebellious since she was a child, fornicating, getting pregnant out of wedlock, shacking up with roguish men, humph, this was bound to happen."

Kadie stopped rocking and stared at Deacon as if she wanted to tell him to shut the hell up, but she didn't say anything. She just sat and simmered in her own sorrow.

"You would think with all the Biblical principles I taught ALL our children that none of them would have turned out like this. I made sure they grew up in church, went to Sunday school, Bible classes. Why would she do this? Why would she turn her back on God?"

That statement struck a nerve with Kadie. She couldn't hold her tongue any longer. She slammed her fist on the table, causing some of Deacon's tea to spill onto the linen tablecloth. Deacon's eyes widened. "I don't believe she turned her back on God," she said. "Yes, she was rebellious, she got pregnant, and maybe she chose the wrong men, but I know ain't no child of mine turned they back on God! And God didn't turn his back on her! As they all became teenagers, you kept trying to treat them like

298

babies. You ran around here shouting Bible verses at them. Anything they did or wanted to do was SO sinful, according to you. When your children needed you the most, you were too busy at the church, teaching bible classes, and being so darn righteous that you couldn't see the forest for the trees.

"You couldn't see that your children needed to talk to you about life and the world. Your only answers were that the world was full of sin and they needed to live right. That was not enough. Johnny and Al went to the Army to get away. Maureen married her way out, but Brenda had already committed the ultimate sin and screwed up her life, so you said, every time you got a chance. You told your baby girl she was ruined after she got pregnant.

"You told her that no man would want her after she had Tia she was not worthy of a good man. So what she do? She took the first man that paid her any attention because in her mind she was lucky to get him."

Deacon was stunned at Kadie's straightforwardness. He sat back in his chair and took a few moments before he spoke while Kadie paced the dining room.

"But, Kadie, I did talk to my children about life. I just tried to do it in accordance to the word of God."

"No, John, you talked AT them. You beat them with scriptures and righteous talk."

"I told Brenda when she got pregnant that God forgave her."

"Yes, you did, but right behind that you told her that she was ruined."

The phone rang, interrupting their conversation. Deacon answered the phone with a gruff hello, but after a few seconds, his mouth dropped open. "What? Brenda's in jail!" he yelled.

"Calm down, calm down," Pap said on the other line. "She *was* in jail, but she's been released and is with Jake."

"So who is this Jake, some hoodlum? Where's he taking her now?"

"She's gone be fine," Pap assured.

Deacon hung up the telephone, explained the details to Kadie, sighed, and shook his head.

"Help her Lord," he whispered, sending a direct request to God.

CHAPTER FORTY-ONE

*T*ia. For days, it was one of the only words in Brenda's mind. She was anxious to see her daughter, but she knew she needed to get herself together before seeing Deacon and Kadie.

"I'm sorry, Mama," Brenda said to Kadie over the phone.

Tears rolled down Kadie's cheeks as she listened quietly to Brenda. She was devastated to learn about all the things that had been going on with Brenda, but she knew that if what Maureen and Johnny were saying was true, it would eventually be revealed. But she also trusted that God would take care of her daughter.

"Don't worry about Tia," Kadie said.

Brenda felt a little better after speaking to her mother on the phone. She never worried about Tia when she was with Kadie. What worried her now was facing Deacon.

She imagined what the confrontation would be like. She wondered if she would cry, scream, or run to the bathroom and vomit after being scolded for what had taken place in her life. She tried not to think too much about it. Kadie told her to take a few days to get herself together.

It was Sunday morning once again. Brenda took the whole week to think and pray. She cleaned her house from top to bottom the way she cleaned her parents' home when she lived there. She knew Kadie would be proud. She made herself some bacon, eggs, and grits and turned the Sunday spirituals on the radio.

The knock at the door startled her.

"Who is it?" she yelled, but there was no answer. With the chain still on the door, she pulled it open enough to peep out. She noticed a box sitting on the floor. She took the chain off and took the box into the house. A card attached to the box read, *Hope you like it, love Jake.*

She rushed into her bedroom and plopped the box down on the bed. Anxiously she untied the red ribbon to open it. A smile illuminated across her face when she pulled the lavender-colored dress out the box. She stood in front of the mirror holding the dress up against her chest. At that moment, she knew it was time to confront every fear she had, including facing Deacon. She hurried to get dressed, putting an extra effort in making herself look pretty.

Brenda took a few seconds to check her lipstick and hair in the rearview mirror before getting out the car and going inside the church. The ushers handed her a church program before she took a seat at the back of the church. Mother Jesse had already led the devotional song, and they were mid-way through the service.

Pastor Pearson was charged up as he preached about forgiveness. "God is faithful and just to forgive you," he said at the end of his sermon. Those words resonated in Brenda's spirit. She felt the sermon was a Word from God for her.

The choir rose for a selection. Pastor Pearson's oldest daughter, Terri, walked up to the microphone to lead the song. Brenda's mind traveled back to her younger years growing up in that church when life was much easier. Tears fell from her eyes as she thought about the pastor's youngest daughter, Darlene, and how much fun they had as girls. She smiled when she thought about Tia. She peered up front, looking for Tia, Kadie, and Deacon. Maureen was there most Sundays with her husband.

Terri continued the song, and the congregation responded with an array of emotional interjections from members of the congregation.

"Hallelujah!"

"Thank you, Jesus!"

"Amen!" Members shouted.

Terri sang the song with a spiritual power that flowed throughout the sanctuary.

Most of the congregation was on their feet, lifting their hands and praising God.

> *All to Jesus I surrender;*
> *all to him I freely give;*
> *I will ever love and trust him,*
> *in his presence daily live.*

> *I surrender all, I surrender all,*
> *all to thee, my blessed Savior,*
> *I surrender all.*

As Terri sang, Brenda stood and made her way to the front of the church where Deacon, Tia, and Kadie sat. She looked back into the congregation and noticed Jake. He his eye at her. She smiled. Next to Kadie sat Maureen and Daniel with their daughter Vanessa.

"Mommy!" Tia said when she noticed Brenda. Tia leaped from Kadie's arms into Brenda's arms. Her tiny feet dangled as Brenda hugged her tight and kissed her cheek. Kadie smiled. Maureen blew her sister a kiss.

"I'm so sorry, Mama," Brenda said. Kadie embraced Brenda.

"I know, baby. I'm just glad you're OK." Brenda handed her baby girl to Kadie as Deacon walked up to greet her. He was emotional, but happy that his prayers were answered. His heart had been heavy because of Brenda, but when he laid eyes on his daughter, a burden was lifted.

"I'm sorry, Daddy." Brenda wept and fell into her father's arms.

"I know, baby. I forgive you, but this is between you and God, and I know He has forgiven you, too," Deacon whispered to his youngest daughter.

Brenda smiled as Kadie gave her a reassuring look. She looked over at Terri as she continued to sing. Terri waved her hand, signaling Brenda to come into the choir stand. Brenda made her way over to Terri, and Pastor Pearson proudly handed Brenda the microphone. Together, Terri and Brenda sang the song like they did when they were little girls in the youth choir. Deacon was elated and pleased his daughter made the decision to surrender her life to God. Kadie and Maureen both shed tears of joy as Brenda and Terri sang the second verse.

All to Jesus I surrender;
humbly at his feet I bow,
worldly pleasures all forsaken;
take me, Jesus, take me now.

I surrender all, I surrender all,
all to thee, my blessed Savior,
I surrender all.

Made in the USA
San Bernardino, CA
10 August 2014